D0027729

CH

It Happened in Tuscany

a novel

Gail Mencini

Capriole Group

It Happened in Tuscany
by Gail Mencini

Published in the United States by

CAPRIOLE
GROUP

an imprint of Capriole Group, LLC, Centennial, CO 80161
www.CaprioleGroup.com

Publisher's Cataloging-In-Publication Data
(Prepared by The Donohue Group, Inc.)

Names: Mencini, Gail, author.
Title: It happened in Tuscany : a novel / Gail Mencini.
Description: First edition. | Centennial, CO : Capriole Group, [2020]
Identifiers: ISBN 9781938592157 (paperback) | ISBN 9781938592164 (ebook)
Subjects: LCSH: World War, 1939-1945–Veterans–United States–Fiction. | Guerrillas–Italy–Fiction. | Women authors–Fiction. | Man-woman relationships–Italy–Tuscany–Fiction. | Family secrets–Fiction. | Tuscany (Italy)–Description and travel–Fiction.
Classification: LCC PS3613.E4795 I8 2020 (print) | LCC PS3613.E4795 (ebook) | DDC 813/.6–dc23

Library of Congress Control Number: 2019906602
10 9 8 7 6 5 4 3 2 1

First Edition

Cover and Book design by Nick Zelinger, *www.NZGraphics.com*
Author Photograph by Ashlee Bratton, *www.Ashography.com*

It Happened in Tuscany is a work of fiction. Names, characters, businesses, organizations, places, incidents, and events either are the product of the author's imagination or are used fictitiously. Though based on the 10th Mountain Division ascent of Riva Ridge in World War II and the inclusion of certain real characters, this is a work of fiction and the author's imagination. Where real-life places and historical figures appear, the situations, incidents, and dialogues concerning those places and persons are fictional or are used fictitiously and are not intended to change the entirely fictional nature of the work. In all other respects, any resemblance to persons living or dead is entirely coincidental.

In honor of WWII military service members:
the Army 10th Mountain Division,
Papa, who served in the Army,
and Gramps, who would want you to know
that he was a Navy man.

Riva Ridge ~ Monte Belvedere
February 1945

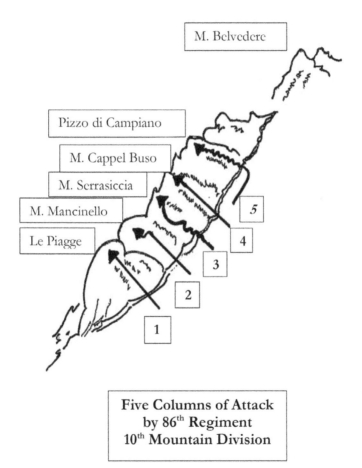

M. Belvedere

Pizzo di Campiano

M. Cappel Buso

M. Serrasiccia

M. Mancinello

Le Piagge

1 2 3 4 5

**Five Columns of Attack
by 86th Regiment
10th Mountain Division**

Province of Siena

1

H^{*igher.*}

U.S. Army searchlights, meant to distract the Germans, reflected off the clouds and bathed the ridgeline above with light. They created hazy moonbeams in the otherwise black sky.

Would these lights—their only protection—keep the men who hugged the base of the mountain hidden? Or would the deadly guns on the ridge blast them once they began their climb?

Higher.

Army Specialist Will Mills, age seventeen, and his platoon brothers faced the most challenging route of the attack on Riva Ridge on this night, February 18, 1945.

Lieutenant James Loose led Will's platoon, which was part of A Company, 86th Regiment. The best mountaineers, they drew the assignment of the gutsy technical climb straight up Pizzo di Campiano on the eastern spur of Riva Ridge.

Will respected Lieutenant Loose, but tonight, Loose turned Will into one of his father's steers being herded up a chute, with a meatpacking plant its destiny.

Climb to glory.

The motto of the 10th Mountain Division.

Will prayed that tonight he would climb to glory. He shuddered. Shuddered from the cold and the dread of what this night might hold.

The Germans had been pushed back to northern Italy by Allied troops, but further progress stalled. Heavy casualties plagued the Allies in the fall and brutal winter of 1944. Mount Belvedere in Italy's Apennine Mountains held the key to piercing the Germans' fortified Gothic Line and breaking into the Po Valley.

General Eisenhower had tagged the soldiers on skis "playboys." The 10th Mountain troops welcomed this assignment, where they could use their rigorous training and prove his label false.

General Hays tasked the men of the 10th with the responsibility of pushing back the Germans from Mount Belvedere.

Will, and the other members of Loose's platoon, needed to take Riva Ridge.

2

Will licked his lips and waited among the five columns of soldiers for their 19:30 go-ahead. He would climb midway in the platoon of men scrambling up Pizzo di Campiano, which suited him fine.

Will had grown up skiing and climbing the Colorado Rockies. At a buck thirty dripping wet, he didn't have much weight to carry up those mountain faces. Years of throwing hay bales, riding horses, and herding cattle on his parents' ranch had sculpted his frame into one both lean and strong.

Will had skied the backcountry of the Rockies and scampered up the peaks. The elite 10th Mountain Division accepted him thirteen months ago because of his mountaineering skills. The Army didn't look twice when Will lied and added a year to his age to make himself eligible for enlistment.

The 10th's best weapon on this climb would be that the Germans considered a nighttime assault up Riva Ridge impossible. Every other attempt by the Allied troops had failed.

A passel of Germans waited for them. The scouting patrols for Riva Ridge spotted eighteen German positions on the ridge, plus at least four observation posts. If the enemy caught wind of them and started firing from their superior position, the U.S. boys wouldn't survive.

Will wished their mountain boots and cold-weather sleeping bags had arrived in Italy with them. It'd be an icy son-of-a-gun stretching out under a blanket on the snowy, wet ground.

He hadn't slept but a lick last night and expected slim shut-eye in the nights ahead.

His arms trembled.

Fear of the Germans' guns caused Will's shakes. His gun stood empty and useless.

The brass had ordered all guns unloaded until they breached the ridgeline. They wanted no chance of anyone pulling the trigger early and spoiling the surprise.

No one spoke. The companies waiting at the base had been ordered into silence.

Ragged breaths of fear, including his own, created steamy puffs in the cold air.

He stood in ankle-deep mud.

He thought about what General Hays said two days ago to the men charged with taking Riva Ridge and Mount Belvedere:

"Remember the mission. No matter what happens, keep fighting, and take more ground.

Your buddy may fall, but don't stop to help him.

Keep fighting. Take more ground.
Always keep fighting."
The mission was more important than the men.

3

Will lined up behind Tom Hermann.

A strip of white adhesive tape stuck to the back of Tom's helmet bore his name. They all labeled their helmets with tape, to help keep the man ahead in sight.

Will looked at his wristwatch, a gift from his grandfather on the day he enlisted. Its luminous dial was hidden. The men taped over their watches, so the glow didn't give away their position.

Tom tapped Will's helmet to alert him. Tom started his climb. From one man to the next, the "time to go" signal passed down the line.

Will stumbled over the tangled brush, which laced the trail. The sound of broken branches to his rear meant the man behind him got snared up, too. Following their orders, they all maintained silence, fearful of jeopardizing their mission.

Every shrub, every tree possibly hid a German, eager to cut down the enemy with his ready gun. Will hunched his shoulders and gritted his teeth, steeling himself for an oncoming bullet.

The line passed a group of trees, a possible Nazi hiding spot.

Will exhaled with three quick breaths.

The hard, slow climb got steeper with each footfall. The men stopped for rest, five minutes at a time.

Tom tapped Will's helmet. Time to go.

His muscles strained from hauling his gear and ammunition, but Will's training prepared him for the slope and the weather.

Hell, he survived the winter "D Series" outside Camp Hale, the damn-near cruel training in the frigid Colorado Rockies.

And the altitude? No problem. The Rockies beat the Apennines by thousands of vertical feet.

In spite of his training, Will's hands quivered. In the D Series, no Germans hid with machine guns and grenades ready to rain down on them.

The path got steeper, dusted with new snow, and icier as he climbed.

They were supposed to reach the ridge after five or six hours of climbing.

Will looked up, but only an eerie light danced in the distance, no ridgeline.

Will came upon a stream frozen solid. The scouting team had placed a rope on the margins of the ice bulge to help with safe passage.

Will followed Tom up the first rope. They skirted the frozen stream on one side and then the other, careful not to cross straight over the ice. Will thanked God and the advance crew for anchoring the life-saving rope to rock.

The path's slope eased for a short distance after the frozen stream. Will clambered over the boulders, not needing his technical climbing skills.

He looked up, but the darkness kept secret whether snow or a trail lay ahead.

Will told himself not to rush. The steepness of the slope lessened, but that didn't make it less treacherous.

The terrain changed again before Will could settle into a rhythm. The mountain alternated between technical climbing and scrambling over the rocks with his hands and feet.

The breaks came more frequently as the climb took its toll. They climbed for ten minutes, rested for five, and then ascended again, eager for the next break.

Will rationed his water. He took tiny sips to wet his parched mouth on only a fraction of the rest breaks.

Fog, with its snaking tentacles, settled in. Will couldn't spy Tom at all now.

Will blinked his eyes. His ice-crusted lashes clumped together and made opening his eyes a downright chore.

His arms burned as if seared by a mighty furnace.

Will didn't have a sense of time, but he guessed it was longer than the six hours estimated.

Higher. Climb higher.

Ten torturous minutes of climbing passed. He clung to his position and rested for five.

Will forced his mind back to the climb. Though rest had eluded him last night, he wasn't sleepy. His fear kept him awake.

A noise ripped through the silent night. Above him, rocks tumbled down the mountain face. Stones peppered the slope, likely dislodged by a foot skidding on the scree.

Will looked up into the fog, but only an eerie mask greeted him.

The only thing he—and likely the Germans—heard was the crash of rocks racing down toward him.

4

Baseball-size rocks skittered on the slope three feet to Will's right. His stomach tensed, but the stones bounced along on their quest for the base, leaving Will untouched.

The explosion from a German "potato masher" grenade and its lingering reverberation cut through the night.

Will's hands tightened on his handholds. His arms shook.

Small arms fire popped above him. Grenade explosions echoed overhead.

Mixed with the sounds of the German attack, a burst of answering fire rang out, likely from Loose and Harry Reining, the two lead men. They must have slapped clips into their rifles after they came under attack.

Their best weapon, the surprise of the assault, was gone.

Silence.

Had the Germans killed Loose and Reining?

Were the enemy soldiers now waiting for the rest of the platoon to climb within firing range?

Or had our boys taken out a German observation group, clearing the way to the ridge for the rest?

A tap on his head. Time to climb again. Climb to the ridge and whatever it held.

Will's burning arms and legs inched him up the slope. The tape on Tom's helmet bobbed in and out of Will's sight.

The silence, except for his own panting breaths, cloaked the dark, foggy night.

A bazooka's thunder broke the stillness.

The volley from a Browning Automatic Rifle answered. One of the men ahead of Will carried a BAR. Will hoped its rounds had found a German.

Silence.

Had the lead men reached the summit?

Silence.

Will looked up into the fog. He couldn't distinguish more than a clump of snow stuck to Tom Hermann's boots.

Higher.

Climb higher.

5

Nine hours of climbing after Loose's troops started up Pizzo di Campiano, Will reached the top of Riva Ridge.

The first twelve men up the mountain got separated from the rest of the platoon and arrived hours earlier than Will. Near where Loose's team breached the ridge, the men said they found two Germans sleeping in a pup tent, and they made sure the Nazis would never wake up.

Loose called the platoon together. "I've got lousy news," Loose said. "The enemy found and cut the communication wire between Cappel Buso and Pizzo di Campiano. Our own wire party climbed ahead of me and got lost. A Company is stranded. We can't communicate with the other troops on the ridge or those at the base."

Loose ordered Will and most of the others into the German foxholes to guard their position. The lieutenant set off with a small patrol to scout the area.

The morning sun lit the ridge. Will studied the clumps of scruffy bushes and rock formations dotting the land around him.

His arms and legs ached from climbing the entire night. He looked down at his hands. His fingers were scraped and battered from digging into the mountain for handholds.

Tom, next to Will in the foxhole, whispered a question. "You all right?"

"Peachy," Will said. "You?"

"Same."

Explosions, one chasing the next, shocked Will. His head jerked toward the racket. Flames and rising balls of gray smoke told the story. Loose and his patrol had discovered a foxhole fortified with ammunition and mortars and set it ablaze.

Another rumble of firepower sounded. Not far from Loose's bonfire, puffy balls of smoke tarnished the alpine air.

For a brief moment, the sound and sight of exploding ammo reminded Will of lying on his back in the grass on hot Fourth of July nights in Golden, watching the fireworks and fireflies. Frigid fingers crept up Will's spine and chased away his memories. The Germans hiding in fortifications along the ridge set off the second detonations to pinpoint the Yanks' location.

The real fight for Pizzo di Campiano was on.

Loose circled back to where Will crouched in his foxhole. The lieutenant wanted to expand the area cleared, and he sent more men out. He assigned Tom and Will an area to search for the enemy and remove hazards.

The sun was warm on Will's face, but chills crept over him. Now he would face the enemy.

He studied the ridge. A bump rose over the ground in the distance.

Tom took the lead. They moved from cover to cover in the direction of the mystery bulge. What would they find? A stand of bushes, a rock formation, or pup tents?

They soon realized the lump was both God- and man-made. Scraggly crops of bushes provided cover for a pup tent tucked between them. Foxholes likely protected the camp.

Tom pointed to the next clump of brush. Will nodded. It was within grenade range of the pup tent. The perfect spot for them to launch an attack against the Germans.

Tom and Will ducked low and dashed toward the bushes. Tom kept the lead, with Will behind and slightly to his right.

Tom stopped. Had he seen something?

Will's search partner leaned right as the whine of a sniper bullet cut the air.

Tom collapsed to the ground.

The bullet aimed at Will had hit Tom high on his body.

Will crawled to him. Blood spurted out of Tom's neck.

Tears burned Will's eyes. He abandoned his friend and forced himself to crawl quickly to the cover at the stand of brush ahead.

Your buddy may fall, but don't stop to help him. ... Take more ground. ... Always keep fighting. The general's command played in Will's head.

"Will ... Help me ..." Tom's feeble voice affected Will like he had shouted through a bullhorn. Tom wouldn't last long.

Will gritted his teeth and yanked out two grenades.

He pulled the pin on the first one. Cocked his arm and heaved it into the patch of brush behind the tent, where the sniper who nailed Tom hid.

Will pulled the second pin and heaved that device toward the front of the tent.

Both blasts hit their marks.

Will put a clip in his Garand M1 rifle.

Tom wasn't crying out for help now. Was it too late?

Will poked the barrel of his gun out of the bushes. He fired at the hidden sniper.

Submachine gun bullets whizzed through the hardy bushes that hid Will. The missiles snapped branches off, and ruffled his jacket sleeve.

The gunner's aim was off, and his stream of bullets pinpointed for Will the enemy's location.

Will shot at the foxhole. He ducked down and pulled out another grenade. Will pulled the pin and threw it toward the hidden gunner.

The bomb burst.

Silence.

Will again fired at the foxhole. He shot at the spot where the tent had stood before a grenade hit it. He directed bullets at the bushes that flanked the tent and followed with fire into the growth hiding the sniper.

Silence.

Will crawled on his belly back to Tom. Blood soaked Tom's jacket. His friend's mouth gaped open, looking like he had tried to utter one more cry for help. Cries for help that Will ignored.

Will shook as he choked back the sob inside him.

Someone called out their code word. Will replied as instructed.

Sam, Charlie, and Ed, men from his platoon, headed toward him, arms at ready, and covered the area that hid the Germans.

Sam and Charlie crept toward the bushes flanking the tent. Ed crouched next to Will with his gun at ready and spoke with only a quick glance at Tom. "Wounded or dead?"

Will's fingers pressed Tom's wrist. Tom's neck was a pulpy mass of blood and tissue. "Dead."

Ed rested one hand on Will's shoulder.

"They're all dead." Sam's voice got louder the closer he walked toward Will. "Two of them in the brush behind the tent. Grenade got 'em. Plus one sniper dead in the shrubs."

Charlie inspected the foxhole. "Two more dead in here."

Ed squeezed Will's shoulder. "One against five. Easy pickings, right? You did it, Will."

Will looked at the ravaged body of Tom Hermann. "We did it. Tom and me."

Ed grabbed Will's left arm. "You've been hit."

6

One of the sniper bullets had nicked Will's left bicep.

"Not much more than a scrape," Will said. "Let's move on."

Will ripped off a piece of his shirt. Ed wrapped the cloth around Will's arm, but Will refused to let anyone waste their precious water to wash his wound.

The platoon cleared their fortified positions on Pizzo di Campiano of Germans, then hunkered into the foxholes.

Combat medics set up shop in a stone building that Loose had spotted on the climb up. Will refused to go see them. No one left the front and went down to the stone building unless their wounds were severe.

Shortly after 15:00, sniper bullets peppered the ground short of the men's positions.

The bursts came at uneven intervals, spray after sporadic spray of bullets. Each time, the bullets hit closer to where Loose's troops hid.

Will's anxiety and fear ratcheted up with each attack.

Darkness fell on the men who twenty-four hours earlier had scaled the ridge. No one had slept since the night before their climb.

The platoon had run out of grenades and their ammo was nearly gone.

Will ate the last bit of his food. The last drops from his canteen hit his tongue five hours before. Will, as others had earlier in the day, now melted snow for water.

Morale sank up and down the line. No ammo. Almost no food. No water. And no sleep for closing in on 48 hours.

Loose, once the wire company found them, called for men from B Company, who'd taken Mount Cappel Buso, to relieve his all but unarmed platoon.

Will's eyes burned from the dry, cold air and lack of sleep.

Sniper fire continued to land closer and closer to where Will crouched. The snipers advanced toward them. Soon they would hit their mark.

Loose went one step further to push back the enemy. He demanded that the artillery gunners bring their fire in closer to their own bunkers. Closer to his men.

The gunners at first refused. They wouldn't be responsible for the "friendly fire" death of some of their own. No, the gunners vowed to keep their rounds far off from A Company.

Loose demanded again that they bring the fire in closer. "The snipers are going to creep in and keep firing until we're all dead if you don't take them out."

A German grenade exploded in the foxhole next to Will's. Will jumped with the explosion.

Closer now, the Germans flung grenades at them. It wouldn't be long until one hit the spot where Will clutched his knife, the only useful weapon in his possession.

Loose yelled into the radio once more for artillery support.

Soon shells rained between the Germans and the foxholes where Will and the others hid.

Their cover artillery fell closer and closer in a tight circle around their position.

Will's guts wrenched with each grenade explosion. His body jerked back as the artillery rounds peppered the ground nearer and nearer to where he crouched in the foxhole. One came within five yards of Will.

Loose screamed into the radio that the last round was close enough.

"Damn near gave me a haircut," one of the men beside Will said.

The barrage of grenades fell silent. The artillery finally succeeded in backing off the Germans.

After two endless days and nights of fighting, a bleary-eyed Will realized Riva Ridge was secure.

"You," Loose pointed at Will, "get to the medic. Your arm's a bloody mess."

7

Will headed back to the ridge to rejoin his platoon after getting bandaged up at the medic shelter.

Lieutenant Loose sent Will off again, this time to escort a German officer down to where other German POWs were held.

Will hated to leave the troops. Being with the guys he'd trained with at Camp Hale gave him more comfort than being restocked with ammo and having a full canteen.

The assault on Mount Belvedere was set for tonight. Will needed to hustle to deliver the prisoner and get back before dark. He wanted a front-row seat to witness the firepower.

Underbrush snaked across the trail Will followed on Mount Serrasiccia. The path dipped below tree line and crossed through a stand of chestnut and oak trees.

Every creak of boughs weighed down by snow and ice, or shudder of snow falling from its perch, made Will jump.

The German, a good ten years older than Will, walked ahead of him. The man didn't act startled at the sounds, which made Will all the more nervous.

Fog settled in over the mountains again. Cold and damp. The mist hid everything more than a few paces beyond the German.

The Nazi officer stopped walking. One of his boots had gotten tangled in the twisting vines. He twisted and tugged his leg to dislodge it.

Cursing in German, the man bent to use his hands to free his foot.

Will stood still, his gun trained on the prisoner crouched ahead.

"Ah," the German said with satisfaction in his voice. He spun upward, flung a knife at Will, and rolled off to the side.

Will fired his rifle.

The bullet hit the German's midsection.

The knife pierced Will's right arm.

The blade jutted out from Will's bicep. Blood appeared around the wound and stained his jacket. The only good thing was that the blood seeped, not spurted.

Will trained his gun on the injured German and walked closer until the nose of his rifle stopped one foot from his enemy's head.

"You don't want to do that," said a man's voice to his right, from somewhere in the trees. He spoke with accented English. German? Italian?

Will pointed his gun in the direction of the voice. Only shadowy trees loomed in front of him, and beyond that, the fog obscured everything.

"Come out where I can see you." Will's eyes darted around. He focused on the sounds. The German's labored inhalations. His own quick, shallow breaths. "Come out, I said."

"Don't shoot me."

"Well, don't shoot me either," Will said.

The man in the woods laughed. "If that is what I wished, you would now be dead."

"I won't shoot." Will aimed his gun in the direction of the man's voice. "Come out."

The crunch of boots moved through the bramble and snow. Will held his breath.

A man with a slight build appeared from the trees. He wore a black stocking hat, a patched brown jacket, and U.S. issue army pants. His face was ruddy, not fair like the German who lay wounded at Will's feet.

The stranger held his rifle in ready position, pointed toward Will's chest.

"Who do you fight for?" Will said. His right leg trembled.

"Italy," the man said. "I am a partisan who fights for the freedom of Italy."

"We're on the same side. Let's both lower our guns." Will stared at the Italian's gun while he inched the barrel of his rifle down.

The Italian edged closer and nodded at Will after both of their guns pointed at the earth.

The partisan pulled out a Beretta pistol and shot the German in the face.

Will jerked away from the noise of the blast. The grenades that burst around him the night before on the ridge still reverberated inside his head like a church bell.

Will gaped at the bloody mess, once a face. True, he wanted to kill the man who had attacked him, but not like that.

Will glared at the Italian. "Why did you do that? You told me not to shoot him."

The Italian grinned. "Because I wanted to kill him myself. Germans don't take Italian prisoners. If they do, it is only to use them in their labor camps."

The Italian pointed at the knife that stuck out of Will's arm. "This is not good."

A wave of nausea passed over Will. His face flushed with heat. He must control the bleeding fast, he realized, or he'd pass out.

The Italian pointed to his hiding spot in the trees. "We can help you. Supplies."

The Italian held out his hand, palm up, and gestured to Will's gun.

Will was too light-headed and weak to dispute handing over his weapon.

The Italian slung Will's rifle over his shoulder. He moved to Will's left side—the one only nicked by a bullet—and wrapped one arm around Will's waist to help him walk.

The fog and trees provided cover for another three partisans. Their supplies were limited but included a flask of a bitter, strong drink they called "grappa."

One of the men removed his jacket and shirt and tore the latter into strips to bind Will's wound. The man who killed Will's prisoner jerked the knife out of Will's arm with one swift movement. Another man held pressure against the wound, and they bound his arm with the strips of cloth.

A few swigs of grappa backed down Will's nausea.

The crack of a bullet ripped through the air. The projectile whirred by and hit a tree. A volley of shots in rapid succession from deep in the woods sent them all to the ground.

The first partisan looked at Will and mouthed one word.

"Germans."

8

Three volleys of return fire stopped the Germans' attack.

Will and the partisans didn't talk or move for ten minutes. One of the Italians crept toward where the Germans took cover.

The man who had found Will knelt beside him with his hand extended. "I am Anthony."

Will shook the man's hand. "Will."

A bird call rang out. The Italians all looked in the direction of the sound.

"Our sign. The Germans left."

The partisans stood and readied themselves to leave. Anthony explained that he and his friends had a truck hidden nearby. They would take Will to Lucca where Will could reunite with the U.S. soldiers.

A group of American soldiers were camped in Lucca, but Will's platoon was on the mountain. He needed to be with them, and Will tried to explain this to Anthony.

"You do not have the strength to hike up there," Anthony said.

Anthony helped Will to his feet. He looped his arm around Will's middle to take the American's weight against himself.

The man who had left to scout the Germans rejoined them, and they moved downhill without speaking.

The lead man stopped and held up one hand. He pointed to the closest trees with abrupt movements.

Anthony pulled Will sideways and deposited him behind an oak tree.

Machine gun fire reverberated around them. Bullets slammed into the trees and brush.

The partisans returned fire, using trees as cover. Anthony pushed Will's gun into his hands.

Will lay prone on the snow-covered ground, his rifle ready to shoot. He couldn't see the enemy. Will propped himself up on his elbows.

His right arm seared with pain like someone stuck it with a blazing poker. He tried to steady himself in spite of his uneven breaths. He squinted over the gun's sight, looking for movement or a flash from a gun.

The telltale flash sparked. Will squeezed the trigger. Once. Twice.

The German responded with answering shots.

A bullet gashed Will's left leg. He gritted his teeth. The pain and loss of blood would soon take him out of the fight.

He slowly inhaled and exhaled one deep breath to steady himself. Tiny adjustment right. Fire. Small adjustment left. Fire.

Silence.

Will heard the pop of a gun. He felt the force of the bullet slam into his left leg, high on the thigh.

His cheek slammed against the cold, frozen snow.

9

Will's eyes fluttered open. The compact shape of conical trees rose above him, backlit by the moon.

His nostrils flared with a scent that reminded him of the pines, spruces, and fir trees that grew all over the Rockies. Here, a different but pleasant fragrance lingered. Cedar?

Will's mind flashed to lying on the snow behind an oak tree. He remembered the sensation of moving and a hard surface under his back. The sound of an engine. The cold night air.

Where was he now? His hand touched cool dirt beneath him.

He tried to cough but moaned with the pain. Will moved his fingers, toes, arms, and then legs. He sucked in his breath when pain shot through one leg. He reached down with his hand, hoping to find his limb.

A splint covered his leg. Gunfire must have hit his limb.

He thanked God that everything seemed to work. Some parts hurt more than others, but he could tolerate pain if all the pieces were still attached and working.

He explored his wounds with his hands. Both arms had been wounded, one worse than the other. Will remembered the bullet and the knife that hit his arms.

A bandage on one cheek. Bandages and a splint on his whole left leg. He closed his eyes and tried to remember what happened. It came back to him in little pieces, like when he fed his dog one tiny treat at a time.

Anthony and the partisans. Attacked by Germans in the woods among chestnut and oak trees. Had he taken out the machine gunner?

Will's eyes canvassed his surroundings.

"You are awake." A woman's soft voice uttered the words.

Will wet his parched lips with his tongue. "Please. Water."

A girl about his age with fine-boned features knelt over him. She wore a black stocking hat that hid her hair, with eyes as dark as night.

Will figured her for an Italian, given how her skin looked tanned in winter.

The girl put her hand on the back of his neck. She tilted his head forward and brought a metal cup to his lips.

She was the prettiest sight he'd ever seen.

10

An unexpected wet kiss in the morning can signal a sexy start to the day.

Or the sign of a dreaded duty.

In this case, the warm breath and rough tongue that flicked up and down thirty-two-year-old Sophie Sparke's cheek was the latter.

Ugh. Bangor's breath was foul. It must be from the leftover bratwurst he ate before bed.

More insistent now, his tongue lapped her cheek, and he whined.

"OK, OK, I'm getting up." Sophie, five feet six inches tall with spunky brown eyes, rolled out of her side of the double bed.

She swept up her curly, long black hair into a ponytail. She plucked a sweatshirt off the floor and tugged it on over the yoga pants and T-shirt she wore to bed. Denver's nighttime temperatures, even in August, could be chilly.

Bangor's whining elevated in pitch.

No. Don't bark.

She bent over the bed and swooped Bangor, her seven-year-old, fifty-five-pound English bulldog, into her arms.

He rubbed his head against her chest and the ever-present drool smeared across her sweatshirt. Sophie slid her feet into slippers, grabbed her key ring, and headed for the door.

In the hallway, Bangor fidgeted in her arms. His wiggling required both arms to hold him. She couldn't latch the door.

"Easy, fella," she said, and gently set him down next to her. She turned to fasten the lock and Bangor, hearing a noise in her neighbor's apartment, let his vocal cords loose.

Bangor stood up. He faced the offending door and barked.

"Shhh, Bangor. I'm almost done."

As quickly as he had started his protective assault on the unseen person next door, Bangor stopped barking.

His head tilted toward Sophie, and he looked at her with his big, sorrowful brown eyes.

The lock clicked. Sophie squatted to lift Bangor.

The only problem was that he squatted first. The smelly remnants of his bratwurst plopped on the hallway floor.

"Can't you control your mongrel?" Will Mills said in his gravelly voice.

Mr. Mills, Sophie's elderly neighbor, was wide awake. He wore what Sophie assumed to be his nighttime attire of boxer shorts and a crew-neck T-shirt, which at one time had been white.

His narrow face, squeezed between his two large ears, bore signs of two things Sophie understood well: lack of sleep and eyes that had cried until no more tears could be found.

"You know what tomorrow brings. Tonight of all nights your dog decides to dump by my doorstep," Mr. Mills said.

Mr. Mills's silver and gray hair, usually styled with a conservative side part, was tousled and stretched his height, yet he stood a full inch shorter than Sophie.

"I'm sorry," Sophie said.

She bent over the dropping and scooped it up with her hand inside one of the plastic bags she carried when walking Bangor. She cleaned the floor with a disinfectant wipe she brought for emergencies such as this, dropped it into the bag, and knotted the top. The sealed bag, however, didn't muffle the odor.

"I'll disinfect the floor a second time when I return, but I better take him outside first."

"Outside?" He gave a disgusted grunt. "It looks to me like you're a little late."

What a crotchety old man.

Sophie sighed. "I said I was sorry."

"There oughtta be a law against people having pets in apartment buildings, damn it."

"Dogs are allowed in the covenants, and you know it. Bangor is old for his breed. Just because a dog, or a person, is old," she said, glaring at the man who had to be north of eighty, "you don't give up on them. Do you, Mr. Mills?"

He lowered his eyes.

Sophie gently picked up Bangor and held the plastic bag with her other hand. When she stood, he stared at her.

"Is that how your parents taught you to speak to elders?"

Sophie's breath caught. Tears welled in her eyes at the thought of her parents. She shook her head and choked out the word. "No."

Mr. Mills retreated into his apartment and closed the door behind him.

Sophie threw the bag into the trash barrel and led Bangor to the grassy slope next to the building. She let him wander over the grass, still damp from the sprinklers. He squatted and attempted to relieve himself twice. He whined with pain on each attempt.

Sophie cried. *Please, don't let him die. I can't bear to lose him, too.*

She returned to her apartment and offered Bangor some water, but he was too exhausted to drink. He fell asleep in her bed with loud, shaking snores, a prelude to his record-setting drool.

The snores made him sound OK, but Sophie suspected that something more than greasy bratwurst caused Bangor's GI distress.

She wiped the hallway floor with a mixture of bleach and water, dried it, and then locked the door behind her for the third time that night—the third trip outside for Bangor. She flopped on the bed next to Bangor and, with her head buried in her arms, let her silent tears flow.

Sophie's crying slowed and she got up, rinsed her face, and took a sip of water. She chided herself. She had to be strong. No more tears.

Notes to self:

Don't ever buy bratwurst.

Be kind to the grouchy old man next door. His problems are worse than mine.

11

Russ, Sophie's ex-boyfriend, loved German food, especially bratwurst, and copious volumes of beer to wash it down.

The day before, she pretended Russ had placed every sketchy-looking leftover in her refrigerator, even though they broke up months ago. This approach helped her clean her refrigerator with gusto. She slam-dunked the leftovers into her waste can with appropriate fist-pumps and celebration.

One stray package of frozen bratwurst left from her days with Russ had escaped her frenzied cleaning and ended up as dinner for her and Bangor.

Russ Grant, age 36, her boyfriend of two years—now her ex—was a V.I.P. at work and the boss's son. Mr. Grant, Russ's father, owned Grand Properties, one of the leading real estate companies in the United States.

Her former boyfriend's status and potential wealth weren't why she fell in love with him, though.

Russ, handsome in a not over-the-top way, oozed confidence. Women stared at him, with his mischievous brown eyes, wavy brown hair, and close-fitting custom suits.

Sophie fell in love with him because he—the sought-after bachelor—wanted her.

Their chemistry in the bedroom? Well, maybe not as great as she expected, but at least good. Some things took practice, right?

Russ was perfect for her.

Perfect, that is, until he broke her heart and said he met someone else.

⌒⌒

Sophie walked around the tiny one-bedroom apartment. The white walls that looked fresh and clean when she moved in now seemed cold and lonely.

Her gaze wandered to the photo of herself on top of Torreys Peak, one of Colorado's fourteen-thousand-foot mountains, attached to the refrigerator door. Sophie's lips curled up in a smile.

She and Russ hiked two 14ers that day, Grays and then its sister peak, Torreys. The photo showed her flushed and beaming, with a panoramic view of mountains and valleys behind her.

When Russ had told her he planned to "bag" all the 14ers, she quipped that she could climb any 14er anytime she wanted.

That was a tiny fault of Sophie's. Something in her made her shoot off her mouth and claim skills and capabilities she didn't possess. He made her prove her boast by taking her up to Grays and Torreys peaks the following weekend, which resulted in this photo.

She proved her ability to scale a mountain. Sophie climbed to the top of both peaks without complaining once, though her new hiking boots caused blisters on both heels and she got light-headed from the altitude.

Sophie loved this picture. She stood with pride on top of Torreys Peak. No Russ anywhere to be seen. When he broke up with her, she tore the photo in half and threw away the piece with him.

Sophie got more than her pretty face, quick mouth, and spunky nature from her maternal Italian grandmother.

Nonna, her grandmother, had displayed a similar picture in a frame on the sideboard in her dining room. Dressed in a pretty white dress with floor-length cascades of lace on the skirt, Nonna smiled, all alone, at the camera.

Nonna caught her first husband sleeping with another woman and chased the two out of her house.

Her grandmother got that marriage annulled in short order and divorced him. Nonna, considered quite a catch at the time, married Sophie's grandfather one year after the divorce was final.

Sophie's feisty grandmother had torn her ex-husband out of her wedding picture. She placed the jagged-edged half-picture in a gold frame and displayed it with pride. "I'm not ashamed of my past," Nonna said.

Sophie wasn't ashamed of her past, either. She refused to give up her job even though staying meant she had to see that snake, Russ, in the hallways.

Sophie yawned. She sank, exhausted, onto the bed next to Bangor.

Flopping side to side, sleep eluded her.

Visions from her past danced around her.

The next day she would do the right thing. She'd made a commitment and intended to honor it.

Her throat constricted and her mouth filled with stale air, the telltale signs she was about to be sick.

Sophie ran to the bathroom.

After rinsing her face and mouth, Sophie brushed her teeth. She looked in the mirror.

Can I really do this?

12

Sophie's exhaustion eventually won over her anxiety, and she fell asleep, only to be soon awakened by her ringing cellphone. Light spilled into the room through the pale green cotton curtains.

Sophie glanced at her phone and groaned. *Russ.* Not only did she not want to talk to him about travel arrangements for his latest out-of-town buyer, but she saw the time.

She was late.

Sophie rolled out of her bed into a stand. "Can't talk. I'm running late." Her curiosity got to her. "Why are you calling me?"

Russ chuckled. "Good morning to you, too."

Sophie gritted her teeth and made a face at the phone.

Russ spoke again in that smooth voice of his. "I'm calling for my father. He didn't have your number and wants to meet you in his office this afternoon at three."

Sophie hated Russ, but she respected Mr. Grant. A meeting with the CEO wasn't optional.

She spoke without thinking about what effect the morning's events would have on her. "I'll be there at three."

"What are you late for other than work? Do you have to take Bang somewhere?"

How dare he assume my only social engagements involve my pet?

And it's Bangor. My dog's name is Bangor, not Bang.

Sophie swallowed the sharp words she wanted to fling at him. "Gotta go." She tossed her phone on the bed.

She was seriously late now.

Sophie checked her purse for the essentials: wallet, lip gloss, comb, and tissues. The sight of a blue passport inside her bag made her think of something else for a moment—her road trip to Niagara Falls next month.

In a few weeks, she and Bangor would head east in her Mazda MX-5 Miata. A few months ago, Sophie splurged on the convertible when she decided to take the cross-country trip.

Her quick mouth got her into trouble then, too. Of course she drove a manual shift, she told the salesman.

The truth? Sophie had no clue how it all worked.

She went home and watched an online video multiple times that night.

The next day, when Sophie sat behind the wheel of the Mazda, she got nervous. The salesman stood next to her, beaming with the joy of a new-car commission. He didn't help her confidence.

She recited the video instructions to herself. The night before, Sophie performed each step in her apartment until she could do them without thinking.

Her hands caressed the steering wheel and she imagined her road trip. *You can do this.*

Press in the clutch with the left foot. Compress the brake with the right foot.

Put the car in first gear. Release the hand brake. Ease her right foot from the brake to the accelerator and press slowly, watching the tachometer.

The engine purred to life. *This is easy.*

The tach needle went from 1,000 to 1,500 to 2,000. The engine revved louder.

The tachometer kept rising.

Sophie tightened her grip on the steering wheel and snapped her foot off the clutch.

The car shuddered and the engine died.

The red heat of shame flushed over her face. Sophie forgot one thing: she should have released the clutch slowly while she pressed on the accelerator.

The salesman coughed, his hand shielding his laugh. He approached the car to offer his suggestions, but Sophie declined his help.

It took three more attempts before the car moved forward in first gear. She drove to the parking lot of a discount store half a block away, never shifting out of first.

In the parking lot, she had practiced starts, stops, and shifting until she was ready for the streets.

She glanced at the old Minnie Mouse alarm clock on her nightstand. *Time to shower. Now.*

Sophie rushed to the closet and pulled out her conservative black dress, the only black dress she owned. She laid it on the bed next to Bangor, her purse, and her phone. She dashed into the shower.

The warm water doused Sophie, but it did no good.

The black dress brought back the memories that haunted her last night.

Putting on the black dress that some adult bought.

Sitting in the church.

The freezing rain at the cemetery.

The double caskets.

The chills from the night before returned and marched with staccato feet over her face, down her arms, and across her spine.

Sophie leaned her head against the hard, cold tile of the shower. She closed her eyes.

13

Mr. Mills had intercepted her four days ago. His arms crossed his chest and a scowl darkened his face.

The night before, Bangor had barked nonstop for two hours.

Mr. Mills vowed to report Bangor to the apartment management company.

He informed her this would be Bangor's third warning, which carried a steep fine and potential eviction.

Mr. Mills gave her an out. He offered her a deal. She could drive him Friday morning, he said, and he wouldn't report Bangor.

Today was Friday. Her day to chauffeur Mr. Mills.

Her neighbor stood in the hall by his apartment, proud and erect in a crisp military uniform. Four brass buttons closed the jacket over his chest, with another fastening each pocket.

"I didn't know you were a veteran."

He nodded. "World War II. Tenth Mountain Division."

Sophie's eyes widened. The legendary Tenth Mountain Division ski troop's grueling training took place in the frigid, high peaks of Colorado.

She'd seen a statue of a soldier with skis over his shoulder when Russ drove her up to Vail on the one weekend they went away together.

"The ski troops?"

"Yes. Now are you ready or not? We're late."

She put her hand on his arm. "How are you doing?"

"How do you think I'm doing?" He clamped his jaw shut and glowered at her. "Your dog's barking kept me awake last night." He blinked his red, puffy eyes. "And today I have to bury my wife."

Sophie suspected crying over his wife's death and mourning her loss kept him awake rather than Bangor, but she didn't argue.

"We can go in my car." She held out her hand to him. "Do you need help going down the stairs?"

"Hell, no, I don't need help. You go on ahead and fetch the car from the lot. You can pull it up to the front."

Sophie nodded. She stepped across the landing and walked to the staircase.

"If he barks tonight, I'm reporting that damn dog tomorrow!"

Would the man ever quit?

The funeral service for Marie was in a Presbyterian church not far from their apartment building.

Sophie had been raised Catholic by her Italian mother but drifted away from church attendance when she went to boarding school.

Churches—like funerals—brought back memories best left buried in the dank, dark earth.

A handful of elderly women dotted the pews. A dozen men with weather-aged faces—in their seventies, Sophie guessed—sat together behind Sophie and Mr. Mills. Only these few senior citizens, the pallbearers provided by the church, Mr. Mills, and Sophie attended the service.

Sophie had never visited a Presbyterian church but found the short service a gentle ushering of Marie into the next life.

Her neighbor stared at the casket, with his back straight and shoulders squared. He didn't sing the hymns or bow his head in prayer. He exhibited as much emotion as the hard wooden pew they sat on.

A group of women from the church hosted a punch and cookie reception after the service in the community hall. Mr. Mills stood at the entrance to the room and greeted each of the funeral attendees. He introduced everyone to Sophie with a strained, quiet voice.

The men, to Sophie's surprise, were members of the "Over the Hill Gang," a group of senior downhill skiers.

Will was a member of the group, one of the men explained, but her neighbor had stopped skiing the black diamond runs with the other elite skiers when he turned eighty-eight.

Eighty-eight. Sophie had no clue Mr. Mills was pushing ninety. He delivered his harsh criticisms of Bangor with the caustic wit and enthusiasm of someone younger.

"Thank you for coming today," Sophie said to the elderly men of the ski club. "Your presence means a great deal to Mr. Mills. It's hard for him to express his emotions today."

Her neighbor scowled at her. "Speak for yourself, Missy," he said in a gruff voice.

Sophie's face reddened, in both embarrassment and anger.

"We're sorry about Marie, Will," one of the skiers said. "She was a peach to put up with you. Even though that damned disease stole her away years ago, you're sure gonna miss her."

Will gave a terse nod in response.

Sophie studied her neighbor's face. Tears brought a glaze to his eyes. He turned his head away from his skier friends and wiped his eyes with a white, folded cotton handkerchief.

Another man cuffed Will on his shoulder. "We'll expect you on the slopes with us again this year. Nothing is holding you back now."

Mr. Mills stepped back, in retreat. "We'll see. I won't promise anything."

The skier shook Will's hand. "That's good enough for today. Just think about it. It's three months until the slopes open." The group moved on to the reception. Sophie saw them stacking their plates high with homemade goodies.

Mr. Mills stared at his friends.

He muttered in a quiet voice. "I may not be here when the snow flies."

14

Following the reception, the minister, pallbearers, Mr. Mills, and Sophie accompanied the body of Marie Mills to Fort Logan National Cemetery.

Sophie had attended only one funeral before. She dreaded the graveside service, but at least it wasn't raining. She swallowed hard and followed the hearse.

Will had refused to pay for a limousine. It was a waste of money, he told Sophie, which was why he bribed her to drive him.

At Fort Logan Cemetery, Sophie drove past rows of engraved white headstones, perfectly aligned front to back and at crisscross angles. Row after row, the simple, curved-top markers lined the cemetery.

Pulling up next to the newly dug grave, Sophie drew in a deep breath and gritted her teeth. She could do this. She had to do it, for Mr. Mills.

Her heart pounded in her chest. She moved to help her neighbor out of the car, but he climbed out too quickly for assistance.

Sophie had never met Marie. Mrs. Mills relocated to an Alzheimer's unit before Sophie moved into the building.

At the grave, the widower refused to sit. He stood telephone-pole straight, his hands rigid by his sides.

The minister finished the final prayer and turned to the widower and Sophie. "Are there any words you would like to say as we send Marie to her final resting place?"

Sophie gulped. She didn't expect to have any duties today other than to drive her neighbor.

Mr. Mills snapped to a military salute. After his hand returned to his side, he quarter-turned and marched toward Sophie's car.

Sophie gulped. She had to say something.

"You can rest, Mrs. Mills. God bless you." Her years of Catholic school kicked in, and her hand moved in the sign of the cross.

Sophie murmured a quick thank-you to the minister and scurried to her car.

On the ride back to their apartment building, Mr. Mills stared straight ahead. Neither one spoke.

I did my part. We made a deal.

Sophie followed Mr. Mills up the stairs. She decided to microwave a box of macaroni and cheese for herself before heading to the office to meet Mr. Grant. Macaroni and cheese, one of the few dishes she attempted in the kitchen, would be the perfect comfort food to banish all thoughts of funerals from her head.

Mr. Mills stopped in front of his door and turned to face Sophie. "I want you to come inside with me. There's something of Marie's I want to give you."

Sophie looked at her watch. She didn't have much time to spend with the grouchy old man, and she didn't want to be late for her meeting with the boss.

"May I come over tomorrow? You must be exhausted."

"You're in a hurry to ditch me. Don't worry, I'll be quick." He opened his apartment door and motioned for Sophie to enter first.

The man buried his wife today, and now he wanted to give Sophie something that had belonged to her. Sophie had no choice.

Two things surprised her about the apartment.

First, Mr. Mills's apartment was cleaner than the models set up to entice people to rent in a brand-new building.

Second, the delicate ivory lace curtains, brocade side chairs, and floral love seat in shades of pink and green froze the apartment in the past, when the late Marie selected them.

"Sit." He gestured to one of the side chairs. Without seeing if she followed his direction, he walked into the bedroom.

Sophie sat, ankles crossed, hands folded over her lap. She didn't usually sit in this manner, but somehow, this chair from another era required formal posture.

Mr. Mills re-entered the room with one hand held before him. He lowered his hand, palm up, in front of her.

Sophie gasped. A necklace rested on his palm. A silver chain held an enormous, sparkly, pear-shaped, bluish-gray gem.

"It's a sapphire. I gave this necklace to Marie for our fortieth wedding anniversary. It's the color of her eyes."

His hand, still cradling the necklace, jutted toward her. "I want you to have this."

Sophie shook her head. "Oh, I couldn't." The variation of color in the gem captivated her. She had never seen a more vibrant sapphire.

"Say thank you and take the necklace. Now." He offered her this lovely gift with a tone more suited to banishing her from his sight.

Sophie glanced up at her neighbor. The determined expression on his face convinced her. He wasn't giving her a choice.

She gently picked up the necklace and cradled it in her hand. The elderly man backed away, to allow Sophie to stand.

What words adequately expressed gratitude for this extraordinary gift from a man she hardly knew? Sophie smiled. "Thank you, Mr. Mills."

He nodded.

"How long were you and Marie married?"

"Seventy-three years." His voice broke. "Damn. I wanted to make seventy-five." He turned away and rubbed the tears from his face.

Mr. Mills crossed the room to the entry door. He turned to face Sophie.

He studied her face like a detective cross-examining a suspect. "A few weeks ago you blathered on the phone outside my door to that slick boyfriend of yours. Something about booking airline flights and hotels. That's what you do at that job you complain to him about, right?"

Now that remark was objectionable on several levels. *Slick boyfriend?* He eavesdropped on her conversations with Russ, who was definitely not her boyfriend. *Not anymore.*

Mr. Mills also accused her of complaining. Sophie might be naïve, or cautious about the unknown, but one thing she had never been was a complainer.

Where should she start to rebut his accusations? She held out the necklace.

"You can have this back. We obviously do not see eye to eye on just about anything. I don't want your wife's necklace."

"I gave the necklace to you. Now be quiet and gracious, and answer my question. You're a travel agent, aren't you?"

Sophie placed the necklace on the entry table and, with effort, peeled her eyes away from the stunning jewel. She looked at Mr. Mills. "No, I'm not. I handle the travel arrangements for my employer and our clients."

He grunted. "Finding a travel agent these days is about like finding a man who changes the oil in his own car. Damn near impossible."

The timing of this question baffled Sophie. "Why do you ask?"

"I want to fly to Italy to find my wife."

15

Sophie's eyes widened with shock. *Mr. Mills wants to go to Italy to find his wife? We buried his wife of seventy-three years not more than two hours ago.*

She could only manage one word. "What?"

Mr. Mills opened the entry door. "Get on to whatever you're doing that is so damned important. You can come by later tonight or tomorrow for your necklace. We can talk about my trip to Italy then."

Sophie wanted an explanation, but even leaving now, she might be late for the meeting with Mr. Grant.

Sophie waved at the office receptionist and made a beeline for her cubicle. She grabbed a notepad, pen, and her laptop and rushed to Mr. Grant's office.

Mr. Grant and his wife had cruised from Venice to Greece and several of its magical islands last year. Sophie made all the arrangements and enjoyed every minute of the planning.

The company's owner assigned the penthouse corner office to himself, of course, and furnished the room with soft leather chairs, a commanding mahogany desk, and bookcases behind him. Sophie loved his office.

Most of all, she loved the full Front Range view of the Colorado Rockies.

She walked into Mr. Grant's office. He looked up from the paperwork on his desk. "Hello, Sophie. Would you mind closing the door?"

The entire office practiced an open-door culture. *Had Russ persuaded his father to fire me?*

She closed the door and walked, eyes lowered, to one of the high-backed chairs in front of his desk. She eased herself down on the supple leather.

Be brave. She looked up at her boss. Startled, her eyes widened. *If he's going to fire me, why is he smiling?*

"Sophie, I want you to work on a confidential assignment for me."

Sophie exhaled. She leaned forward. "Of course, I'll help. Where are you headed?"

"Not me." He rubbed his palms together. "Mrs. Grant and I are giving Russ and Angela a honeymoon fit for a prince and princess."

Sophie gulped.

"I want you to make all the travel arrangements, but you can't tell anyone, especially Russ. I want to surprise them. I've told him we'll pay for the honeymoon as part of their wedding gift, but I want to keep the details secret from the lovebirds."

Lovebirds.

Sophie steadied herself. She asked in a level tone, "When do you think they'll set the date of the wedding?"

"Everything's set. Angela's parents reserved a prestigious venue for the wedding and reception. The block of hotel rooms for the guests is locked down, too. The wedding will be Labor Day weekend next year."

He chuckled. "Russ said he liked Labor Day weekend because after the wedding, his darling Angela will never need to labor, except when having his babies."

Sophie felt queasy, and her mouth filled with dry, suffocating air.

If the lovebirds found time to investigate and book everything for the wedding, they've probably been planning this for a year.

Russ broke up with me the day before Christmas. How could they have fallen in love so quickly and gotten all this arranged? Sought-after venues are booked a year or more in advance.

The truth slapped her in the face. Russ started dating Angela long before he broke up with Sophie.

Sophie stood and smoothed out the creases in her skirt.

Her anger kept her voice steady. "Booking a honeymoon trip is outside of my expertise. I will find two highly regarded travel planners and give you their names."

"Sophie, you know Russ better than most people. I'd consider this a significant personal favor if you'd handle the arrangements."

"I can't do it." She took one backward step toward the door.

His eyes narrowed. "Can't or won't?"

"Both." Sophie turned and walked to the door.

Mr. Grant spoke to her retreating form. "You would be wise to reconsider—right now—before you walk out that door."

Sophie turned to face him. "I quit."

16

The next morning, in spite of her sleepless night, Sophie jumped out of bed. She hoped the veterinarian could give her tips on how to care for a bulldog with bowel issues—both for her sake and Bangor's.

The bulldog's bathroom needs had risen over the last month. A week ago, she booked an appointment with Bangor's vet.

Bangor acted as though he were the one without sleep. She carried him in her arms.

Light pooled beneath Mr. Mills's door. Sophie tiptoed by his apartment. She couldn't stand to hear her neighbor launch into a tirade on how to train her dog.

What an angry old man. He may not be a dog lover, but why does he take every opportunity to chastise me?

Sophie touched Bangor's nose—warm and dry, not a good sign. When she scratched his head between his ears, he didn't open his eyes or grunt in satisfaction. No wag of his tail, either.

Sophie sighed with worry. *What is wrong with Bangor?*

Sophie stood beside Bangor in the vet's "dog" room. A bulletin board on the wall displayed thank-you notes and photos of grateful dog owners nuzzling their four-legged family members.

Bangor stood on the raised examination platform. His body trembled with fear.

He usually liked his vet visits, for the new smells in the waiting room and the treat he received while she paid the bill. Not today. When they approached the office front door, Bangor pulled back on the leash and whined.

Does Bangor sense this visit is different from a routine check-up?

Sophie stroked his back and spoke in a soft, comforting voice. "It'll be OK, Bangor. After we're done here, you'll be better."

She prayed this visit would make her words come true.

The veterinarian, a plump, middle-aged man with laugh wrinkles that framed his eyes, entered the exam room. "Good to see you, Sophie. So our buddy here is having some difficulties, is he?"

Sophie recounted the progression of Bangor's GI issues while the vet examined and gently palpated Bangor. When he pressed against Bangor's belly, the miserable dog whimpered.

"I'd like to do an ultrasound on Bangor. We'll have a better idea of what's causing his problems."

Sophie suspected what that meant: a sizable bill and the possibility that something serious plagued Bangor.

She didn't hesitate. "Can you do it now? And may I stay with him during the exam? He'll be scared."

Sophie had two options for Bangor.

Choice one, with a low success rate given the metastases of the tumors, was expensive surgery. This option would cause pain and terror for Bangor, and Sophie couldn't have afforded enormous vet bills when she had a job, much less now.

Tears tumbled down her cheeks. She chose the second option.

Sophie made an appointment to put Bangor down on Monday.

17

Cancer riddled Bangor's body. Sophie carried him up the stairs to her apartment.

The vet recommended she offer Bangor as much water as he wanted, feed him warm rice, and give him two days of love.

Sophie returned to her apartment with puffy, red eyes. She cooed to Bangor, gave him his favorite dog treat, and moved him to her bed for a nap. Sophie stretched out on the bed next to her devoted dog, rested one palm on him, and cried. Bangor moaned and moved away from her hand. Her tears started anew.

She picked him up the way the vet did and positioned him on his doggie bed.

Sophie heard a knock on her apartment door. She opened it to find Mr. Mills, dressed in rumpled khaki slacks and a white V-neck undershirt.

"How's Bangor?" He had given his usual grimace the day off. Rather than demonstrate concern, however, his face held no expression.

"What?"

"Didn't you take that dog to the vet?"

The nosy neighbor had snooped on her again and listened to her phone calls. The typical sounds of life—voices, a dog's bark, water running, a cell phone ring—traveled through the thin apartment walls.

Her eyes welled with tears. "Tumors spread throughout Bangor's body. I need to put ... put him down."

Mr. Mills scowled. "Who was this vet you took him to?"

Sophie gave him the doctor's name and explained that the apartment manager had recommended him.

His scowl returned, and his tone was skeptical. "Hmph. I guess the vet might be OK."

"He was voted the top canine veterinarian in Denver the past three years." Sophie had noticed the framed magazine articles on the wall of the clinic's waiting room.

"Sorry to hear about Bangor." His words were proper, but his tone of voice sounded like she asked the time of day or directions to the restroom.

No wonder he's grouchy. He doesn't have a kind, empathetic bone in his body.

Her neighbor gave one dismissive nod, turned, and retreated into his apartment.

⌒

Sophie tossed and turned in her bed. Her eight trips outside with Bangor served as a depressing reminder of the appointment she faced on Monday.

On Sunday, when Bangor wasn't asleep, he exhibited rare good humor. He refused to eat but happily rewarded her with a steady stream of sloppy, wet kisses.

How can Bangor be loving and content when his body has betrayed him? Why does he act so happy? Isn't he hurting?

The nagging woodpecker of her conscience attacked all night.

Does Bangor have a chance to survive without the surgery?

Is putting Bangor down another thoughtless, selfish mistake that will forever haunt me?

18

On Monday morning, Sophie gave Bangor a bath and then took a shower to rid herself of the wet dog smell.

She stood in front of her closet and wondered what one wore to march her best friend to the death chamber. Sophie shuddered. She chewed on her lower lip and fought back the tears.

She looked in her closet and felt worse.

The closet still held the tight, low-cut dresses she bought during her days with Russ.

Sophie hated herself for changing her style to please Russ. She grabbed as many garments as she could hold, carried them out to the space that doubled as an eating area and a great room, and flung the clothes to the floor.

She returned to the closet, jerked the remaining "Russ" clothes out, and dumped them on the pile in front of her TV.

Sophie considered herself average in the looks department. She'd call herself pleasant-looking, maybe even pretty. Certainly not beautiful.

Her large brown eyes were the best feature in her oval face. Sophie was most comfortable in simple tops and T-shirts that didn't cling to her body.

She visualized an imaginary horizontal line halfway between her neck and her breasts. Except for her one cocktail dress, in her mind, the neckline of Sophie's shirts should not dip below the line of demarcation.

She eyed the heap of garments. She bought them because Russ admired those styles. Sophie thought they made her look like a lady of the night. A trip to Goodwill was on her docket. It would be more productive than curling up and crying over Bangor. Sophie nodded with satisfaction. Her closet looked bigger without the suggestive clothes in it.

The comfortable clothes she put on did nothing to lift the dark fog of her mood.

Sophie called for Bangor to join her for a ride. He trotted over to her and looked nothing like a dog headed for his last outing. She fought back tears.

Her neighbor surprised her. He stood in front of his apartment door with an unreadable expression on his face. Mr. Mills wore a pressed, long-sleeved plaid shirt, khaki slacks, and brown shoes that gleamed from a fresh polish.

"You're headed somewhere," Sophie said. "Go on ahead. I'm going to let Bangor walk out of here the last time on his own four legs."

"After you." He gestured for her to go ahead down

the stairs. "I'm going with you. You shouldn't have to be alone for this."

Sophie stared at him with shock.

"What?" Mr. Mills said. "What's so surprising? I had a dog myself once. Got hit by a car and died. Losing him tore me up for weeks."

He gave a curt nod and motioned to the staircase. "After you, Miss Sophie."

19

They pulled into the clinic's parking lot. Mr. Mills turned toward Sophie. "Should I stay in the car, remain in the waiting area, or come inside the exam room with you?"

"In the room with me, please, but maybe off to the side." She had never put a pet to sleep and didn't know what to expect.

He nodded.

In the dog room at the vet's office, Mr. Mills stood in the back. Sophie sat on the floor with Bangor and scratched her dog's favorite spots. She looked up when the door to the treatment area opened.

Her eyes widened as the doctor entered the examination room with a broad smile.

Her face heated with anger. *How dare the veterinarian forget the purpose of her appointment?*

"I've got great news, Sophie," the vet said.

"Do you mean Bangor's tumors won't kill him?"

The doctor knelt in front of her and petted Bangor. "If the tumors shrink, Bangor might have a chance. There are no approved drugs on the market that can reduce the size of his tumors. Surgery, as I explained Saturday, is risky because the growths are too diffuse in his abdomen."

His words confused Sophie.

"I made a few phone calls. A research team at Colorado State University is working with a prototype drug that might work to shrink the tumors."

Sophie sat up straighter. Her words rushed out. "Can we get this drug for Bangor?"

"No. We can't get it in the office. If Bangor participates in their study, though, they could try it on him."

"I will drive him up to Fort Collins and they can give Bangor the drug." Her voice rose with hope.

"It's not that simple, Sophie. The only way the CSU research program can give Bangor the drug is if you sign him over to them."

"What? I have to give Bangor to them?"

"Yes. For liability reasons. They received a research grant to study the use of this drug but can only treat animals the research lab owns. There is also a precondition that, absent the treatment, the subjects would be put down.

"Bangor would be medicated. He would not be in pain. If no positive results are seen, he'd be put down."

Sophie stroked Bangor's head. *Do I have the strength to sign away my ownership of Bangor and all rights to him? Can I, in good conscience, absolve CSU of any liability for whatever they do to Bangor? Can I bear to be absent when my best friend is ushered out of this life?*

Sophie leaned her head down until she was nose to nose with Bangor. She asked him what to do. *Is the pain too much, my friend? Or are you willing to endure it for a while longer for a chance to live?*

Sophie knew it was her decision and hers alone.

A hand reached down to stroke Bangor's back, a hand veined and spotted with age and exposure to the Colorado sun. "Are these good people in the CSU lab?"

"Absolutely," the vet said.

"Will they use Bangor as a pin cushion for their needles or run unnecessary tests or labs on him?"

"Never."

"Here's the big question." Mr. Mills's voice rose in volume. He sounded like he was grilling a raw Army recruit. "Can you promise Miss Sophie that Bangor will not suffer, either with this treatment or if they have to put him down because the drugs don't help?"

"I know the person well who is in charge of this study. I promise."

Sophie looked at the doctor and nodded. "I'll sign the forms."

After she completed the paperwork, the veterinarian encouraged Sophie to take as much time as she wanted. "Knock on the interior door when you're ready for us to take Bangor."

Sophie leaned down and rested her head against Bangor's still torso. His steady breath showed he clung to life. She had to do this for Bangor. It was his only chance.

She straightened to a sitting position and drew in a deep breath. Sophie felt Mr. Mills's calm hand on her shoulder.

He helped her to her feet. She walked to the door and knocked.

Bangor stood and padded over beside her. He leaned against Sophie's leg.

Tears spilled from her eyes.

The door opened. Sophie nodded to the tech and looked one more time at Bangor. "Good luck, buddy. I love you."

20

Mr. Mills insisted they stop at a diner on the way home. He ordered a slice of pie and a cup of black coffee. Sophie wanted only a glass of iced tea.

He let her speak first.

"Thank you for coming with me, Mr. Mills. I did need someone with me today."

He nodded.

The waitress brought his pie and their drinks.

She had a panicky thought. "Do you think, if Bangor gets better, they'd let me visit him?"

Mr. Mills scratched his chin. "It might take some time for them to run their tests, but I bet you can."

Her spirits rose a little. "Right. I'll call them in a week."

He shook his head. "You may want to give them a month. Let them try their drugs. Didn't the vet say they'll give you a report once a month?"

"Yes."

Mr. Mills focused on his pie, eating one slow, deliberate bite after another. "You can measure a restaurant by their apple pie. It's true."

Sophie sat in silence and stared at her iced tea. The monster in her belly tried to gnaw its way to freedom.

His fork clinked against the plate. "That's the way it is," Mr. Mills said.

She looked up at him. He had eaten his pie and drunk half his coffee.

"The way it is with pets." Mr. Mills fingered the handle of the coffee cup. "When you love a dog they are part of you forever. They grab onto a piece of you, and unless you find a way to deny that love, they're always there. Waiting to be reunited with you."

Sophie blinked. His face broadcast an intensity that caught her off-guard more than his words.

His expression and tone of voice made Sophie wonder if he spoke about loving a dog or a woman.

21

The next day, Sophie woke up from a fitful nap when someone knocked on her door.

Mr. Mills, dressed in the same plaid shirt and khaki slacks as the day before, stood in the hallway. "Thought somebody ought to check on you to make sure you're OK since you stayed home from work."

Will he ever stop spying on me?

She sighed. "I didn't sleep well last night."

"That's understandable." Mr. Mills inspected her face. "You're not sick with the flu or another contagious disease, are you?"

Sophie shook her head.

"Good. Why don't you come to my apartment for a snack? A nibble might get your mind off your dog."

Socialize with Mr. Mills? The prospect sounded as pleasant as letting a dentist attack her mouth with a drill. Sophie knew she needed to start moving out of her catatonic mourning for Bangor. His face showed sincere concern about her, as doubtful as that seemed.

She nodded. "Thank you. I haven't eaten all day."

She stood in front of his door thirty minutes later. The door opened before she knocked. The man anticipated her actions in an eerie way.

He invited her to sit at the round wooden kitchen table.

Mr. Mills stood behind one of the chairs. "Would you like a glass of water?"

"Yes, please."

Mr. Mills withdrew a glass from a tidy cupboard, filled it with water from the tap, and offered the tumbler to her.

Sophie thanked him.

"How about a snack? I have canned smoked oysters and saltine crackers. Would you like both?" Mr. Mills smiled like he had offered a delicacy.

Not the snack she expected. Cheese and crackers, and maybe a glass of wine, had been her hope. "Uh, yes. Thank you."

He nodded, extracted a box of crackers from the cupboard, and brought it to the table. He opened the can of oysters and put the can and a box of toothpicks on a plate. Mr. Mills grabbed paper napkins and two salad plates from the cupboard.

Simple hospitality, shaped by manners learned from his deceased wife, or perhaps his mother.

Mr. Mills motioned for Sophie to help herself.

Neither one spoke for a few minutes.

Her curiosity took control. "Mr. Mills, may I ask you something about an earlier conversation?"

He nodded. "Go on, Miss Sophie."

"Please tell me why you want to go to Italy."

"Will you help me if I do?"

"I'll make no promises, but I won't help you if you don't explain your reason for going."

Her neighbor lowered his chin and sat with his hands clenched in front of him.

Sophie attempted to hide her impatience. "Do you want to see something, or someone, specific when you go to Italy?"

"Yes."

Dammit, Sophie. Ask open-ended questions, not the kind deflected with a simple "yes" or "no."

Too tired and too emotional to play cat-and-mouse, she asked her burning question: "You're going to see a woman, aren't you?"

He nodded.

"Please tell me about her, Mr. Mills."

"You can call me Will." He pushed up from the table, walked to the bedroom, and returned with a faded black-and-white photograph.

He handed the photo with scalloped edges to Sophie. Some of her grandparents' photographs were on the same type of paper.

Will's photo featured a smiling young woman, perhaps 15 or 16, with long dark hair, a tiny waist, and a full-skirted dress. She leaned forward in a sexy pose over an outdoor bistro table in what appeared to be a European city.

Sophie turned over the photograph. Beautiful script revealed the name of the woman in the photo and the date it was taken: Francesca Polvani, June 7, 1945.

"You met Francesca during the war?"

"Yes. I met Francesca. And loved her."

Sophie spoke in a quiet voice. "And you married her in Italy?"

He shook his head. "Loved her, yes, but it was wartime. Impossible to have a wedding."

"I thought you told me she was your wife."

A shadowed, angry look took over his face. "When in the hell do you imagine I said that?"

"When we came back from the cemetery." As soon as she uttered the words, Sophie regretted them. The pain over losing Marie must boil in him underneath the surface.

"Hell, we buried my wife that morning. Don't you think I was half crazy at the time?"

"Of course. I'm sorry, Mr. Mills. I may have misheard you. It's been rough for us both."

He gave one curt nod and blinked. "It's Will. You should call me Will." His face had closed down like a stone wall surrounded it. The discussion ended, as did any questions about going to Italy to find Francesca.

Sophie studied the photograph. "This is Francesca? She's beautiful."

As quick as his defense had gone up, it disappeared. "A real beauty and full of spunk."

"What happened to her?"

Will shook his head. "I don't know. I left with my division."

"You want to find her now, all these years later?"

Will nodded.

Sophie tried to hide her judgment of the man who had buried his wife and only a few days later wanted to find an old love. She wondered if her neighbor's mental capacity had slipped.

He pulled another photograph from his shirt pocket. He handed the picture to Sophie.

The photo featured Francesca, but this time she was not in a sexy pose.

Here, Francesca had her hair piled up on top of her head in a haphazard way, the hairstyle of someone who had no time to tend to her appearance.

It was clear why she looked that way. In her arms, a fuller-faced Francesca held a bundled infant.

Will nodded. "She said the baby was mine."

22

Sophie looked at the young woman and infant in the picture. She forced herself to keep her voice level. "What do you think, Mr. Mills?"

"Will."

"Is it possible you fathered this child, Will?"

"Hell, I don't know. It's possible." His face reddened. He rubbed his eyes. "When I left Italy, I promised to come back to get her after the war. Everybody said that to their wartime girls." He bowed his head. "I was young, foolish, and full of myself."

"What happened?"

"I didn't know she carried a baby when I left. We were together only a short time."

"How did you meet?"

Will took a deep breath. "My division fought in the Apennine Mountains." A haunted look crept over his face. "Terrible, terrible fighting."

Sophie waited in silence.

He gazed out the window. "The officers pushed us hard. Climb up this godforsaken mountain, and if we were lucky enough to survive it, they'd have us snowshoe and ski down the next. Miserable conditions. We fought not only the Germans but also the weather."

He faced her with haunted eyes. "We lost scores of men on that mountain, and even more as the troop advanced. I was damn lucky to be alive."

He swallowed and spoke with slow, even-toned words. "I got separated from the others and wounded while marching a prisoner out of the mountains."

Sophie suspected Will never talked about his days in the war. She didn't speak, afraid he would stop talking if she said anything.

He looked at her and nodded. "Italian partisans took me with them to care for me."

"Lucky for you," Sophie said.

"Damn lucky. Francesca was the sister of the guy who found me, an Italian who'd been drafted by the Germans but refused to go. He hid in the woods and helped anyone who managed to escape from the camps."

"Did Francesca nurse you back to health?"

He smiled. "Best incentive ever to heal—a gorgeous, gun-toting babe as a makeshift nurse."

Sophie leaned forward over the table, eager to learn more.

"First, though, I needed to convince her to like me. She held no fondness for the Yanks. We bombed the harbor cities in Italy, you see."

He nodded with confidence.

Sophie imagined him as an eager young soldier. "You charmed her."

"I told her the truth. I fought in Italy to stop the Germans and to liberate the Italians."

Sophie smiled at the thought of her grouchy neighbor as a smooth-talking charmer in his youth. "Why did you leave her?"

"It was my duty to rejoin my unit, or at least the U.S. Army. The war ended, and then I was stateside again."

"When did you learn about Francesca's baby?"

"By the time I got these pictures in her letter, more than a year after the war ended, I had married Marie." Will shook his head. "It was too late."

She touched the back of his hand with her fingertips. "I'm sorry."

His voice grew softer. "I sent letters to the main church in the city where she mailed hers from. I wanted to send her money to help with the baby. I never got a second letter from Francesca."

"So you want to go to Italy now to find her and the child?"

Will nodded. "Will you make flight reservations for me? And whatever the hell else I need—trains, car, and hotels?"

Sophie studied his determined face. *Will has one more mission to complete.*

She hated to burst his bubble, but he missed the obvious. Sophie rested her palm on his forearm and spoke in a quiet voice, to cushion the sting of her words. "Do you have any idea where to even begin looking?"

"Hell, no. But I know for certain I won't find Francesca if I continue to rot away in this little apartment. The only way I can find her is to do the one thing I swore never to do when I left. I need to put my feet back on the ground in Italy and start turning up rocks."

A World War II veteran going to a country he visited over seventy years ago, searching for a virtual needle in the haystack? How can I let Will go on this harebrained journey?

"Who will go with you?" Sophie asked.

"Not a damn soul."

23

Sophie's mobile phone rang. It was the office, the place she used to work until she quit in a huff. Sophie excused herself and stepped out into the hall.

"The company will mail your last check," said Emily from the HR department. "I want to verify your address. Because you didn't turn in your resignation with proper advance notice, you will forfeit your accrued unused vacation and bonus."

Sophie's meager savings would now have to pay her bills while she looked for a new job.

She had whispered her plan to Bangor every night. The two of them would take a long, winding road trip up the East Coast, all the way to his namesake, Bangor, Maine.

Tape held a picture of a pretty red-and-white-striped lighthouse to her bathroom mirror. The magazine photo represented their last East Coast stop: a lighthouse, the ocean, and a park for Bangor to play in.

After visiting the lighthouse, they would drive west to Niagara Falls and Canada, an opportunity to use her new passport.

Now, Bangor was gone, and with him, her dream.

She returned to Will's kitchen with tears in her eyes.

A map of Italy covered the table. Will hummed and drew tiny circles with a pencil around several towns midway on the map.

He looked up at her. "Did something bad happen at work?"

"Yes."

"What is it?"

"I quit my job Friday. They called to tell me that they're not going to pay me the month of vacation or the bonus I'd earned."

Will slapped his hand against the table. "They can't do that. Want me to go talk to them?"

She shook her head. "It won't do any good. The HR person told me I forfeited the pay because I didn't notify them ninety days before leaving."

He nodded. "You strike me as a hard worker and a sensible girl. If you didn't give them proper notice, I bet you had a damn good reason."

"I did."

"There is a solution for you."

"What's that?"

"You should come to Italy with me."

"Right," she said, with sarcasm drawing out the word.

"I'll bet you've never been to Europe."

"Other than Colorado, or states I've driven through, my trips have been to Las Vegas, Chicago, and a boarding school in Virginia. Nowhere else."

"It's a shame you haven't traveled much." Will looked wistful. "Marie and I visited national parks across the U.S. We didn't make it to all of them, though. Once Marie started slipping, she didn't enjoy riding in the car. It was confusing for her."

The only national park Sophie had seen was Rocky Mountain National Park in Colorado. The depressing prospect of a life unfulfilled washed over her.

Will bent low over the table and studied the map.

Sophie pushed up from the table and walked to the door. She and Will held one thing in common. They were both alone in this world.

For Will, his dream of finding Francesca gave him hope.

Sophie had nothing.

24

Sophie wanted to stay sequestered in her apartment for the rest of the day, but her only food was a bargain-priced can of pink salmon. After the oysters with Will, she couldn't face it.

When it was time for dinner, she left her apartment for the sandwich shop on the corner. She thought a filling meal might soothe her battered heart.

Sophie ordered a Philly cheesesteak sandwich, chips, and a sweet green tea for herself. Remembering the meager offerings in Will's kitchen, she doubled her order.

The prospect of what life would now look like—no Bangor, no vacation, no job—crushed Sophie's spirit. The only thing that kept her from burying herself in her bed for the long haul was that her troubles were nothing compared to Will's. He lost his wife.

Sophie opened her apartment door and deposited her food and tea on the small square table beside the entrance to her galley kitchen.

She returned to the landing and raised her arm to knock on Will's door. At that moment, he opened it.

"I brought you food." Sophie held out the bag of food and tea.

"Thank you for dinner, Miss Sophie. What is it?"

Sophie described the take-out meal to him.

He stepped back and swung his door wide open in an invitation. "What about you? Where's your food?"

The man had buried his wife only a few days ago, with his only remaining family—using the term loosely—an ocean away. He wanted her company.

Being with Will, who clung to the improbable hope of reuniting with his lost love, made Sophie even lonelier. *Can I share my meal, intended to give me solace, with a person who gives me no comfort?*

Her parents had taught her to be considerate and think of the other person's point of view.

Sophie sighed. She went back for her sandwich and joined Will.

They ate in silence. Their only communication was when Will smiled and nodded at her between bites.

He wiped his mouth with his napkin. "Best meal I've eaten for a month. Thank you most kindly. May I pay you back for the cost of it?"

"No, thank you. It's my treat." Sophie stood and cleared the trash away.

"Did you think about it? About helping me find Francesca?"

Curled up in bed the night before, Sophie had considered his offer. He dreamed of a romantic adventure, to look for a lost love all these years later. She wished someone—just once—would love her with that kind of enduring passion.

"You need a travel advisor. I can research travel agents who specialize in travel in Europe and Italy." Let someone else break the harsh reality to him—a trip to Italy was reckless. Why did she have to squash his dream?

"No. You should do it. We can plan together where we should go from Francesca's letter. Get clues on where to find her."

"There is no 'we.' I'm not going with you."

Will looked away. He pressed his hands against the table to stand and moved to the window, staring outside.

Sophie moved to stand beside him. She saw nothing remarkable outside to warrant his attention. His eyes focused straight ahead. Sophie got the impression he was somewhere far away.

The poor man misses his wife.

Another thought hit Sophie, one that made her ashamed. *He put aside his grief and own needs and went with me when I thought we were going to put Bangor down. Why? Because he recognized I needed company.*

She had dismissed his idea of traveling to Italy as ill-advised and minimally researched. But the biggest obstacle? A European trip would be too physically demanding for him.

Sophie suspected something else. Keeping alive the idea of Francesca, and planning a trip that would never happen, might give Will a reason to live. A reason to hope and dream.

Sophie patted his back as if he were a child needing to be soothed. "I'm sorry, Will. I can't go with you, but I'll help you find a qualified travel advisor."

He spoke without looking at her. "Don't bother. I'll come up with a solution myself. Besides, you've proven you don't know anything about love. Look at the deadbeat you squandered your time with. That slick guy from your office."

He spied on me when I dated Russ. He must have heard our angry breakup. Will's words pierced her chest like a blazing hot poker. Will knew exactly how to hurt her.

Sophie walked to the door. She had suffered enough hurt over the last few days. Could she bear any more?

She reached for the doorknob.

"Wait," he said, "Don't go. You're right. I should hire someone to help me."

She turned around and looked at him. The words spilled out of her. "I don't know anything about love?"

She shook her head. "I'm not interested in helping you anymore. I suggest you spend your time looking into someone who will shop and cook for you instead of chasing a ghost."

"Francesca is not a ghost." His lower lip trembled. He wiped his mouth and chin with one shaking hand. "I'm going to find her, with or without your help." He pointed to the door. "You can let yourself out."

25

Back in her apartment, Sophie flung herself on her bed. She dared not scream out her frustration. Will heard every voice or noise in her apartment.

She pounded her fists against the pillows. The pummeling did nothing, however, to ease her frustration.

Sophie curled up into a ball on the center of the bed.

This would be an excellent moment to vaporize. Disappear. Sophie could not think of one thing she wanted to do or one person she wanted to see.

The precise rapping at her apartment door meant Will stood on the other side of it.

Sophie had no doubt he'd stand there until she opened it.

Will held an opened envelope in front of his chest. Facing her, on the back of his repurposed mail, Will had drawn a tulip. The smile on his face and the picture of the flower said it all.

"My sincere apologies, Miss Sophie." He bobbed the flower side to side. "Forgive me?"

The thought of the octogenarian attempting to charm her into forgiveness melted her resolve. She held up her hands in surrender. "Fine. I'll help you find a travel agent, but nothing else. Got it?"

"Thank you," he said. Removing a twenty-dollar bill from the envelope, he pressed it into her hand. "You can use this to pick up lunch for us tomorrow. After we eat, we can start planning where to look for Francesca."

She smiled. "That sounds nice." Much better, in fact, then spending the day alone in an empty apartment. "I'll research travel agents tomorrow morning."

Given Will's age, finding anyone willing to talk to him would be a challenge. Maybe she could find a tour group that specialized in elderly travelers.

The prospect of reading Francesca's letter enticed Sophie, and helping Will plan his trip would be a welcome diversion.

Job hunting—the last thing she wanted to do—might soon be a critical task, but it held zero appeal.

❧

The next morning, Sophie called agencies that specialized in European travel. She told them a gentleman in his eighties wanted to visit Italy.

On her first call, the man—in a perturbed tone—asked Sophie to remove him from consideration after only ten minutes of conversation. They did not, he explained, offer overseas guided travel services to octogenarians.

On the second call, Sophie started by revealing Will's age—in his eighties, but in good health. Sophie didn't inquire about fees, figuring it was Will's business, not hers. The woman agreed to meet Will and offered to visit him after lunch.

Sophie went back to the diner where Will had his apple pie and picked up the meatloaf "blue plate special of the day" and apple pie for Will. She got the fried chicken lunch plate for herself.

Will answered the door after one knock.

When she shared the news that a travel agent would visit them after lunch, he grew agitated. After her hours of Internet research and telephone calls, his lack of gratitude surprised her.

Only the clinking of knives and forks touching plates broke the stillness. Will picked at his food.

When the travel agent knocked on the door, a dark expression shadowed Will's face.

Sophie's hope of outsourcing the planning of this folly to their visitor dimmed when the woman laid eyes on Will.

The woman's shape resembled a bowling ball topped by short-cropped silver hair. "Mr. Mills," the woman asked, peering at him through narrowed eyes, "how old are you?"

"Ninety-one, but I'm not dead yet, if that's what you're wondering."

Ninety-one? I thought at Marie's funeral Will's friends told me he was in his eighties.

The woman frowned.

Sophie did a mental calculation. She counted back from the end of World War II. Ninety-one would be right if he had enlisted as a teenager toward the end of the conflict.

"Mr. Mills lives alone, still drives himself, and," Sophie swept her hand to draw the woman's eyes to the clean, tidy apartment, "as you can see, is self-reliant."

"Ninety-one?" The woman shook her head. "My company has a policy about overseas travel for anyone over the age of eighty. You must obtain the written approval of your physician before we do any work." She glared at Sophie. "It's for their own health and safety."

"Do I have to write my name on my coat, too, as I did in primary school?" Will snorted and scowled at the woman, who stood a head taller than he did.

She stared back at Will.

Yikes. If Sophie didn't act fast, the travel agent would decline the job and leave. She wanted a gradual letdown for Will, not an ax blow.

"Will," Sophie said, "you mentioned your physician commented on your excellent health. Can't you call his office and ask him to say that in a brief letter?" Sophie glanced at the travel agent. "That'll do, won't it?"

The travel professional nodded, although her face broadcast her lack of enthusiasm for the idea of having Will for a client.

"Mr. Mills can request the physician's letter tomorrow," Sophie said. "He will forward it to you upon receipt."

The travel agent walked to the door. She turned to face Will. "Why not stay in the United States? There are scores of lovely places here to visit. It would be much easier to accommodate someone of your age."

"I want to go to Italy!" Will's voice rose in volume. "Last time I checked, Italy isn't in the United States. I guess that means I need to go to Europe, doesn't it?"

The travel agent's angry face turned scarlet. "I don't need a geography lesson."

"I don't need a babysitter."

The woman's face tightened. "I don't need a grumpy, ninety-one-year-old man for a client." She stomped into the hall and slammed the door behind her.

Sophie's heart sank. If this woman wouldn't agree to plan Will's trip, his dream of finding Francesca would end.

26

Sophie turned to Will. "Why did you do that? Antago-
nize her?"

Will looked pleased with himself. "She's an imbecile.
It would have never worked. I guess you'll have to take
me."

"No. I can't."

"You don't have a job anymore. What's holding you
back?"

"Money."

"I'll pay for your expenses."

"I need to find a job."

"You can do that when we return."

"No."

"Why not?"

Sophie drew in a deep breath and exhaled it in a slow
stream. "I. Don't. Fly."

She held up a hand to stop the inquiries. "I won't fly
with you across the ocean. It's not happening, Will, so
please stop asking."

His face crumpled.

Will walked to the window and gazed outside. September winds gushed through the tree branches, accelerating the annual transition into fall.

"I'll find someone to go with me if you'll help me plan the transportation and hotels." His eyes pleaded. "Please?"

Sophie was torn between the wrong of perpetuating his hopes and the crime of dashing them. Will needed a purpose and goal for living. He needed the time to be able to face and tie up the frayed pieces of his life.

Although she doubted the wisdom of her decision, Sophie reached for the pad of paper and pen she brought. "Tell me about Francesca and what she was like when you met her."

"She's Italian and claims she bore my child. That's all the details you need to know. Let's talk about where to look for her."

Sophie cocked her head at him. She pushed back from the table. "Do you want me to help you or not?"

Will slammed his palm against the table. "Look, young lady, don't be snippy with me!

"I'll tell you what you need to plan my trip: where I met her, what I know about where she or her family lived, where her letter was mailed from, and anywhere else I might want to go in Italy. But we won't talk about how I felt about Francesca or what she was like. That's private."

"Fair enough. Then let's start with her letter."

"No. I'll tell you what you need to know. Her letter is private."

No letter. No details. How could Sophie plan an itinerary?

He took a deep breath and blinked several times. "First, I want to go to the American Cemetery in Florence."

Sophie shook her head. "I didn't know there was an American cemetery in Florence."

Will nodded with one firm bob of his head. "The U.S. doesn't ask for reparations from the countries they liberate. Nope. We only ask for land where we can bury our fallen."

Sophie spoke in a tender voice. "Are some of your friends from the Army buried there?"

Will's face was guarded. "My division, as I told you, had heavy losses in the Apennine Mountains. The 10th Mountain Division helped end the war in Italy and never lost a battle. Not one." To emphasize his point, he crossed his arms over his chest and gave a decisive nod of his head.

Sophie could tell he didn't want to say more.

The only way to show him the foolishness of his plan was to go along with him. *When he can't find someone to accompany him and guide him on the trip, he'll abandon the idea.*

Sophie wrote options on her pad.

Fly into Florence to see the cemetery?

Fly into Rome or Milan and then train to Florence?

"The initial stop seems pretty straightforward. I imagine you could get a cab or bus that would take you from the airport or train station to the cemetery."

"Damn straight. Those Italians know we liberated them and they'll welcome a vet like me."

Sophie wasn't as convinced about that as Will, but she kept her opinion to herself.

"OK. After the cemetery, where next?"

"To find Francesca, of course."

The poor man hadn't a clue of how difficult it might be for someone his age to navigate around Italy alone, much less find a woman he'd lost track of seventy-five years ago.

Will nodded with a broad smile. "I can't wait for her surprise when she sees me."

Sophie knew she didn't have the heart to deflate his vision. "Where do you think you should start looking?"

Will shrugged.

She set down her pen and covered one of his hands with hers. A soft, calm voice dampened the sting of her words. "I know you realize that finding Francesca will be quite difficult. Perhaps impossible. I respect you for your determination to try. I'd like to help you, but you've tied my hands. Let me look at the letter Francesca sent you. I might see a clue that you missed."

Will glared at her with fierce eyes. "Let me tell you something, Missy. I grew up on a Colorado ranch and spent my summers bull riding in rodeos. The Army placed me in the 86th Division because of it."

His eyes lit up. "I wanted to ski with them, of course, but it was damn tough to get into the ski troops. Three interviews or more were required. I had no patience for that, so I signed up with the mule busters. I didn't have to compete with those college boys from out East to ride mules."

He chuckled. "Didn't take long, though. The officers found out I could climb a rock face and race down a ski slope with the best of them, and that was all it took. No more mule busting for me."

He stood and walked to the hall closet. From it, he pulled an old pair of wooden skis and propped them up against the wall.

Will next pulled out a set of skis that, to Sophie's eye, looked similar to those Russ had used to ski at Vail. "See these?"

Sophie nodded.

"Until Marie's Alzheimer's got so bad, I skied every Wednesday, and sometimes Thursdays, too, until the end of the season."

Will tucked the skis into the closet and turned to her with fierce conviction. "If a bull-riding ranch kid can climb and fight in the Italian mountains and ski the Rockies until he's eighty-eight, then he can sure as hell try to find the woman he loved and his child."

Will has grit.

"Of course you can." *This is a doomed quest.*

Will walked into his bedroom and closed the door.

Sophie wondered if he was going to come out again, or if he was dismissing her.

The bedroom door opened, and Will returned to the table carrying one pale gray envelope.

He placed it in the center of the table and covered it with his palm.

"If you look at this, then we have an agreement. You'll help me plan my trip. And you promise to never tell anyone about Francesca and me."

Sophie rested her palm over his hand. "I promise."

With his eyes square on hers, Will handed the precious letter to Sophie.

27

The thin envelope held stamps priced in lire, canceled by a post office in Montepulciano, Italy.

The sight of the tiny white inner envelope, filled with jet black baby hair, sent her reeling. *Francesca mailed her infant's lock to the father of her baby.*

When Sophie's fingertips touched the wispy black strands, it turned a child in a faded photograph into someone real. This baby would now be a grown man or woman. Will's child.

"Will, do you have a family member or friend who would want to travel with you?"

"No family. Marie couldn't have kids. My older brother passed seven years ago. Marie was an only child, not that I could ask her kin to help me find another woman."

"What about friends? Someone you skied with?"

"Nope." He scowled. "What's the matter? Don't you think I can handle a trip to Italy? Hell, it's peacetime now, except for those damn terrorists who are trying to ruin everyone else's lives. I handled Italy during the war, remember."

Will bolted out of his chair and stomped to the kitchen. He poured himself a glass of water. His hand trembled hard enough to slosh water over the rim of the glass.

Will placed the glass on the counter without drinking. He gripped the edge of the sink with both hands and bowed his head.

Sophie's eyes widened with alarm. "Will? Are you OK?"

"Fine." But he didn't move from his position braced against the sink.

"Will?" She leapt to her feet and stepped toward him.

Will waved to decline her help. He released his grip on the sink and turned to face her.

He spoke with deliberation. "When I left Italy, I left more good men who died there than I deserved to know in a lifetime. Leaving ..." His voice broke.

He sucked in a big breath. "I swore ... I swore on my mother's life I would never walk on Italian soil again. A bullet meant for me killed the man next to me. I all but died there, too. That's why, once I set foot on American soil, I gave up the thought of going back for Francesca. I was afraid I'd die there if I returned to Italy. I'm an American. I want to croak in my own country."

"Of course you do." *You needn't worry about being out of the country because the truth is that no respectable guide will fly with you to Italy.*

She stared at the envelope. Francesca mailed the letter in 1945.

Will outsmarted Sophie. Two hours after she presented him an itinerary for his trip to Italy, which she considered hypothetical, he booked airline tickets into Florence for himself and Sophie.

When she looked away, he'd gotten her identification details from the passport in her purse.

"I paid for business class tickets." He smirked. "Now you don't have to worry about it being too taxing for an old coot like me."

Sophie was stuck.

She would never forgive herself if she refused to go and Will died in Italy, all alone and brokenhearted.

Three weeks later, Will and Sophie boarded a plane, the first of three that would carry them to Florence, Italy.

Sophie tossed and turned the night before they left with nightmares about flying to Italy. She hadn't been in an airport or airplane since she was eight years old. She insisted on traveling only on the ground, by car, or train.

She considered taking a medication that would put her to sleep on the flights but realized it wasn't an option. She had a responsibility to Will.

Instead of sleeping through the overnight flight on the seat that fully reclined, Sophie gripped the armrests with white-knuckled hands during the slightest turbulence.

She gritted her teeth and clutched her hands together on the takeoffs and landings.

Three flights and seventeen hours after they left Denver, Sophie and Will landed in Italy.

Americans, headed to Europe for holidays or business, filled the majority of the seats on their flights. But now, as Sophie and Will edged their way through the crowded lanes of people headed to the ground transportation area, it was evident that she and Will were indeed in a foreign country.

The melodic sound of Italian surrounded her, peppered with voices in English, German, Spanish, French, and languages that she could not identify.

The Italian women of all ages wore neutral colors: white, beige, and black. Not like the vibrant colors on the passengers walking the corridors of Denver International Airport.

Ahead, a stern, solemn uniformed police officer staffed the hallway to ground transportation. The officer held a fierce-looking submachine gun in his hands.

Sophie's eyes widened.

Will grabbed her elbow and picked up his pace.

Does he think I want to stop and chat with a gun-toting officer?

Sophie didn't make eye contact with the police officer and walked by with a purpose to her stride. True, he was in the airport for security, but the sight of his gun frightened her.

What did I get us into?

28

At the taxi queue, Will's face grew stern. He handed the driver, a dark-complexioned, scruffy man, a paper with the address of their hotel in Florence.

"Shouldn't take more than thirty minutes to get there," Will said. "It was a long flight. We're not interested in a scenic route."

Sophie was surprised, but she said nothing.

As he watched the driver load their luggage into the rear compartment, Will whispered to her, "I asked one of my ski buddies to email the hotel and find out how far it is from the airport."

Her neighbor surprised her. *What else had Will investigated?*

The taxi driver wove through the airport roads, past alternate routes that listed in Italian the outlying destinations—Genova, Livorno, Roma, Ancona, and Milano—and merged onto a highway headed to Firenze.

I hope Firenze is Italian for Florence.

The taxi soon darted through the streets of Florence, which got narrower and busier as they approached the ancient city center. Sophie held her breath in the busy intersections. Cars whizzed side by side at alarming speeds. The driver of one vehicle could adjust the side mirror on the next. Vespas and other scooters darted between the lanes and cars.

Don't the scooter drivers realize they're putting their lives at risk?

The noise of engines revving and horns honking reverberated off the stone walls of the buildings.

The driver slammed on his brakes and swerved to the curb.

"Yes, this is it," Will said. His voice sounded calm, but his pale face and hands that gripped the edge of the seat told Sophie he shared her feelings about the cab ride through Florence.

The narrow hotel front was constructed from large stone blocks, with the hotel name etched in an inlaid stone above the door.

The online travel site Sophie had used described it as a four-star hotel with excellent reviews. Sophie sighed with relief. The hotel looked every bit as charming as the website photos.

When Sophie stepped out onto the cobblestone street, a wave of relief and exhaustion hit her. She had planned for them to walk through several parts of the city center today, but after the flights, all she felt like doing was curling up in a bed.

If they were granted early check-in, she and Will could shower, unpack, and freshen up before a minimal walking tour. Sophie could rally for a brief stroll through the historic district, but she worried about the wisdom of a longer meander through Florence.

The problem? Will looked even worse than she felt.

29

Sophie and Will entered the lobby, a small room with a single upholstered armchair, a blue-and-yellow ceramic umbrella stand, and a standing-height wooden check-in counter. A desktop computer on a small built-in desk was visible through a doorway off to the right behind the counter.

Twenty wooden cubbyholes lined the back wall behind a smiling Italian woman in her forties. The desk clerk was lovely, with a broad smile, wavy shoulder-length black hair, and brown eyes. All of five feet two inches tall with delicate bones, she likely weighed less than 110 pounds.

At the sight of her, Will straightened his back and quickened his step.

Sophie smiled at the sudden change in her travel companion's spirit.

The woman walked around the counter to stand in front of Will. The clerk cupped his hand in both of hers and introduced herself in English as Chiara, the hotel manager.

Will's chest puffed up as he introduced the two of them to Chiara.

When she stood in front of Sophie to shake her hand—again, a two-handed greeting—the Italian's eyes locked on the mustard stain on the front of Sophie's white shirt. The mustard was the product of Sophie's lapse in judgment. She put mustard on her airplane sandwich, and she planned to wear this and three other shirts—washed only when necessary—for three weeks.

"After you have unpacked your luggage, bring your shirt to me," Chiara said in a kind voice. "I will help you with that stain. Come, come. Let me register you. Passports, please. I will keep them here." She held out her hand, palm up.

Panic gripped Sophie. The woman wanted her passport, the item Sophie considered more precious than money or credit cards. "If you need to make a photocopy, I can wait here for them."

"You go to your room now." Chiara studied the faces of the two Americans. "The photocopy should be ready before dinner."

This gave Sophie an uneasy feeling, but she and Will handed their passports to Chiara, who slipped them inside a folder on the counter.

Chiara pulled out two room keys and handed them to Sophie and Will. "Your rooms are on the *primo piano*, the first floor, up one flight of stairs."

Will looked confused.

"This," Chiara swept her hand to indicate the lobby, "is the *piano terra*, the ground floor. One floor up we call the first floor."

Will nodded and cradled the key fob. A narrow brass lady, three inches long, was attached to a key. As long as the brass lady, the key resembled one belonging to a treasure chest or castle door.

Sophie held her key and fob in one palm and ran her fingers over the worn brass figure. This beautiful item had likely been used for decades, perhaps centuries.

In spite of her exhaustion, Sophie had no intention of resting now or allowing Will to sleep.

She had read that the best way for Americans to beat jet lag was to walk and tour your first day in Europe, eat early, and try to sleep until morning.

Sophie knew Will must be exhausted. Except for his spark of energy on meeting Chiara, the poor man looked disoriented and drained.

They agreed on a time to meet for sightseeing.

After unpacking, showering, and changing her clothes, Sophie knocked on Will's door.

She got no response.

"Will, it's Sophie. Are you ready to go out?" She knocked louder.

Silence.

Her rapping intensified.

No sound came from his room.

She ramped up the volume even more.

The door swung open to reveal Will, who looked rested. "I'm not deaf. I heard you the first time."

"Why didn't you answer the door?"

A devilish grin split his face. "Think about all the reasons I might not have been able to come to the door." He nodded his head. "Do you want me to explain the dirty details to you?"

Sophie's face flushed crimson. "Uh, no. Let's leave it unsaid."

He chuckled. "Let me grab my camera, and then I'll be ready."

When he returned to the door, he held a saddle-colored leather camera case. "Let's go."

30

In the lobby, Chiara turned away from the computer and moved to the counter. "*Buonasera*. Did you bring your shirt?"

Sophie handed it over. "Thank you. It may be hopeless. It's mustard." She wrinkled her nose.

"I will try." Chiara turned and grabbed their passports out of the cubbyholes that held room keys.

Our passports sat in those cubbyholes for anyone to grab if Chiara left the front desk. Do Italians not worry about identity theft?

Sophie noticed that another guest's blue passport rested in one cubby and a burgundy passport lay in another. She decided it must be the customary practice here, but it still made her uneasy.

A lean, middle-aged man entered the lobby from the stairs that led to the rooms. He wore slacks, a crew-necked shirt, and a blazer. Chiara smiled and exchanged his key for the red passport.

"*Grazie*," the man said.

"*Prego*," Chiara said with a smile and tip of her head.

That man acts as if it's normal to leave his passport in a lobby cubbyhole.

Two things struck Sophie. She felt ignorant for not being able to speak any Italian, and second, she knew little about the etiquette of traveling in Europe.

"We're headed out to explore for a little while and then will stop for an early dinner. We're tired from the long flight," Sophie said. She showed Chiara the restaurant recommendation in her guidebook. "This restaurant is nearby, isn't it?"

"It is not far. Many of our American guests go there." Chiara looked down at the guest registry.

Will's hands searched his pockets, looking for something. He leaned toward Sophie and patted her back with his fingertips. "I left my extra rolls of film upstairs, I'm going to go up and get one before we leave for our walk."

"Would you like me to go up for you?" Sophie said.

"I walk the stairs every damn day in our apartment building. I can manage here."

He disappeared up the stairwell.

Chiara ran her fingers over their names in the registration book. "Mr. Mills is your, uh, grandfather?"

"No. We're not related."

Chiara scowled.

Sophie's face reddened as she realized what Chiara assumed. "Mr. Mills is my neighbor. We're friends, but nothing more." Will was hardly her friend, but that was the simplest explanation. "Will was one of the brave soldiers who liberated Italy at the close of World War II."

A shadow fell over Chiara's face. "Firenze and Italy suffered from the war. Many civilians died. Your country destroyed many ancient buildings and railroads."

The words Sophie wanted to say filled her mind. *The Nazis caused the destruction of Europe and the murder of six million Jews. That's why the Americans fought here— to liberate the European countries and stop a madman. By the way, Miss Uppity, what country did Italy side with during the war?*

Not wanting to offend their host, Sophie watered down her words. "Germany was responsible for the destruction of Europe during the war, not America."

Chiara scoffed. "Hitler bombed every bridge except the Ponte Vecchio. That one he spared because of Mussolini. But it was the Americans, not Germany, who hit us the hardest after Mussolini surrendered.

"Our war should have been over. Instead, children were made orphans, and women, like my mother's sister, had their homes destroyed by the Allies."

Sophie's eyes widened. *America bombed Italy after Mussolini surrendered?* She looked at Will, who had returned to the lobby.

He nodded to confirm Chiara's claim. Will spoke quietly. "It was necessary. We entered the war to defeat Hitler. The bombing was necessary to cut off Hitler's supplies and liberate Italy, though it hurt the very people we came to help."

Chiara stared at Will. "That is what the Allies told my mother and my aunt with their pamphlets. Bombing must happen to liberate Italy." She shrugged. "Maybe yes. Maybe no."

Sophie, eager to change the subject, placed one of the hotel's walking maps in front of Chiara. "We are eager to see your beautiful city. Would you please show us how to walk to our restaurant?"

Chiara's head lowered as she drew on the map the route from the hotel to the restaurant. She slid the diagram across to Sophie. With one curt nod, Chiara dismissed them and retreated to the small office.

Sophie wondered whether they'd receive the same chilly reception from all Italians. A lack of cooperation from the Italians they met would doom their search for Francesca.

31

Sophie and Will turned right on the sidewalk, following the route Chiara had drawn. Will moved around Sophie, inserting himself between Sophie and the street.

Their hotel sat across the Arno River from the Cathedral of Santa Maria del Fiore, known as the Cathedral of Florence. Sophie had read in her guidebook that the main cathedral in an Italian city is referred as the Duomo, which means the Cathedral.

With their limited time in the city, Sophie wanted to see the famous cathedral featured in skyline photos. "Let's walk to the Duomo first."

Sophie showed Will its location on their map of the ancient city center. "Our restaurant is very close to it. We might even have time to look inside before dinner."

After a few blocks, they reached the Ponte Vecchio, the medieval stone arched bridge that Chiara mentioned. Sophie had read about Florence in her guidebook on the plane. "This bridge is known for goldsmiths that line both sides of the bridge. It'll be fun to window-shop on the way through."

"I'm not interested in gold. I'm only interested in finding Francesca and getting something to eat." The old grouchy Will had returned.

Sophie consulted her guidebook as they approached the Arno River and the Ponte Vecchio. She refused to let grumpy Will ruin her first glimpse of Florence.

She read aloud—whether he cared to listen or not was his choice. "Ponte Vecchio means 'Old Bridge.' It dates to the age of the Romans. In the 1300s, the bridge was reconstructed using a revolutionary technique. Segmental arches, less than 180 degrees, supported it to prevent bowing."

She glanced at Will. His face showed no interest in the structure's history.

Having read about the row of jewelry stores on the bridge, Sophie expected high-end shops like Tiffany's or the independent jewelry designers in Denver's Cherry Creek area, with their window displays of unique jewelry pieces. Instead, the tiny shops' windows held only a few thin necklaces and pairs of earrings.

In front of some of the stores, vendors stood with tables displaying their gold jewelry. Sophie asked one gentleman whether his pieces were fourteen- or eighteen-karat gold.

"My jewelry," the vendor said, "is eighteen-karat gold. Only the finest gold is sold on the Ponte Vecchio."

Sophie sighed. No window-shopping now. The mission was to keep Will moving.

Sophie had studied the walking map of ancient Florence on the plane, fearful they would lose their way. The brown signs that marked walking directions to the historical sites, however, made navigating toward the Duomo easy.

They walked over the few blocks to Via dei Georgofili and then followed Via Lambertesca to the Uffizi Gallery courtyard. There, they turned left and strolled toward the Duomo.

The Uffizi courtyard opened into a beautiful, open piazza, with the Palazzo Vecchio on one side. Tour groups and people strolling arm-in-arm filled the open space. The chatter of tourist voices created lilting layers of sound.

Will's hand tightened on her arm. "Keep one hand on your purse and watch for gypsies."

Sophie stopped and took it all in. A rush of excitement tingled up her spine.

She wanted to stay in this piazza for hours. Watch people. Listen to the languages being spoken around her. Wander over to one of the cafes with tiny tables and have a gelato or espresso or glass of wine.

Italy. She was here. Never had Sophie imagined a trip to Europe.

"It's not much farther to our restaurant, is it?" Will said.

"No. We're close."

Sophie studied her map. The distance from where they stood to the Duomo was farther than the first leg from the Arno River to this piazza. A taxi for their return to the hotel might be necessary.

When the sea of people walking ahead of them dispersed into another grand piazza, Sophie saw the Duomo. She drew in her breath and stood in awe of its beauty and majesty.

Beside her, Will gave an appreciative whistle, his focus on food put aside for a moment.

The Duomo held court in the center of a piazza that swarmed with people and voices. Ringing the Duomo, broad spans of stone separated the cathedral from the cafes with tables out front for alfresco dining and the open doors of luxury tourist shops.

The shops with colorful leather coats and purses beckoned to Sophie, but her feet catapulted her toward that looming architectural wonder, the Florence Cathedral.

The clay-colored dome designed by Filippo Brunelleschi was a striking landmark of the city that had flourished during the Renaissance.

The exterior of the building looked like white-and-gray marble from where they stood, a beautiful contrast to the colorful dome. As Sophie and Will drew closer, to Sophie's delight, she discovered the exterior walls were not white and gray but pink, green, and white marble in intricate inlaid patterns.

The Duomo was a summer breeze ice cream cone with the delicate pastel shades and precise patterns of color, topped by the majestic, striking dome. No picture could do it justice.

"There's the line for entry," Sophie said and pointed at the queue.

The line snaked along the entire length of the Duomo.

Will's steps slowed. His feet scraped the stone with each footfall. Her elderly neighbor edged forward with a shuffling, dragging step.

It would be inconsiderate to ask Will to wait in a queue to enter the Duomo. She grabbed his arm. "Let's go to the head of the line. I want to ask what time they open in the morning."

He nodded and licked his chapped lips, dried and cracked by the overseas flight.

"Excuse me," Sophie said to the man who monitored when and how many people entered the cathedral. "What time does the Duomo open to visitors in the morning? We just flew in and are too tired to wait in line."

The man smiled. "You two may go now if you wish. Exceptions are made," he tilted his head at Will, "for special cases."

"Thank you, thank you," Sophie said.

The man stepped back to allow Sophie and Will access to the doorway.

Will grunted. "Good thing I'm with a pretty girl. That Italian would've made me stand in line, but for you? He lets you cut in front of all those people."

Sophie opened her mouth to correct his misconception, but the sparkle in Will's eyes made her swallow her words. "I guess if I'm the ticket to cut in line, that means you buy dinner tonight, doesn't it?"

"You bet I will."

32

Inside the Duomo, cooler air welcomed them. The high arches of the white Gothic ceiling were crisscrossed with gray stone. Brilliant pops of color from stained-glass windows pierced the walls of the vast pale cavern. The magnificence of the exterior dwarfed the beauty of the subdued inner space.

The voices of other tourists—many of whom strolled with audio guides plugged into their ears—did not override the peace of this holy place. Except for a handful of weddings and the funeral for Will's wife, Sophie avoided churches.

But standing here, inside this beautiful, centuries-old cathedral, made Sophie think about God. Some of the artisans who built this masterpiece likely believed in a higher being and perhaps even credited their inspiration and vision to God.

Elaborate mosaic patterns of white-and-gray and brightly colored stones composed the floor of the Duomo. Will trailed Sophie as she walked to what she most wanted to see, the underside of the dome.

The construction of the dome was long an engineering mystery. This dome, with no visible support, had been built using two domes and lifting mechanisms invented for that sole purpose.

While the dome's construction itself was a marvel, the intricate underside was a work of art. Giorgio Vasari designed frescoes of the Last Judgment to grace the inner dome of the Duomo.

Sophie would have loved to see the dome's artwork up close, rather than from the floor of the cathedral. She longed to look out over Florence from the height of the dome but knew that to be impossible. For those views, she and Will would have to climb the 463 steps to the top.

Perhaps the next time in Italy, she would climb the steps to the dome.

Her thought shocked her.

I haven't recovered—physically or emotionally—from the flight, and I'm contemplating my next visit? No. Not happening.

Sophie recalled her anxiety on the plane before departing Denver and thought about the long flights home. Her breathing quickened. Icy prickles raced from her extremities toward her heart.

A wave of nausea hit her. Light-headedness caused her to sway.

Someone's firm hand gripped her biceps.

Her head spun to see who touched her.

Will's eyes bore into her. He spoke in an even tone.

"Come on, Miss Sophie. You look pale. Let's go over to those benches. We're both tuckered out."

He moved with deliberate steps in a slow, steady cadence, guiding her to sit down on the bench.

He placed his palm against her forehead. "You don't have a fever. That's good."

Will sat down beside her on the marble bench.

Sophie closed her eyes and walked her mind through the steps she learned from her child psychiatrist, which were designed to enable Sophie's body to hit "pause" when blood rushed from her head.

The mental exercises worked.

She glanced at Will, expecting to find him sleeping.

He sat with his back straight, his palms resting on his knees, and his eyes wide open.

"Thank you for taking care of me," Sophie said.

His eyes studied her face.

"I'm OK now. Thank you." She smiled at him. "You're a gentleman."

"My momma drilled basic manners into me when I was a young cub on the ranch. She was a good, hard-working, God-fearing woman. She vowed to make sure that no son of hers would be ignorant of manners and make a fool of himself."

His mother raised Will as a gentleman.

On sidewalks, he positioned himself between the street and me.

When he isn't cursing at me, he watches over me, like

his "protection" in the airport and here, at the Duomo, when dizziness threatened to bring me to my knees.

But the lessons only somewhat stuck with Will. A gentleman would never abandon his child and the woman he got pregnant.

And a gentleman wouldn't complain about an old, dying dog.

Is Will a true gentleman? Sophie held doubts, but Will at least passed some of the tests. *Not like Russ.*

"Will, I think it's time we go to dinner. We can eat a little something and get a cab back to our hotel."

Will coughed into his elbow. He pulled a white, pressed handkerchief from his pocket and wiped his mouth. After he had finished, Will folded and returned the cotton cloth to his pocket.

"Dinner is a great idea." Will stood and offered his hand to help Sophie rise, the proper action for a gentleman.

33

Customers occupied many tables in the restaurant, though it had opened only fifteen minutes earlier.

Pride filled Sophie. She—the woman who got her first glimpse of the Atlantic Ocean last night—found a trendy restaurant in Florence, Italy.

A male host led them to a small table in the back.

A waiter appeared and thrust two menus at them. In a brusque voice, he said, "With or without gas?"

Sophie turned red.

Will chuckled. "I'd say we're without gas. What do you think, Miss Sophie?"

"Water," the waiter said. "Water with or without gas?"

Sophie's red face turned crimson at her misconception of the waiter's question.

Will frowned. "Without gas." He looked down at the menu. The waiter bustled off to a foursome who occupied a nearby table.

"Not very friendly," Will said. "Must be because they're busy."

Sophie glanced at the menu, and then turned it over. It was printed in English, with prices listed in U.S. dollars, rather than euros. She listened to the cadence of voices around her.

She strained to filter the speech patterns. The language she heard spoken by the patrons was English. *American English.*

Sophie swiveled her head and took in the dress and appearance of the customers. She noticed the guidebook she used for the trip rested in a place of honor on top of one-third of the tables. Other Americans studied different well-known travel publications.

Tour books written in English dotted the room.

Her lower lip trembled. *That's why it's packed. It's full of Americans. Americans who eat too early by European standards.*

"I think I'll have chicken under a brick," Will said. "Didn't you tell me that is their specialty?"

Sophie nodded. Her appetite fled as she wondered if all her research for the trip was flawed.

"I think chicken will be perfect for curing my travel stomach."

Sophie looked at him. Tears dampened her eyes. "I'm s...sor—"

"Starving?" Will's eyes brightened. "Me, too. How about two chickens? I'm so hungry I might even eat the brick." He reached across the table and patted the back of her hand.

Sophie looked around as plate after plate of flattened chicken scooted by them on the arms of waiters, destined for other tables. Her spirits sank further. "I thought I found a typical Italian restaurant."

"This is great for tonight. The good news is that if we happen to feel like something else tomorrow, I'll bet there are a whole slew of restaurants in this city."

Sophie had made a poor choice for tonight's meal, which might have explained Chiara's reaction when Sophie asked for directions. It did no good to take her disappointment out on Will.

"I agree." She forced a smile. "About everything but the brick. There's no way I'm eating a brick, though I must admit I'm starving. How about it? Let's order the chicken."

When their waiter arrived, Will surprised her by also ordering two glasses of the house wine.

"I'm in Italy with a beautiful woman. You're in Europe for the first time. We need to celebrate."

A glass of wine—precisely what Sophie needed.

Sophie's chicken dinner satisfied her hunger and, although not extraordinary, the meal was better than she feared.

Tomorrow I'll ask Chiara where the locals eat.

34

Sophie hailed a taxi after dinner. She was too exhausted to walk back to their hotel, and she imagined Will felt the same. Will's shuffling step when they left the restaurant worried her.

She tried to talk with him during the drive, but his eyelids drifted shut.

Did I overdo it on the very first day with our walk to the Duomo?

The next morning, sounds of movement from Will's room traveled through their joint wall. His footsteps outside her door meant he was headed down to breakfast. Sophie rushed to finish.

She entered the ground floor breakfast room and was pleased to find a bright room with six small tables. A self-service buffet of cold food lined the opposite wall.

A pleasant-looking woman in her forties walked into the room from a side door and carried steaming coffee cups to a middle-aged couple, who were seated at the back of the room.

Will stood by the smorgasbord, filling a plate and chatting with the man she saw yesterday in the lobby. Will waved at Sophie.

"Good morning, Miss Sophie," Will said in a cheery tone. His face beamed with an uncharacteristic smile.

Will introduced her to his new friend, a businessman from England. The man declined Will's invitation to sit at their table, saying he needed to look over notes prior to his morning meeting.

Sophie filled a small dish for herself from the modest but appetizing array of choices. She chose a wedge of cantaloupe, a whisper-thin shaving of prosciutto, one thin slice of salami, and two rectangular slices of a cream-colored cheese.

Sophie eyed the crusty Italian ciabatta at the end of the table. Its sweet, toasty aroma tantalized her.

No bread in the morning. I'll have some tonight, but I can't have bread with every meal or I won't fit into my clothes.

The prosciutto hit her tongue, and a sigh escaped Sophie's lips.

Will grinned. "Good, isn't it?" He shook his head. "I forgot how delicious the salami is in Italy. 'Course when I had this before, it was wartime. We sure didn't have a spread like this. Whatever I ate, though, beat my K rations all to heck."

"What was in a K ration?"

"Well, let's see." He scratched his chin and leaned back in his chair. "Canned meat, which we all hated, hard biscuits, bars of fruit and cereal, and instant coffee."

Sophie looked at her food and shuddered from the image of the food he described.

"They did throw in a couple of things to compensate for the miserable food, like cigarettes, gum, and sugar tablets. Oh, and pills to treat the water so we wouldn't get the runs."

"Ugh," Sophie said. "I guess you'll enjoy the food on this trip, won't you?"

"Yep. I already am. Even the chicken last night whipped the K rations."

Sophie's face reddened.

"Don't take it personally, Miss Sophie. We'll do better today."

"Still up for the American Cemetery?"

He nodded. "Tomorrow we'll head south to find Francesca."

Sophie downed the rest of her food and then pushed up from the table.

"Let's go."

Another graveyard with Will. I'll get through this, but certainly not my choice of how to spend a day.

35

Chiara stood at the front desk. She held up one hand. "One moment, please." She ducked into the back room and emerged moments later with Sophie's shirt.

"Here." She held out the top to Sophie with a self-satisfied expression on her face. "See? The mustard is all gone."

"Thank you." Sophie recalled what she learned from her infamous guidebook and said, with a tentative voice, "*Grazie.*" She pronounced the word "Graat-see."

Chiara cringed as if fingernails had scratched a blackboard.

Determined to conquer the pronunciation, Sophie asked Chiara for help and tried to mimic Chiara's intonation. "Grah-tzee-eh."

Chiara smiled. "Better."

"We would like to visit the American Cemetery in Florence today. I think it is on a bus route. We might be more comfortable, though, if we have someone take us."

"This is possible. Would you like me to call a private driver?"

"Yes, please."

"It might take thirty minutes or an hour for a driver to come. I will call your room when I am successful. A taxi will also go to the memorial, but a car is better."

"*Grazie.*"

"*Prego.*" Chiara turned her focus on Will. "Do you have a friend buried there?"

"Yes. It's why I need to go. To pay my respects."

Sadness marked his face. Sophie knew that there was more to his story than he'd told her.

Here was Sophie's opportunity to explain why they were traveling together. "Mr. Mills doesn't have a family and is too old to journey by himself."

"I'm not too old!" Will said. "You're used to making travel arrangements. That's why I brought you along. Maybe you should stay in the city center and shop or something today. I can handle myself." His voice bristled.

Sophie turned to look at him. "I want to go with you. I'd rather see interesting sights and memorials than go shopping."

"Do what you please. I'll manage."

Chiara stepped from behind the desk and crossed the lobby to a shelf displaying flyers for tours in and around Florence. She picked up a couple of brochures and extended them to Sophie. "Perhaps the following day, you might like a tour. I can arrange these for you."

Sophie shook her head. "No, thank you. Tomorrow we head south from Florence. I arranged for a driver, who will arrive at nine in the morning."

"Where do you head next?"

"Montepulciano," Will said. "We're going to find a woman."

Chiara's eyes widened.

Sophie thought she needed to clarify. "We are here to look for the woman Will met during the war. He loved her all those years ago."

Chiara's face brightened. "You kept in contact. How wonderful!"

"Nope," Will said and slapped his hand against the counter, "but we're gonna find her. Aren't we, Miss Sophie?"

"We're certainly going to give it our best try."

"We're going to find her." He uttered the words through pursed lips. "We will."

Chiara reached out and patted Will's arm. "You are a romantic." She bobbed her chin in a proud nod. "It is what an Italian would do."

Will's voice rose. "We will succeed!"

"Bravo," Chiara said.

The woman had warmed to them. Now was Sophie's chance to pick her brain. She asked for dinner recommendations for tonight.

Chiara pulled out a walking map.

"Here," Chiara circled the hotel's name on the brochure, "is where we are situated." She pointed to the street guide. "Here is the Ponte Vecchio, and here," she tapped with her pen at a street on this side of the bridge, "is Osteria Armando. The food is quite good. It is one of my favorites near the hotel." She wrinkled her nose. "Not like the place you went last night."

"I hope not." A flush crept over Sophie's cheeks.

Chiara offered the diagram to Sophie. "Please tell them that I sent you. You will enjoy the restaurant and the food.

"*Grazie.*"

Chiara's face lit with a wide smile. "*Prego.*"

36

Chiara was true to her word.

A black car and a driver, dressed in a black shirt and slacks, picked up Will and Sophie an hour later. Thirty minutes after leaving the hotel, they entered the grounds of the Florence American Cemetery.

A somber cornerstone on each side anchored the metal lattice fence, which featured ornate gold at the center. Prickles raced up Sophie's legs.

Sophie and Will got out of the car and walked toward the grassy meadow of graves.

On the west border of the property, Sophie saw the dark green of a forest on the hillside above the memorial. The tall, thin spires of cypress trees reached toward the heavens.

They crossed the bridge to where U.S. soldiers rested.

Neither Sophie nor Will spoke.

Ahead and on either side of them, the solemn markers that guarded the fallen spanned the hillside in symmetrical rows. Pristine white marble Latin crosses, interspersed with headstone posts topped by the Star of David, crisscrossed the hallowed ground like a massive choir of angels.

Sophie gasped. *Thousands of headstones.* She'd seen pictures of the vast burial ground at Normandy, but viewing in person these hills dotted with gravesites made the war of her grandfather's generation suddenly real.

She fought her urge to turn and run away. She handled Marie's funeral. She could do this, too. Will needed her.

Sophie looked at Will. "Some men from your division are here?"

Will nodded.

Will had told her the 10th Mountain troops never lost a battle but incurred a high percentage of casualties. This holy place evidenced the war's toll.

Will clasped his hands in front of himself. "I'm going to Tom Hermann's grave. He was in my unit."

"Do you know where to find his gravesite?"

"Yes. One of my ski buddies did the research on the Internet for me. He even printed out a diagram."

Will pulled a folded sheet of paper from his pocket. He studied it without asking for help or advice, twisting his head back and forth as he matched landmarks to the map.

Sophie squashed her impulse to peer over his shoulder and offer assistance. This was something Will had to do by himself.

"Was Tom Hermann a close friend of yours?"

"No." Will strode off. His mission was to find Tom. Sophie wasn't a part of the team.

Not a friend? Sophie knew that despite what he claimed, something propelled Will to find this man's resting place.

Sophie followed Will. His rigid cadence turned the elderly man's shallow steps into a slow-motion march.

They passed one large section, and then, at the next, Will counted each row as he strode past. He turned and faced the left section.

His lips pressed together in a narrow line. He stood motionless at the edge of the row.

Will stepped forward with a slower pace, moving along the graves with an even stride. His head bobbed slightly as he walked by each fallen fighter.

Sophie walked several paces behind him. Pinpricks did a centipede walk up her legs. She glanced at the names on the headstones beside her.

These men left someone behind. Their loved ones were far across an ocean. Mother, father, friend, sweetheart, wife, or child. Someone grieved for those buried here.

Will paused and his head turned to read the inscriptions.

His shoulders straightened and he moved in a brisk walk to a burial plot farther down.

One crisp quarter-turn and he faced the headstone. He saluted.

Sophie stopped and watched from a distance.

Will talked to the soldier in the ground. He removed something from his pants pocket, kissed the small object, and moved to the marker.

Will leaned on the arm of the cross to drop to one knee and placed the contents of his hand at its base. He bowed his head, folded his hands, and prayed. Will used the gravestone to support him when he stood.

He resumed his position at the foot of the grassy vault and saluted again.

Will returned to where Sophie waited. "OK. I'm done here. Let's go to the memorial."

Sophie walked beside him, burning with curiosity. She wanted to know what Will left for the man he claimed wasn't a close friend.

They neared an intersection with another paved path. She eased a packet of tissues from her purse into her palm.

Sophie tossed the pack behind her and said, "This is an impressive sight, isn't it?" She gestured to the tall pylon presiding over the memorial. She hoped her voice would cover the sound of the tissues landing on the soft grass.

Sophie waited until five more rows were behind them. "I can't believe the number of Americans interred here. This is just one of many cemeteries on foreign soil, isn't it?"

"Yes. Over 4,400 American warriors from the U.S. Fifth Army are buried here. That includes 355 soldiers from the 10th."

"So many for the short time you were in Italy."

"Too damn many."

37

S he sniffled, to set up her excuse. She rubbed her eyes with one hand. "I lost my tissues. I must have dropped them. I know I had them when you stopped to pay your respects to Tom Hermann." She waved him ahead. "You go on. I'll dash back and see if I can find them. I can catch up."

Afraid he would offer his starched handkerchief, Sophie turned and jogged back to the row where she tossed her tissues.

Sophie ran past the packet and went to Tom's grave. She saw Will move steadily forward. *Please don't turn around.* She knelt and looked at the object on the grass.

It was a Bronze Star attached to a blue-striped red ribbon.

Did Will give his own medal to Tom Hermann?

Sophie stood and sprinted back. She bent down beside the plastic pack and pretended to tie her shoe.

She intended to jog up to Will, but her side hurt. She settled for a quick walk.

Will stood by the pylon. A lovely sculpted figure topped the tall column.

"I found it," Sophie said with labored breath.

"You didn't have to go through that charade, Miss Sophie. I know you did that on purpose. You're a terrible actor and a worse liar. You could have merely asked what I left with Tom."

Sophie felt her face flush. Will *had* been evasive when she asked if he'd known the man well. "OK, I'll ask you straight up. Was that your Bronze Star?"

"Yep."

"Why did you leave it there?"

Will met her gaze with a steady look but revealed nothing. "Tom died of battle wounds. I imagine his next of kin got a piece of metal for his sacrifice."

Sophie was frustrated with his cat-and-mouse game.

She jammed both of her fists onto her hips so that her elbows jutted out to the sides.

"Will," Sophie said in a stern, disciplinarian voice, "That's enough. You've accused me of lying and called me a terrible actor. Now you're dancing around my question."

Will snapped at her with the voice he used when he had threatened to report Bangor to the apartment manager. "I'm not dancing!" Will's tight face glared at her.

Sophie sighed. She knew it was her responsibility to de-escalate the situation, even though she thought his actions justified her response.

She inhaled and exhaled a slow, deep breath to calm herself.

"Will," Sophie said, reaching out and touching his forearm, "I apologize for being so insistent. Whenever you're ready, I'd love to learn why you left your medal on Tom Hermann's grave."

He nodded in a curt acknowledgment.

She waited.

OK. You don't want to tell me now. But I won't forget.

Sophie pointed to the memorial. "Are you ready to go on?"

Will nodded.

They stopped by the low fountain. The murmuring water encouraged visitors to pause and reflect.

Will sat on the bench. He lifted his left hand and shielded his eyes. His head tilted forward. Will's other hand rested on his thigh. Both his arm and leg trembled.

Exhaustion? Emotion? Sophie bet either one might apply.

Will lowered his hand from his eyes and motioned for her to join him on the seat.

She sat next to him, with a small span between them.

His face had turned the dusky gray of the Rocky Mountains clinging to their last moments of sunset.

Will spoke slowly with quiet words. "Tom and I were sent ahead to search and clear an area. We were within range of the enemy, headed for the best cover we could find."

Will's right hand clamped tighter on his leg. "A sniper saw us. Tom stopped and leaned in front of me an instant before the sniper's bullet flew."

Will turned to face her. He bit his lower lip. "Tom took the slug that should have been mine."

He swiped at his eyes with the back of his hand. He swallowed with difficulty. "Tom called to me for help. But I followed my orders. I protected myself and blasted those Germans with everything I had."

The proud, brave veteran sat stiff-backed beside Sophie. "By the time the fight was over, Tom was gone."

He turned to look at Sophie. "Tom took the hit and I didn't help him." Will's chin dipped once, and then he pushed himself up to a stand.

Teardrops trickled down Sophie's cheeks.

He extended a hand to help her up.

"Thank you," Sophie said, "for sharing your story. I can't imagine how hard it is for you to recall that horrific day."

Will muttered something Sophie couldn't quite understand. It sounded like, "That wasn't all."

In a firm voice, born of the steel that makes a young man volunteer for hazardous, life-threatening, body-punishing duty, he continued. "I said I'd tell you why I gave him my Star. Tom got one, too. His Medal of Honor, though, went to his surviving family.

"I figured after freezing, climbing, damn near starving, battling the peaks and the Germans, and then saving another guy's life, Tom deserved his very own medal."

Sophie's tears blurred her vision. "He did."

"I better move before I get too creaky." Will clapped

his hands once. "Miss Sophie," he said with forced determination, "let's finish the tour."

They walked up to the third tier of the memorial, the highest level. Two open courts created a frame on the north and south ends. The south atrium served as a forecourt to the chapel.

A rectangular pool faced with travertine sat in the center of the open court. It featured one spray of water that jetted toward the sky.

Will edged toward the connecting wall between the two solemn courtyards. The granite Tablets of the Missing were inscribed with names. Names of the 1,409 missing in action in the region, on land or at sea.

Will stopped a couple of times during his somber walk along the wall. Each time, he moved closer to the wall to read it better. Once, he removed his glasses, rubbed his eyes, and leaned closer to the name before him. His fingers traced the inscription on the cool stone. His head bowed.

Sophie didn't intrude on his pensive stroll. It was apparent Will had lost friends to death as well as that black void of "missing in action."

He walked over to rejoin Sophie. "I'm ready to go."

Sophie had a hunch Will harbored more secrets about those war years. Secrets that caused him pain. Or shame. Or both.

38

Will knocked on Sophie's door five minutes ahead of the agreed time to leave for dinner.

"I'm starving. How about you?" Will had showered, shaved, and, no doubt, napped after their emotional trip to the cemetery.

"Me, too." Sophie had been afraid she wouldn't sleep after seeing the thousands of graves that morning. She was wrong.

She had struggled to keep her eyes open during the ride back into Florence but had felt it was her duty to stay alert. Sophie collapsed on her bed for a nap as soon as she returned to her room.

She finished freshening up and rushed downstairs.

Will stood by the reception desk, visiting with the heavyset man who had taken over for Chiara. On top of his blue-and-white-striped, short-sleeved shirt, a navy blue sweater rested on the back of Will's thin shoulders. The arms of the cardigan hung straight down across his chest.

Sophie had taken note of the Italian men with sweaters draped over them the night before when she and Will walked to their disastrous meal. It was evident that Will had also noticed.

She walked up to Will and patted one shoulder. "You're looking very dapper this evening."

Will had decided he needed only two pairs of pants for the journey, khaki slacks and blue jeans. Tonight, he wore the khakis.

In the Denver airport, Will had insisted on stopping to have his brown dress shoes shined, one of the many revelations about the terminal Sophie learned. The variety of food stands, sports bars, and stores selling sundries, clothing, luggage, and books shocked her.

A glance at her scuffed black ballerina flats made Sophie regret the lost opportunity for a polish.

Her jean skirt and knit shirt made Sophie feel underdressed. She hadn't brought anything sporting a logo or a saying, but a wrinkled pullover top couldn't match his crisp-looking outfit.

"Did you iron your shirt?" The words blurted out before Sophie could stop herself.

Will grinned. "A fella's gotta always look good. Never know when, or where, we'll find Francesca."

A pin pricked Sophie's heart. She doubted they'd find Francesca in Florence or anywhere else. *What will the disappointment do to Will?*

The aromas that filled Sophie's nostrils when she entered Chiara's recommended restaurant pushed aside her worries about Will.

The warm, soft light from wall sconces and candlelit wooden tables embraced her and beckoned weary travelers inside.

The milky-white, rough-plastered walls and a travertine floor resembled the pictures Sophie had seen online of Italian trattorias. Burnt umber cushions topped the ladder-back chairs. The restaurant's decor was a reflection of the Tuscan color palette.

The tempting aromas of savory meat and freshly baked bread brought a growl to Sophie's stomach.

She felt Will's eyes on her.

Will nodded with a wistful smile on his face. "That smells like the last meal Francesca cooked for me before I left for the port."

How can he remember the smell of food he ate over seventy years ago?

A dark-haired twenty-something beauty interrupted Sophie's thoughts by showing them to a table. "Please enjoy your evening." She held out a chair for Sophie.

Sophie slumped against the back of the wooden chair with relief. She looked around the room. Unlike where they dined the previous night, the room was empty of guests, except for one other table.

An elderly couple, both short and plump, sat at the table closest to the kitchen. The woman's hands flew through the air as she relayed a story in Italian to her companion.

Sophie saw the man raise one finger as a young male waiter walked past. The server moved to the man's side and bent low. Sophie could not hear their conversation.

The young man rushed into the kitchen.

A man swathed in a long, white apron over a pale green shirt and black pants stepped out of the kitchen. He walked up to the couple and visited with them.

The apron-clad man moved to a side table covered with bottles of spirits, cordial glasses, and thin champagne glassware. He opened a bottle that had been chilling in an ice bucket and filled two flutes.

He picked up the stemware and presented one each to Sophie and Will. "Would you care for a glass of Prosecco?" he asked in English.

"Yes, please," Sophie said. "*Grazie.*"

"*Prego.*" The man smiled at Sophie.

The chef, with a glance and nod at Will, moved one step closer to Sophie. He angled in toward her and described their specialty, Pappardelle al Ragù di Cinghiale—noodles with a sauce of cinghiale—which, he explained, was wild boar.

A solemn look replaced the chef's smile. "Many restaurants carry this dish, but ours is most special. We use only homemade pasta, the best tomatoes, and the most delicious *cinghiale* in Italy."

Sophie leaned forward as he elaborated on the entree. Will's admonition about flirtatious Italians popped into her head and made her press back against the chair frame. "That sounds delicious."

The chef kissed the tips of his fingers and sent the kiss airborne with a flick of his hand.

"Thank you." Will's voice was pleasant. "We would like to look at a menu, though, before we decide."

"Of course."

The woman who had brought them to their table stood by the kitchen with the server, who was in his mid-twenties.

The chef retreated into the kitchen.

"*Buonasera,*" the waiter said and handed Sophie and Will menus. The dishes were listed in Italian with an English translation written below.

He smiled at Sophie and gestured to the paper of heavy stock, printed in a handsome script. "Please. Look over our excellent offerings this evening. Then I can answer questions about the preparations and suggest some of my favorites to you."

"We'll look at it now, thanks," Will said.

After he and Sophie were alone, Will rested against his chair back and raised his eyebrows at her. "Old, young, doesn't matter. Everywhere we go, this will happen."

"What?"

"The men will flirt with you."

"What? They're not flirting. They're doing their job."

"You've got it wrong, Miss Sophie. That cook came out for one reason only. He heard a beautiful American was in the restaurant and he wanted to check you out for himself."

"No. Chefs do that all the time. They go out and visit with the customers."

Will chuckled. "Didn't you notice he was only talking to you?"

Sophie brushed off his remarks with a flip of her hand. She tried to ignore Will's smirk.

Will pulled a three-by-five unlined index card from his shirt pocket. It was covered with writing on both sides. He studied it without speaking and then pocketed it.

The waiter appeared and asked if they would like something else to drink.

Will spoke up. "Would you pick out a bottle of Chianti that you think we might like, please? Not the house one. Something mid-range, please."

Will then rattled off the names of three Chianti producers and said that they would like something similar.

After their server disappeared to fetch it, Sophie spoke. "I didn't realize you were a wine expert."

Will chuckled. "I know as much about wine as I do about flying a plane. I can only tell the difference between one that tastes like dessert and one that makes my lips pucker."

Will patted his pocket. "One of my ski buddies gave me suggestions on how to order wine for a pretty lady.

Since I'm planning on taking two pretty women out to dinner in Italy, I figured I better study up."

"Two?"

Will blinked. "Why, you and Francesca, of course."

39

For the first time since they left Denver, Sophie relaxed.

She had walked on and off three airplanes between Denver and Florence—something she never imagined doing. The flights were behind them and, other than the mustard on her shirt, nothing bad had happened.

They were within two short blocks—easy walking distance—of their hotel.

The server appeared with a bottle of Chianti and presented it to Will, and then poured a small portion into Will's glass.

Will sipped the wine. He nodded to the server.

After the man filled their goblets and disappeared into the kitchen, Sophie spoke. "You handled that like a pro."

Will grinned. "Good. Now lift your glass, Miss Sophie."

He picked up his glass to toast hers. "To finding Francesca."

Sophie forced a smile to her lips in spite of her doubts.

Their waiter slid a small platter in front of them. It

held two slices of grilled bread topped with sautéed mushrooms flecked with green herbs.

"Compliments of the chef," the man said. "Fresh porcini with thyme and parsley from our garden." He retreated to the back of the room.

One word came to Sophie's mind to describe the lush flavor of the appetizer: *Seductive.*

He returned to take their dinner requests. The man nodded with a pleased expression and placed a shallow tureen in front of each of them.

"This is today's soup. It is perfect for a night that is turning cool. The chef sent it for you. For dinner, I recommend the Pappardelle with *Cinghiale.*"

He bent a fraction closer to Sophie. "Would you like to order this pasta dish?"

Sophie stifled a giggle. "Absolutely."

"As would I," Will said. His eyes twinkled and his lips curled up in a smile.

The attendant left. Sophie said in a whisper to Will, "We didn't have much choice, did we?"

"No, we didn't. It's what I wanted anyway. This chicken soup," he gestured toward the bowl in front of him, "smells a whole lot better than that canned stuff I eat when I get a cold."

She relished the rich chicken broth, with its golden hue and savory taste. Small, delicate puffs of tortellini, stuffed with cheese and spinach, swam in that soul-nourishing stock. The subtle flavors of the pasta floated across Sophie's tongue.

Will finished his first. After Sophie placed her spoon across her empty dish, the waiter reappeared beside her.

"Did you enjoy the Tortellini in *Brodo*?"

"I practically licked it clean." Sophie flushed crimson, embarrassed at her words.

The waiter chuckled and his fingertips brushed her shoulder.

Her face got hotter.

He cleared their bowls and soon came back with dishes that held long, wide pappardelle noodles. The brick-colored topping was sparsely clumped across the noodles compared to how American chefs would serve such a dish.

Small brown morsels of meat and red pieces of tomato speckled the ragù. Will leaned over his plate, closed his eyes, and breathed in the complex aroma.

He straightened in his chair. He dabbed a handkerchief at his eyes to dry his tears. "Francesca tracked and shot a wild boar in the woods. We didn't have noodles because there was no flour or eggs. She said her sauce was no good because too many ingredients were missing. But it was like this."

His eyes locked on Sophie's. "We *will* find Francesca."

Can he actually remember the smell of that wartime feast with Francesca?

Sophie sighed with delight when she tasted the Pappardelle with Cinghiale. A momentary feeling of guilt about the calories she was consuming hit her, but she got over it in a hurry.

No boyfriend anymore. No dieting needed.

Sophie hated herself for how she changed when she was dating Russ. She struggled with trying to lose weight but did it to please him. She bought scores of sexy clothes that weren't her style. Sophie became the woman he wanted, even though it felt like a betrayal to herself.

Why do women believe these actions are necessary to please a man? Shouldn't the reason for me to diet be because I decide it's good for my health? Or buy cute clothes because they make me confident and smile?

After a small, light salad of field greens and a glass of limoncello, Sophie noticed Will's eyes drooping.

Time to go home.

Tomorrow they would start the search for Francesca.

40

The September morning had not yet found the warmth of the day. The sun hid behind cotton puffs of clouds.

"Fine day, isn't it?" Will attacked his breakfast with delight and even helped himself to seconds of the cured meats and melon.

Their driver showed up on time, and now with Florence soon in the rearview mirror, Sophie wished there had been time to explore the city known as the birthplace of the Renaissance. *When will I ever have another chance?*

"I wish we had gone to a site with a panoramic view of the Duomo. Will we drive by somewhere that I could take a photo?" Sophie said to their driver.

The driver, in his fifties, beamed. "Of course. As you wish. I will take us on a route through Firenze that will give you a place for your pictures and a most excellent view of the Duomo."

After only a short drive, the black Mercedes turned onto a street lined with buses pointed uphill. A brown historic landmark sign pointed ahead with the legend "Piazzale Michelangiolo."

"Follow the people and you will come to a beautiful piazza, the Piazza Michelangelo, where you can view the glory of Florence. This most beautiful spot was created by Giuseppe Poggi in 1869.

"His museum honoring Michelangelo was not completed, but this is one of the best views in Florence. I will wait nearby. Here is my card; call me when you wish to leave, and I will meet you back here."

Sophie asked Will to go with her, and although his demeanor signaled this was a waste of time and energy, he obliged.

The view from the piazza was spectacular. Sophie led Will to a low stone wall at the edge of the terrace where tourists waited to take their turn for a photo. The ancient city center was the backdrop, with a spectacular view of the Duomo's terra-cotta-colored dome, the Arno, and the Ponte Vecchio.

"Go," Will said, gesturing to the edge of the piazza. "I'll take your picture. No arguing."

"One of me alone and then I want one of both of us. Then you alone, too."

He took a photo of her with his camera and another on her phone, after she showed him how. The couple waiting their turn behind them offered to take pictures of the two of them together on both devices.

Will moved in beside her for a photo. Sophie said, "Let's say 'Francesca' and that'll make us both smile."

It worked. The photos on her phone showed two

smiling people with the dome of the Florence Duomo to their side.

The photos of Will standing alone revealed a grumpy man eager to be on his way.

⁓

Their driver drove out of Florence and headed southeast on the A1/E35 Autostrada.

Thank God I'm not driving. The drivers here drive much faster than the I-25 traffic in Denver.

She glanced at the cement barricades that lined the road and narrowed its width. The barricades created a deadly funnel through which the speeding cars raced.

Will's exuberance dimmed. His bony hands clutched the seat edge.

Sophie forced herself to look beyond the blur of the barricades.

Rolling hills with neat green rows of grapevines broadcast that this was wine country. She saw a circular road sign that featured a black rooster with the words "Chianti Classico."

Will nudged her in the side with his elbow. "That's the kind of wine we drank."

Neither of them was an expert, yet Sophie and Will had fun the night before as they tried to guess the flavors in the wine. They giggled over possible terms and decided it held a hint of cherry.

Smaller white signs marked the names of villages near the freeway: Greve in Chianti, Radda in Chianti, and Castellina in Chianti. They left the Autostrada at the exit for ValdiChiana and followed white signs in the direction of ValdiChiana, Bettolle, and Sinalunga. The driver slowed as they approached a small town.

Low, white industrial-looking buildings lined the outskirts of Bettolle. Their car skirted the edge of the village and soon left it behind.

They traveled farther from the Autostrada. The softly undulating fields graduated to rolling hills. They passed a vineyard with green, trim rows of grapes. Olive trees bordered the vines, with silvery puffs of leaves at their crowns.

Clumps of trees now banded the road, creating green canopied tunnels over the tight turns. The winding road climbed toward a striking Renaissance hill town at the crest. The colors of the town's buildings changed as they drew closer.

Sophie's first impression of the city that rose above the landscape was of coral-colored buildings, each seeming to run into the next.

The car drew closer to the village on the hill and the colors began to separate. The ginger-colored roof tiles and burnt-orange chimneys contrasted with the golden ocher of the walls.

The walls themselves morphed into shades of gray and mustard-colored stone, both interspersed with warm pinks, tans, and ocher.

They entered the town and drove around the edge of the buildings. Their driver explained that many ancient cities in Tuscany restricted automobile traffic on city center streets. The car crept through tight, right-angled turns. The pavement gave way to bumpy cobblestone streets.

The driver parked in a packed-dirt lot filled with twenty cars. He got out and removed their suitcases from the trunk of the automobile.

"Your hotel is a short walk up that hill. I cannot drive there. It is prohibited. I will help you with your luggage." He smiled. "Welcome to Montepulciano."

41

The narrow passage from the parking lot led up a steep hill and curved to the left. An archway straight ahead at the top of the hill marked the entry to what looked like a wine shop.

"Vino Nobile di Montepulciano" the sign above the door read.

"This is the entrance to the caves of a well-regarded producer here in Montepulciano," their chauffeur said. "It is a very famous wine from this region. You should visit this place during your stay here."

The end of the cobbled path opened into a beautiful square, anchored on one side by a cathedral. A tall bell tower rose up next to the church. Their chauffeur asked for directions from a man walking past them.

From her research, Sophie thought their lodging was near the piazza, and she was correct. She and Will followed their driver down one of the streets that branched off the square. They walked along the line of attached buildings, and after a distance of about a city block, they approached a hotel.

The front of the building stood out from those on either side.

Not grayed and drab from years of weather, dirt, and probable lack of care, the building in front of Sophie stood colorful and proud. Almond-colored border stone surrounded the windows and complemented the salmon color of the mansion.

"This is it," their driver said. He deposited their luggage close to the hotel entrance.

The elegance of the twin door panels with their bulky black handsets and massive brass door knockers belonged in another century. A work of art on their own, the back plate of the knockers featured the face of a man with the ears and mane of a lion. The hinged moving piece attached to the sides of the face where a human's ears would sit.

Sophie reached for the knocker, eager to feel the smooth metal in her hand, the weight of its swing, and the strike on the doorplate.

The knock rang with a solid thud. Sophie wondered, looking up at the four-story house, whether they would hear the knock deep inside the building.

Two elderly women with brilliant white hair strolled down the street. Both shorter than Will, they stopped and silently stared at the Americans.

Sophie smiled at them, but their stoic faces did not respond. The women walked away with scowls across their faces. Surprised by this reaction, Sophie wondered if the women considered them "Ugly Americans."

The large door creaked as it opened. "*Buongiorno,*" said the barrel-chested, balding man who welcomed them to the mansion. The older man approximated Sophie's height and wore wireless round glasses, which mirrored the shape of his head. "I am Vincenzo. Welcome to Villa Lombardi, my home."

Will's hand shot in front of Sophie to shake his hand. Will introduced the two of them to their host.

Will paid the chauffeur and thanked him. Their driver wished them a good stay in Montepulciano, turned, and walked back toward his car.

Vincenzo put their luggage in the lift, said he would ride up with it, and instructed them to wait for the lift's return. They could ride it up to the second floor, which, he explained, was two levels up from the street.

Sophie thanked Vincenzo. With all of the walking ahead for Will and her, taking an elevator whenever possible seemed wise.

The tiny lift returned. Sophie and Will got into the empty elevator and pushed the button for the second floor. It crawled upwards. The elevator opened into a room with small bistro tables for two or four, lofty windows that bathed the room with light, and a long wooden counter topped with gray-streaked white marble.

Platters of pastries resting on tatted lace doilies lined one end of the bar.

The doilies dredged up a warm yet painful memory for Sophie. Her mother gave Sophie a cedar chest when she was five. It had been her mother's girlhood "hope chest," a place to store heirloom linens and gifts for her future marriage.

Inside this chest in Sophie's apartment, waiting for her someday wedding, she kept doilies with similar delicate knotted lacework. They had been handmade by Sophie's great-grandmother.

In the crazy dichotomy that was her life, next to the doilies, Sophie kept the electronic device cords that multiplied like rabbits, yet mysteriously existed without a partner apparatus to charge.

42

Will's room was compact. His bathroom, bed, and sitting area could all fit inside Sophie's small combined kitchen and living space in Denver.

Sophie's room was nothing short of glorious. The sprawling room featured a "large bed for two people," which seemed smaller than an American queen bed, and a dresser with a curved mirror attached. On top of the chest was another tatted lace doily resting beneath a small lamp topped with a linen shade.

A polished dark wooden floor scattered with throw rugs welcomed her into the spacious bedroom. On one side of the room, a wooden bench, coat hooks, and a large armoire provided additional storage for her clothes.

A small café table and two wooden chairs sat along another wall. It was the perfect place for her to set up her notes and maps for their quest.

The bathroom? Sophie sighed. Definitely *not* the highlight of her room. One could call it a "walk in, back out" space.

The tiny area held a bidet, toilet, white pedestal sink, and a shower. Sophie appreciated that the shower had a door, rather than a curtain, but the enclosure, barely three feet by three feet, would make shaving her legs a nearly impossible task.

For this trip, she had followed the advice from a travel blog, which was lucky. Sophie splurged on a hanging foldable cosmetic bag sided with clear plastic for easy viewing of the contents. It was perfect for cramped quarters. Without it, unpacking her toiletries would have been dicey at best.

Sophie explored her room further. A narrow door off the bedroom opened into a sitting area.

She smiled with delight.

The covered sitting area was a verandah that opened to a central courtyard and the sky. Sunlight filled the space with light and promise. This private retreat, furnished with a wicker loveseat, chair, table, and two large terra-cotta pots stuffed with red geraniums, was her favorite part of the entire suite.

Guilt washed over her. *Will is paying for this hotel. He should have the premium room.*

She went to visit Will and offered to switch rooms.

"No. Not a chance, Miss Sophie. What the hell would I do with all that space? But," he winked at her, "after we find Francesca, I might take you up on that offer."

I should have been firmer in saying "no" when he first asked me to help. Will truly believes we'll find her. I allowed him to have false hopes.

Sophie finished the last of her unpacking and tucked her suitcase and carry-on into a corner of her bedroom.

Her stomach growled. She hadn't eaten since they left Florence.

She found Will in the breakfast room with an empty dessert plate in front of him.

He grinned at her and pointed to the platter of pastries on the bar. "I can vouch for the square ones with apricot. Mighty tasty."

Sophie shook her head. "I want to explore the town. We can start looking for Francesca."

Will jumped up from the table. "Let's do it."

Outside, the warm autumn sun filled the piazza with light. A large church—the city's Duomo, Sophie guessed—dominated one side of it. More people were here now. Every age was represented in the piazza, mostly Italian, but Sophie also heard snippets of English conversations in the buzz of voices.

Two young women in short, tight skirts strolled by them, their rapid-fire, sing-song Italian words musical in tone and rhythm.

Three elderly Italian men stood in front of a majestic medieval stone building. A tall turret stretched to the sky from the roof, and arched windows lined the second floor, with a balcony across the center two openings. A businessman, dressed in a sports coat, entered the building.

Sophie gestured down the street that fell away from the piazza on the left. "Let's try this street. The road is crowded with people. I'll bet we can find a restaurant."

Half a dozen steps later, Sophie realized Will hadn't moved with her. He stood frozen in the piazza.

Sophie walked back to where he stood.

Will's arms hung by his sides.

"Will? Are you OK?"

His head slowly pivoted toward her. "I don't know where to start."

Sophie nodded. "I know. It's overwhelming."

He nodded.

"This city," Sophie swept her arm to encompass the lively square, "is a great place to start. Francesca, or at least her letter with the Montepulciano postmark, *was here.*"

She linked her arm through his. "First, let's find some food."

Sophie put up a brave front, but Will's fears mirrored her own.

Sophie also worried about Will's health and about his emotions if they couldn't find Francesca. She held fears about the adequacy of her arrangements for this trip overseas. *Did I plan for any and all emergencies?*

43

They wandered into a small restaurant, where they each ordered an individual pizza and a small bottled water. The food and fluid gave them energy and lifted their spirits.

Outside again, Will stepped in front of a couple in their sixties. He held up the photograph of Francesca holding her baby.

"Do you recognize this woman?" He didn't bother with pleasantries or a smile.

The couple shook their heads and brushed past him.

Will stomped over to two young girls in their teens. He thrust the image in their faces and barked out his query.

The girls backed away from Will with a frightened look in their eyes.

No wonder, Sophie thought. Will was a gruff old American man and, although slight in frame, looked threatening as he growled out his questions.

"Will, stop." Sophie put her hand on his shoulder and squeezed firmly. "I think we should take another approach. Let's walk down this street and stop in every shop and restaurant until we get to a dead end, or six blocks, whichever comes first.

"We can reward ourselves with a cup of espresso or a glass of wine when we reach that point. Then, we'll turn around and hit each of the establishments on the opposite side of the street as we head back up to the piazza."

He nodded. "Let's do it."

Halfway down the street, businesses and restaurants began to shutter their doors for the afternoon closure.

Sophie and Will turned around and walked back toward their hotel.

They hadn't planned on the stores closing for the afternoon. *One more thing that I didn't know about Italy.*

She proposed they have a drink of some sort back at the hotel and rest. Then, at 5 o'clock, or as the Italians said, at 17:00, start searching where they left off.

After their rest, they encountered a new problem: The farther from the piazza the stores were, the less English was spoken by the shopkeepers.

Sophie left Will to rest on a wrought iron bench outside a shop that sold pottery and household decorations.

She trudged back up the street to a housewares store they had stopped at on the way. The young woman tending the store spoke excellent English.

Sophie asked the young woman for her help with a written translation of their query.

I am Will Mills. This is a picture of a woman I met at the end of World War II. Her name was Francesca Polvani. I appreciate any help you may offer. Do you know this woman, her family, or someone who looks like her?

Sophie walked back down the street, hopeful that the written question would bring success. She tilted her head back, enjoying the afternoon sun on her face.

Sophie could feel the sun's warmth on the cobblestones beneath her thin sandals. The sound of Italian voices headed for shopping peppered the narrow street.

The angle of the sun cast shadowed light on the bench.

Will was gone.

44

Sophie dashed into one store after another.

No Will.

Where can he be? Did he trip on the uneven stones and injure himself?

The sound of laughter and female voices speaking English drew Sophie's attention. A cluster of middle-aged women stood outside a business farther down the street. It sported a red awning over its large front window.

She rushed over to them. Perhaps they had seen Will.

"Excuse me," Sophie said. "I'm looking for my friend. He's an elderly American. He's a bit shorter than me, has a lean build, and gray hair. Did you see him?"

"He's inside with Margherita," one of the women said. She was younger and thinner than the others. "She runs the cooking school here, where our group had a lesson and lunch."

She said to her friends, "Let's go, shall we? Our wine tasting is next." She turned toward the piazza and motioned for the others to follow.

Sophie walked under the arched entrance to the school. The hefty mahogany-colored doors stood wide open, encouraging visitors to enter.

To Sophie's left, a long wooden table occupied most of the space in a dining room, surrounded by simple chairs. The table held a bouquet of wildflowers, but nothing else.

Aprons with the embroidered skyline of an Italian hill town, presumably Montepulciano, decorated the left wall. The saying below the apron's horizon read, "*Cucinare è Amore.*" A center plaque on the same wall in a curly script translated: "Cooking Is Love."

To the right sat the most captivating kitchen Sophie had ever seen.

A butcher-block counter lined the right wall, stretching beyond the edges of the large windows that faced the street. Thick oak legs held up the bench and the lower shelf. Black cast-iron skillets, substantial stainless steel pasta pots and bowls, and oval roasting pans blackened from use filled the lower shelf.

The center island would suit an upscale Denver restaurant kitchen. A bar suspended over the metal table held hooks, which gripped copper pans, long-handled stainless steel spoons and ladles, and metal whisks.

More counter space, two deep sinks with tall faucets on hoses, and two dishwashers lined the back wall.

The jaw-dropping allure, however, was on the left side of the kitchen.

The enormous wood-burning fireplace, with a stone hearth and surround, reminded Sophie of the gaping mouth of a whale. The flames of a wood fire danced behind the arched six-foot opening.

Long poles with hooks and square spatulas the size of extra-large pizzas leaned against the wall on one side of the firebox. Neatly stacked firewood bordered the other side.

Sophie had seen wood-fired ovens in Denver and Boulder, but nothing could match the rustic beauty of this fireplace.

Two armchairs, diminished by the dramatic oven, sat unoccupied off to one side.

Sophie's culinary skills were limited to removing the lids from cans of tuna and preparing macaroni and cheese from a box. This kitchen, albeit intimidating, made her want to take lessons.

But where is Will?

45

A rounded woman in her fifties entered the kitchen using a back door. Her penny-colored hair complemented her freckled alabaster skin. She didn't look Italian at all, except for her broad nose and almond-shaped eyes.

"*Buongiorno*. May I help you?"

"I'm looking for my American friend, an elderly gentleman. He is thin and nearly my height."

"*Prego*. He is, I think, in our garden. Come. I will show you." She spun around and motioned for Sophie to follow her through the door at the rear of the kitchen.

Sophie was surprised at the charming, light-filled patio. It was a sunny garden, hidden from view in the middle of an ancient city center. The outer perimeter of green shrubs and wispy plants softened the stone-paved space.

Will sat at a long, rough-hewn wooden table in the center of the courtyard. A vine- and flower-decked pergola offered shade.

Stacks of salad plates, cruets of olive oil and vinegar, and baskets of sliced crusty bread adorned the table's center.

Sophie studied Will's face. "Are you all right?"

"Of course I am. Don't I look like I'm OK?"

"You look marvelous. I was worried about you. You disappeared on me, you know." She sat beside him. "It's pretty here, isn't it?"

"I suppose so."

"Look." Sophie gestured to the greenery. "Lush bushes, herbs of more varieties than I can name, and," she pointed overhead, "vines and flowers to offer shade."

The woman who showed her to the courtyard appeared with two goblets of water.

Sophie and Will thanked the woman but let the glasses of tap water sit untouched. They had agreed, except in the case of a dire emergency, to drink only bottled water while in Europe.

"I am Margherita Baggi, and this is my cooking school." Their hostess beamed with pride.

Sophie smiled at the woman and introduced herself and Will. "I heard from the ladies leaving your class how wonderful you are and how much they had learned. Your kitchen is beautiful."

"*Grazie*. You should come to a class. Both of you. You will like it."

"Perhaps in a day or two," Sophie said. "We've only just arrived today."

Margherita nodded in Will's direction. "Perhaps you should rest today and start your touring tomorrow."

"That's an excellent idea." Sophie turned to her travel companion. "What do you think, Will?"

"I think time's wasting." He pushed up from the table but immediately swayed backward and plopped back down on his chair. He grabbed the glass of water in front of him and drank half of it.

Sophie's eyes widened with dismay, but she didn't say a word.

"Let me bring you something to eat. You must be hungry." Margherita hustled back to the kitchen before Sophie could explain they ate lunch a short time ago.

Margherita returned with a plate of thin slices of prosciutto and salami, sliced Pecorino Romano, and figs cut in half to showcase their glistening boysenberry-colored flesh.

A warm aura spread over Sophie. A fig tree grew in her Italian grandparents' backyard. This simple gift of a fruit that she rarely saw in grocery stores conjured up the smiling faces of her grandparents and their inviting home.

Now, she and Will were here, in a foreign country where they couldn't speak the language, chasing a dream. Worries snaked into her mind. *What kind of trail do we have to follow? A single postmark from seventy-five years ago. How will we deal with it if Will gets travelers' diarrhea from the water?*

"Rita, I got more flour. Only five kilograms. Hope you can make it last until they get the delivery." The man who spoke entered the courtyard from the narrow rear alley. His unruly hair the color of a football and puffy, red face made him resemble a Scot who'd been in the sun too long.

The Scot was in his early fifties, with a belly that caused his belt to rest low on his hips. Over his bulbous nose, his eyes matched his hair.

"Well, hello, Luv." He grinned at Sophie. His voice sounded American, with a trace of a British accent.

"Hi." Sophie smiled.

Will nodded at the man who was at least four inches taller and seventy pounds heavier than him.

Sophie turned toward their host. "Margherita, do you have—"

"What is this?" Margherita's hand flicked the air at the man. "You could only find five kilograms of double zero? What do we do here? We teach tourists to make pasta. No flour? No pasta. If you no find it here, then maybe tomorrow you should go to Perugia."

The man laughed. "Not likely." He then moved closer and whispered something to Margherita.

Margherita shook her fist at him, but her face wasn't angry.

Sophie suspected this type of bantering was common between them.

Margherita looked at Sophie. "You would like something?"

"Bottled water, please, if it's not too much trouble. I'm happy to pay you for it."

The man walked into the kitchen and came back with two bottles of water. He offered them to Sophie.

"Thank you. What do I owe you?"

"For you, Luv—"

"Nothing," Margherita said in a firm voice. She shot the man a silencing look.

He winked at Sophie.

"This man," Margherita said, "is Joseph. I've tried to get rid of him for almost ten years." She wrapped an arm across his shoulders and kissed his cheek.

He grinned at Sophie. "Joe. Joe Able. An able-bodied man for all your needs, and a fellow American."

Margherita gave him a playful spank with the dish towel tucked in her apron.

Sophie handed Will both containers of water. "Thank you." She introduced herself and Will to Joe.

"What are you doing here besides eating our food and drinking our water?" Joe's question was rude, but this man with his disheveled appearance looked more a jokester than someone nasty.

Sophie patted Will's forearm. "We can leave now if Will is up to it."

"Up to it? Hell, I'm always ready," Will said in a loud voice.

"We've got another lesson in an hour." Joe scratched under his unshaven chin. "Unless you want to help with the lesson, you should leave."

Margherita turned to Sophie with a warm smile. "Do not listen to this impolite man. You stay as long as you want."

"I'll bet you can't boil water, much less make spaghetti," Joe said.

"You'd be surprised. I make great pasta." Sophie was lying. "I'm practically a gourmet cook, in fact."

Right. Gourmet cook indeed. On occasion, Sophie cut up a rotisserie chicken from the store and added it to her macaroni and cheese.

Joe nodded and sucked on his teeth. "Good to know. We'll know who to turn to if we need a backup for Margherita."

"Let's go." Will stood. The bottled water apparently perked him up.

Sophie vowed never to travel anywhere without bottled water nearby for each of them for the duration of the trip.

Will and Sophie walked toward the door that led to the kitchen.

"Good-bye, Chef Sophie," Joe said.

No classes for me. Sophie refused to let this jokester find out she knew nothing about cooking. Her culinary skills didn't even stretch to deciphering the menu in the fancy restaurants Russ had taken her.

46

Back at the hotel, she and Will sat in the breakfast room. He nibbled on another pastry, and she sipped the espresso that Vincenzo made for her.

Sophie eyed her travel partner, wondering if he ate as many sweets back home. She told herself to put the pastries out of her head, as thinking about Will's intake of sugar would only give her one more worry.

Sophie finished her espresso in one gulp. "Let's plan our attack for tomorrow. Crowds of people gather in the large square by the Duomo, the Piazza Grande. Our search should start with the arteries running off it.

"I'd like to find someone to help us translate. What do you think about enlisting Joe? He speaks both languages and knows the town and residents."

Will chuckled. "I suspect he has time to do it. I'm willing to bet Margherita is the workhorse."

"Let's pick him up a gift from one of the shops near the Piazza Grande. We can ask Joe for his help after their class is finished."

Vincenzo made no attempt to hide his eavesdropping.

He recommended they take a bottle of the local Vino Nobile di Montepulciano to Joe.

"This wine is the best," Vincenzo said. "It is DOCG and one of Italy's most important wines. I will sell you one from our special collection."

"I'd like to visit a store," Sophie said. "I want to learn more about the different varieties of local wine."

"The wines of Tuscany are the best." Vincenzo shrugged. "Of course. You wish to purchase *vino* from a tasting room." He approached their table. "Let me draw you a map to the excellent establishment owned by my cousin."

Sophie smiled. "That would be lovely."

Vincenzo drew the way to his cousin's business, which was farther than they previously walked. Today's search took Sophie and Will past several wine shops and tasting rooms. *Of course, he wants to give his cousin our business, regardless of whether it is out of our way.*

Sophie convinced Will to rest while she went shopping. He objected at first, but when she promised to suspend the Francesca search until he rejoined her, he agreed.

The first shop Sophie passed looked pretty but too expensive. The racks inside were constructed of wood, and on the plate glass window gold lettering declared the store's name and hours.

Too fancy and too pricey.

Sophie walked farther. This street off the Piazza Grande continued for the distance of several city blocks without visible crossroads intersecting it.

The cobblestone street was barely broad enough for two vehicles to pass. The narrow lane was reduced even more by the vendors' displays outside their shops, parked motorcycles and scooters, and the cars that people set down anywhere, ignoring the signs forbidding parking.

On her right, Sophie slowed beside a leather goods store she hadn't noticed earlier. The colors of the leather caught her eye. Montepulciano was a small village off the interstate highway, yet these hues were ones she hadn't seen in the States.

One in particular made her peer closer.

The wallet, fastened by a snap closure, mirrored the coloring of Bangor's collar—red, green, white, and blue. Sophie fell in love with the braided neckband, which showcased the colors of the Italian flag, for her mother's ancestry, combined with the Union Jack, for her father's heritage.

How is Bangor? It's about time for the lab to send me an update. What does it mean that I haven't heard any-thing? I'll email them when I get back to the hotel.

Sophie pulled her eyes from the attractive display and spotted another wine store a short distance ahead.

The door was open. Inside, the bottles stood upright on open wooden shelves. The room occupied a smaller space than the shop she passed earlier.

A thin man in his fifties with hair more gray than black sat in the back watching a small television. He stood when Sophie entered.

"*Buongiorno,*" he said.

"*Buongiorno.*"

"May I help you find something?"

"Yes, please."

He walked close to her. "Red? White?"

"I would like a ..." Sophie had practiced the name so she wouldn't have to look at the paper in her pocket. "Vino Nobile di Montepulciano."

"You're asking for the best, you know. Very famous. The grapes are all grown in this area. You know about it?"

"Only that."

"It is made with a minimum of seventy percent Sangiovese grapes and up to thirty percent from other varieties authorized for the Tuscany Region.

"Vino Nobile di Montepulciano was the first wine in Italy to receive the DOCG designation." His pride was evident. He explained what DOCG stood for and the prestige of the honor. "Our wine is controlled by the government, you see. The law requires a maximum yield per hectare of 80 quintals."

"Maximum yield?"

"Oh yes. This ensures quality. Let me show you what to look for."

He pulled a bottle from the shelf and pointed out the official-looking neck strip with the initials "DOCG."

"This wine must be aged for two years to be labeled DOCG as well as meet all the other requirements. For a *Riserva*, it must be aged for three years. This," he pointed to the word on the label, "is a *Riserva*."

He returned the bottle to the shelf. "How much would you like to spend?"

"Would you please recommend bottles in a range of prices?"

He pulled three bottles down from the shelf and stood them on the counter in front of her.

Sophie did the euro-to-dollar conversion in her head. The prices surprised Sophie, as she expected their gift to cost more.

Her main exposure to wine was the expensive bottles Russ had ordered in restaurants. *One of several things he did to impress me when we first dated.* It was empowering to learn something about wine. *See, Russ, I'm not as unsophisticated as you thought.*

She purchased the middle-priced bottle and hoped her gift would be sufficient to enlist Joe's help.

47

Sophie hoped Joe would not only be their interpreter in the Montepulciano shops but in the surrounding towns as well.

Joe sat outside in front of the cooking school. Through the doorway, Sophie saw Margherita sweeping the kitchen floor.

"May I join you?" Sophie said.

Joe nodded.

Sophie sat on the far end of the bench and shifted on the seat, allowing her to turn to face him.

"Are the classes for the next week all booked?" A deceptive question, she knew, but after his banter earlier, it was fair.

He stroked his chin. "You're in luck. They are, but let me try to persuade Margherita to work you into a class or two."

He clapped his hands together. "Tell you what. I'll find a spot for you in one each day. By the time you leave Montepulciano, you'll be a gourmet cook."

Sophie forced a smile. "Well, I might learn a thing or

two about the regional cuisine, but I fear they would be too basic for me."

An utter lie, but I have no time for lessons.

Sophie spoke each word distinctly. "I came to ask you for help."

"Margherita is a better teacher than me."

"No, I'm not asking for lessons. I need an interpreter and someone familiar with Montepulciano and the surrounding area."

"A tour guide?"

"Not exactly."

She explained their search for the long-lost Francesca. She gave Joe the Vino Nobile di Montepulciano. He nodded in appreciation.

Without saying anything else, he rose and walked inside.

Sophie peeked into the kitchen.

Joe held the bottle behind his back with one hand and circled Margherita's waist with the other.

Margherita laughed. Joe slid around Margherita and presented the bottle of wine to her.

She responded with a kiss. He murmured something in Italian.

Joe strolled back outside with the walk of a lazy lord grudgingly going to speak to a serf. He sighed, demonstrating that the mere conversation with Sophie took effort.

"I might, for a small fee," he said, "be able to help you as a guide and interpreter. Margherita has a car we can use.

"I need to help run things in the school, though. Tomorrow I shop. I'll be in and out of Montepulciano. The day after may be possible."

"Of course. I understand. Thank you."

"Here is my info," he said, handing her a business card from his wallet. "It lists my mobile number. You can figure out when you'd like to book me, and I'll see what I can do."

Sophie thanked him. Printed on it were the name, address, and website of the cooking school and Margherita's full name. On the back in crooked handwriting, it read "Joseph Able" and a phone number.

To say Joe was of lesser importance to the school than Margherita was an understatement.

I'm pinning my hopes on him?

48

Sophie dragged her feet up the two flights of stairs. Her tired legs felt like someone had strapped ten-pound weights to her ankles. *All this walking up and down hills and stairs counts as exercise, doesn't it?* Russ repeatedly said she needed to lose weight. *Was it true, or merely another of Russ's lies?*

Don't think about Russ. Memories of him only demoralize me.

She headed directly for the breakfast room and found Will chatting with Vincenzo, who stood behind the bar wiping the counter. An empty espresso cup sat in front of Will.

Sophie greeted them both, then asked Vincenzo for a glass of wine.

"You are tired, no?" Vincenzo said.

Sophie's flushed cheeks deepened in color with embarrassment.

"Sit, please, Miss Sophie." Will stood and pulled out a chair at his table.

Sophie slumped down on the chair.

Will patted her hand. "We might have luck tomorrow."

"Joe might be able to help us, but not tomorrow. We're on our own again." Sophie fought to keep her discouraging thoughts to herself.

Vincenzo appeared beside them with a carafe and two glasses.

Sophie gave Vincenzo a weak smile and murmured her thanks. *I feel like I need more than one glass of wine, so it's good he brought a carafe.*

He stood beside the table for a minute or two and then drifted back to his position behind the counter, picking up his cloth to wipe it clean. The countertop, however, couldn't be soiled in the five minutes since he last ran a rag over the smooth surface. He wanted to eavesdrop.

She spoke in a lowered voice to Will. "What makes you think we might be more successful?"

"I've been trying to remember everything about Francesca."

Sophie waited. She'd discovered in their brief time together that pressing Will to reveal his thoughts didn't speed him up.

"Francesca's a gritty one."

Sophie took a big swallow from the goblet. This producer's vino seemed lighter and thinner than what they drank at dinner the night before. She should find out from Vincenzo what he served them, so she could avoid it.

Sophie nodded at Will, encouraging him to continue.

"After the men went off to war, the women here coped alone."

"American women did the same."

Will's lips pressed together, and his eyes narrowed. "The difference is that the war was fought here. In the Italians' hometowns and over their farms and in their forests. Not some foreign place an ocean away."

Will tapped out a rhythm with his fingertips against the underside of the table. Sophie couldn't identify the song, but the tune was fast-paced. He gazed out the window while his fingers drummed to the music playing in his head.

"Will," Sophie said, "please tell me how Francesca was 'gritty.' "

Will's head pivoted back to face Sophie. "Her older brother got drafted as soon as Italy entered the war. Her father ran a butcher shop here in Montepulciano before the war started."

His voice hardened. "The Nazis rolled through here. Even though the countries sided together, the Germans took whatever they wanted from the Italians. They emptied the butcher store of everything of value.

"Her father taught Francesca how to cut meat and she helped run the business. The two of them went at night to the woods. They'd hunted before, of course, but now the wild boar, rabbits, and birds they shot were all that they had to sell."

Sophie sat forward in her chair. "Francesca and her father worked here during the war?" *Why didn't you tell me this before?*

Will nodded. "They closed their shop in 1943. Damn Nazis swept through here, again and again, each time taking everything as provisions for the troops."

Emotion streaked Will's face. "She told me what happened after her father gave up the store. He fell ill and couldn't get out of bed. She had to hunt alone. She went for several days, freezing and sleeping on the ground in the forest."

Will shivered.

"When she killed something more massive than she could carry, she hid the game and ran back into town. Her family owned a cart for the heavy loads, but no horse to pull it. Francesca and her mother loaded the kill and pushed the wagon to town.

"She, a little wisp of a girl, skinned and butchered her kill and delivered the meat in the wee hours to the starving people of Montepulciano.

"No one could pay her, except with vegetables they had canned, or olive oil harvested from trees outside of town."

He shook his head and gazed at Sophie with wet eyes. "She was a hero in Montepulciano." His voice trembled. "They should know her."

Sophie squeezed his hand. "Of course they should. They must." She tried to control her excitement. "Now we have a place to start. Butcher shops. Maybe a relative runs the place now, or the owner is someone who bought it from her family."

She jumped up and rushed over to speak to Vincenzo. She invited him to join them for a glass of wine at their table and signed for a new bottle on her tab.

Once their glasses, including one for Vincenzo, had been filled, Sophie explained that Francesca worked in town during the war. She pelted Vincenzo with questions.

"How many butcher shops in town are operating in the same location as they were during the war? Did you know the families who owned them before the war?"

Vincenzo pushed his glass toward the center of the table. He stood and crossed his arms over his chest. "I know these things you ask, but I will not help you. These people did not butcher only animals and fowl. They butchered *people*, too."

49

"You lie!" Will sprang to his feet.

Sophie grabbed his arm. Will balled his hands into fists.

Vincenzo slammed both palms on the table and sneered at them. "I speak the truth. Ask the people of this town if you wish. No one will help you. No one."

The hotelier stomped out of the room.

"What the hell does he know?" Will said.

Shaken but not about to discard their only lead, Sophie agreed. "Tomorrow we'll go up and down the streets and ask questions at every store that sells fresh meat. I can do it alone if it's too taxing for you."

"Hell no, you're not! Tomorrow I'll beat you walking up and down these streets. This is my girl you're talking about."

Sophie disagreed with him. Will would tire quicker than she would. She only hoped he wouldn't exhaust himself for nothing.

The next morning before she showered, Sophie sent a quick email to the lab at CSU and asked about Bangor's reactions to the trial medication. *Bangor's a fighter. He must be OK.*

Will knocked on Sophie's door fifteen minutes early. Thankfully, she was dressed, but she hadn't finished putting on her makeup. Sophie opened the door. Will had pressed his collared shirt and, by the looks of it, buffed his shoes until they glistened.

"Good morning, Will. You're early. I'm not quite ready yet."

"I want us out of here before that lying S.O.B. opens the breakfast room. You're beautiful as you are."

He gazed at her. His voice softened. "Marie always hated to go out without her eyes done." He nodded. "Put on your mascara, and then we're hitting the road. I'll wait for you outside."

"Right. Mascara and downstairs. I'll be there." She couldn't agree more. Sophie had no desire to see Vincenzo this morning.

She shuddered. *Did the beautiful young woman in Will's photographs dismember a man?*

Sophie dashed to the bathroom for the fastest application of mascara ever. No time for moisturizer, foundation, blush, or eyebrow pencil. Good thing she didn't know a soul in Italy, other than Will, Margherita, and Joe.

They stood at the counter in the small bar across the piazza to drink their espresso, which was half the price that Vincenzo charged them. They each ordered a ciabatta roll with thin slices of mozzarella and tomato inside.

"A meal to go," Will said to her as they munched on their sandwiches. "Beats American fast food all to hell, doesn't it?"

Sophie tucked two extra bottles of water in her shoulder bag. They would likely be walking farther today. She didn't remember any meat markets close to the Duomo.

"Let's start down this way," Sophie said, and gestured in the direction they had entered the city. Near the Teatro Poliziano, next to its colorful posters, they turned to follow Via di Cagnano.

A few steps along the cobblestone street, a stone stairwell sloped down under an arch built into the ancient bastion on the left. It was a shortcut from an outer side road to the Piazza Grande.

She would watch for it on the way back. Will would need every shortcut they could find.

Will walked down the street with an energetic bounce in his step and his arms pumping. "We're going to prove that lying bastard wrong. Oops, sorry about the swearing, Miss Sophie."

She fell in beside him. "Don't worry. Some nasty things came to my mind about him, too."

Will quipped about the businesses they passed.

The street continued to run downhill from the piazza, which troubled Sophie. Eventually, they'd have to work their way back uphill.

Sophie pointed out a charming trattoria next to a small bed and breakfast hotel. She stopped to look at the posted menu. It listed pizza and half a dozen pasta dishes. The tiny restaurant looked clean and welcoming. "We can walk here later and stop for dinner."

They agreed that the weather that day, warm and mid-70s, was perfect for their walk. What Sophie and Will didn't talk about was that they had yet to see one meat market.

After they walked awhile in silence, Sophie could hear sounds of a busier road nearby. Beyond a curve in the street, slow-moving vehicles and scooters crossed the street on a wider, intersecting road.

Awnings and picture windows of tasting rooms, restaurants, and bars lined the sides of the street.

Sophie's heart ached with disappointment. *No markets selling fresh meat here.*

50

An invisible rope pulled Sophie and Will to the colorful window of a gelato store on the corner.

The colors alone beckoned them—pale green pistacchio, white limone, blush fragola, chip-flecked stracciatella, deep brown cioccolato, and many beautiful hues with names that Sophie couldn't decipher.

They stepped inside.

"*Buongiorno.* May I help you? Would you like a taste?"

"*Buongiorno.* Thank you." Sophie smiled at the attractive, thirty-year-old woman with big, dark eyes and tight curls of black hair that spilled out of a high knot on her head.

Will grinned like a six-year-old. "You bet."

He turned to face the Italian. "Miss, please describe these. They all look delicious."

The woman smiled and pointed out the flavors: Pistachio, lemon, strawberry, chocolate chip, chocolate, double chocolate, orange, hazelnut, mocha, almond, raspberry, mixed berry, mint, vanilla, peach, and caramel.

Sophie's mouth watered at the choices and the vibrant display.

Will spoke first, with a broad smile on his face. "I'd love to sample your chocolate, hazelnut, and peach if that is not too much trouble."

The woman smiled. "Not at all."

Will took each of the plastic tasting spoons in turn and settled on the hazelnut.

Sophie sampled the lemon, almond, and raspberry. She chose the almond, a flavor not carried by her favorite ice cream store in Highland, a trendy neighborhood not far from the apartment building where she and Will lived.

"Thank you. How long have you been in Montepulciano?" Sophie said.

"Ten years ago I moved here from Florence, where I had gone to university."

Sophie decided the direct approach was the best. "We are interested in visiting butcher shops. Could you help us locate where these are on our map?"

"Stores where they cut their own fresh meat, or also markets with food ready to eat?"

Sophie and Will exchanged glances.

"Both, if you would, please," Will said. "I suspect the butchers in town give a woman as beautiful as you all the best cuts, don't they?"

She smiled and batted her eyes. "That I do not know."

"What is your name?"

"Tessa."

Will shook her hand. "I'm Will, and my pretty friend is Sophie."

Sophie shook Tessa's hand. *Ninety-one years old and still playfully bantering with young women. He must have been quite the ladies' man when he was younger.*

He pulled his street map out of his back pocket and extended it to her. "Tessa, would you please mark the butcher shops with a little "x" and the markets with a dot?"

"Of course I will do this, and you," the clerk gestured to the cafe tables and chairs outside, "should go and enjoy your gelato before it melts."

Sophie's gelato definitely tasted like almonds, but with a creamy freshness that popped in her mouth. She had devoured a third of her small dish when she saw that Will had barely eaten any.

Will scooped gelato onto his spoon and gazed at it with appreciation. He placed the spoon in his mouth, closing his lips over it. He noticed Sophie watching him and blushed.

Sophie rested her hand on his arm. "Don't be embarrassed. I'm the one who should be for gulping mine down. You're savoring it."

Will's face turned sorrowful. "This dish of gelato is good for me. It helps me forget. Forget what a coward I am."

"What do you mean? You're not a coward. You're a war hero."

Will's pained eyes rebutted her words.

Tessa appeared beside their table. She looked at Will's face and stepped backward. "*Scusi.* I interrupt."

"No," Will said. "I'm an old man with too many memories. Please, sit with us."

"It looks like you brought our map," Sophie said, trying to lighten the mood at the table.

"Yes." Tessa pulled a chair over from a neighboring table and sat down.

"Here," Tessa spread the folded street guide out. "There are two butcher shops, here" she touched a spot on the guide "and here." The second one was in a section of town far from where they were. "The markets" she pointed out four "as you see. These two" the ones that were closest to the Duomo "have more items to take and eat on a day trip. They cater to visitors.

"These on the outer edges of the town are for residents, with staples we use in cooking. They also have cured meats plus foods that are easier to purchase than preparing ourselves."

Will's face brightened. "Thank you, Miss Tessa. This is helpful. We sure appreciate it."

Tessa stood.

Sophie jumped to her feet and impulsively hugged Tessa. "Thank you. This is perfect."

Will scrambled up and reached in his pocket for the photograph of Francesca.

Sophie shook her head at him, thinking Tessa was too young to have seen Francesca.

There was no stopping Will, though. He showed Tessa the old picture. Not surprisingly, Tessa did not recognize Francesca and had never heard of her name or family.

Sophie was eager to head to the butcher shop closest to the gelato shop.

They threw away their trash, thanked Tessa again, and walked outside.

Six leads here in Montepulciano. *Will one bring us to Francesca?*

51

The first establishment was a small shop, with glass cases along one side. Those in the rear held raw meat and poultry. The man tending the counters spoke English. He glowed with pride when Sophie inquired about the shop's history.

"My father was a tailor," the man said. "He worked here fifty years and his father's family for generations before. I added these ten years ago." He tapped the top of the refrigerated case. "Everything inspected. *Perfecto*."

Tailors occupied this space. It wasn't a butcher shop during the war.

"What meat will you want today?"

Sophie remembered her delicious dinner their second night in Florence. "Wild boar."

"Come the day before your meal. I'll give you cooking tips." He thrust out his chest.

Will stepped forward until he stood closer to the clerk than Sophie.

"Thanks for the help. My friend knows how to cook, though, so she won't need advice. Appreciate the help." Will nodded to the man.

They went outside. "Strike one," Will sighed. "Dang it."

"We have several more leads."

"I'm not discouraged about this place, or even upset at how that guy made goo-goo eyes at you. It's that." Will pointed to the uphill road that led to the Duomo.

Sophie glanced around. She didn't see anything resembling a taxi or bus. She doubted the ride-sharing services she used in Denver had made their way to the hill towns of Tuscany.

Sophie and Will walked back to the busy thoroughfare. She knew what she had to do.

Half an hour after her call, an older model, dusty, blue four-door Fiat pulled to the curb on the narrow side street.

Joe got out of the car.

"You called. I came." He looked cheery. Joe's hair was tousled and his face as red as the first time they saw him.

Joe ushered Will into the front seat of the car and held open the door behind Will for Sophie.

"What model of car is this?" Will said in a gruff voice.

"This beauty is a 2005 Panda, second generation. One of the best-selling models ever in Italy. Pandas are used by the Italian army and some police forces. It's a fine car."

At one time it probably was a beautiful car. Joe might be correct about the army and police forces choosing the Fiat for official use, but his car had seen its share of wear over the years.

Joe headed up the hill, alternating his focus between Will and Sophie. He barely glanced at the unforgiving stone walls or occasional pedestrian.

"Is this the vehicle you use when you take tour groups?" Sophie asked.

An elderly woman carrying a large grocery bag in one hand and the leash to a small scruffy dog in the other walked toward them on the right edge of the street. The dog zigzagged back and forth from the wall into the street.

"I take this or rent a van." Joe pivoted back to look at her.

"Joe—look out!" Sophie pointed at the woman and her dog.

He swerved left, and the woman jerked her dog's nylon lead to pull him to safety.

Sophie looked out the back window to verify that the woman and her dog were safe. The woman turned around to look uphill at them. She shook her fist and cursed. The dog stood at his owner's feet, wagging his tail.

Bangor's goofy, loving face filled Sophie's mind. Her stomach cartwheeled. The veterinarian lab hadn't responded yet to her request for information about Bangor.

52

Joe took Sophie and Will back to their hotel. He offered to drive them to the markets farthest from the Grande Piazza after they had rested. "We can stop for a coffee afterward," he said.

"I'm pooped, Miss Sophie. I'm not hungry." Will smiled. "Must be all those pastries I ate today. You can go with Joe now."

Sophie was desperate for any clue that might lead to Francesca and agreed to Will's suggestion.

Joe whistled beside her in the car. He glanced over at Sophie. "How come your boyfriend didn't come along to Italy?"

Sophie felt the heat creep over her face. She pushed aside her embarrassment and spoke with false confidence. "I'm single."

She astonished herself. Her words sounded confident. Strong. Independent. Much better than "I don't have a boyfriend because he dumped me."

Joe's eyes took a slow assessment of her body. "Are you gay?"

"No." Sophie lifted her chin. "I like men, but I'm single."

She saw the market ahead. "That's it. You'll interpret, right?"

"Of course." He motioned for Sophie to walk in first and then sauntered in behind her.

"*Buongiorno*," said the man standing in front of the glass displays.

Joe's hands flew in front of him as he spoke in quick words to the merchant.

The shopkeeper was in his forties and wore snug indigo jeans. His white T-shirt clung to him like a second skin, and black chest hair curled over the shirt's V-neck.

Cured meats rested in one arm of the refrigerated glass cases, and prepared sandwiches on ciabatta bread, salads, and pastries sat in the other.

Narrow shelves in front of the sandwiches held fresh fruits and vegetables of vibrant hues. Sophie marveled how the produce—grape clusters with tiny round orbs, red Roma and cherry tomatoes, long yellow-green pepperoncini, and glossy, deep purple eggplants—was arranged with the eye of an artist.

Joe waved his hand in Sophie's direction while asking questions of the shopkeeper.

The merchant directed his short responses to Joe, but his eyes remained locked on Sophie.

Joe picked up three eggplants.

The storekeeper scowled at Joe.

Joe responded by juggling the eggplants.

The seller threw up his arms and cursed.

Joe caught the fruit with soft hands and eased them back into their tray.

The retailer shooed Joe and Sophie out into the street with booming Italian words and a jabbing finger.

That attempt for information was a bust.

Joe hadn't mentioned Francesca's name to the merchant, and Sophie had no chance to show the photograph. The shopkeeper made it clear that no one should touch the produce, let alone juggle the vegetables.

Tears dampened Sophie's eyes. She inhaled a deep, slow breath, and steadied her emotions.

She excused herself from Joe and made the excuse that she wanted to shop for a purse on the way back to the hotel. He motored away.

Good riddance.

She wanted to go—alone—to the other market on the outskirts of the city, as it was not far from where she stood.

She berated herself for trusting Joe, a shyster who took advantage of fellow Americans needing help in a foreign country.

Sophie's stop in the next store also failed. The current owners bought it five years before and didn't know the store's history.

We're getting nowhere. Will and I may need a new plan, but what?

53

The next morning, Sophie slept through her alarm. The first thing she did was to check the email on her phone. *The lab responded.* Her hands shook when she opened the message.

Bangor showed no progress with the experimental medications in the first month. We will continue the same protocol for at least two more weeks and determine our next course of action at that time.

We are understaffed and will not be able to respond to your queries in the future. Our goal is to update you every four to six weeks as the clinical trial proceeds. Lab resources are prioritized on clinical research rather than correspondence.

Sophie closed her eyes and pictured Bangor standing in her apartment, wagging his tail at her. Tears filled her eyes. *Bangor showed no progress. They also made it clear my queries aren't welcome.*

She wrapped her arms around herself and thought of Bangor as a puppy. He loved to sleep in the crook of her arm when she lay on her sofa and watched a movie at home. He snuggled in and flopped over—belly up and legs spread—safe and secure in Sophie's arm.

Fight, Bangor. You can do it. Fight.

She glanced at the digital clock on her phone. "Ugh, I am so late."

Sophie had no choice but to minimize her makeup, as she had done the day before. She had intended to "doll it up" for the shopkeepers she would meet, but sleeping in cost her.

Sophie, Joe, and Will met in the Grande Piazza. Sophie arrived last.

To her relief, Will asked Joe to drive him into the country around Montepulciano. A ride would give Will an opportunity to sit and have a restful day.

Sophie wanted to visit the last markets in Montepulciano alone. She could walk much faster without Will, and Joe wouldn't be along to act like a goof and anger the owners.

The sunny new day brightened her spirits. Sophie had a list of questions written in Italian by Joe, Francesca's photo, a smile, and an American Midwesterner's determination.

Joe and Will hurried off after they drove Sophie to Montepulciano's second butcher shop. This store was housed in a more recent addition built outside the town walls.

Sophie soon learned this business started in the 1950s, and the owners had moved here from Siena. *Zero for two on the butcher shops.*

Sophie walked back inside the ancient town. Her route took her by the two remaining markets that sold cured meats. The first was a repeat of the others and also opened after the war.

A nasty blister developed the day before on the back of her right heel. The cute sandals, Sophie decided, weren't adorable if they caused a raw foot. Today she wore her ballerina flats and covered her blister with a cotton adhesive pad Will gave her.

The last business was a short distance from the main piazza. She stepped inside. The aroma of freshly baked artisan bread hit her nostrils and made Sophie's mouth water.

Long wooden shelves filled with bottles of olive oil, balsamic vinegar, and wines crossed the left side of the store. Overhead, whole prosciutto hams and different varieties of dried meats hung from the ceiling above the counter, some with a white powder casing on the outside. Crusty bread in a variety of shapes and sizes peeked out of diamond-shaped wooden cubbyholes on the back wall.

Sophie followed her nose to the rear counter like a hummingbird drawn to the smell of sugar water in a feeder.

A woman in her fifties turned to face Sophie. "*Buongiorno.* May I help you? You would like some bread?"

The answer in her head was a resounding "yes," but Sophie declined.

"I will cut you a sample." The woman sliced a thick chunk from the low, broad loaf on the countertop. She offered the piece to Sophie. "This is a ciabatta. A crunchy crust and large crumb."

How can I refuse such a gracious offer? Sophie thanked her and bit into the bread. The juxtaposition of the firm, chewy crust and the soft interior was a perfect combination.

Sophie usually didn't eat bread. She used a visual trick of imagining hunks of bread, rolls, muffins, and biscuits stuck to her hips, where starches ended up on her body.

In college, Sophie knew the cause of her "freshman fifteen." She ate an English muffin every day for breakfast. Her "hourglass frame" quickly turned into a diamond on her lower half, large enough to warrant naming rights.

Sophie tried to conjure up her baked-goods-on-the-hips visual before she devoured the entire piece but couldn't do it. Her body craved carbs after walking around Montepulciano.

"Delicious," Sophie said to the woman. "*Grazie.*" Sophie tore her eyes from the wall of bread before she weakened and bought a loaf. She stepped away from the counter. Three Italians who entered the shop after Sophie—a young couple and an older woman—moved to the bread counter to place their orders.

The two glass cases on the left held varieties of cheese, rectangular slices of pizza Margherita, pasta salads, olives, marinated red peppers, sun-dried tomatoes, grilled vegetables, and sandwiches built with a thick slab of fresh mozzarella cheese, green pesto, and sliced raw tomatoes.

Sophie wanted to eat everything.

A man a little older than Sophie walked in from the back room. He held something that resembled salami. "Miss," he said, "would you like some soppressata or prosciutto? A sandwich we make fresh?"

Sophie shook her head. "No, thank you. Maybe tomorrow my friend and I will come and have you make something for us."

"A picnic, no? There are many wonderful spots to picnic in the countryside near here."

"You might be able to help me with one thing." Sophie moved closer.

"Yes. Of course."

"This is a lovely market and has a prime location close to the piazza. I'd love to learn its history. Are you the owner?" She suspected it was someone older, but flattery would only help to foster his cooperation.

"No. Angelina's family owns it. I work here. Me?" He tapped his chest. "I am the boss of sandwiches."

Angelina, the woman who offered Sophie the ciabatta, wandered over. The man changed places with Angelina to help the other customers with their bread orders.

"You ask about our business?" Angelina's face brightened into a wide smile, showing crooked front teeth. "Are you a travel writer or tour operator?"

"No, just a tourist interested in Montepulciano."

"Why?"

Sophie lied. "I am doing research for an article on the history of the town businesses, from the start of World War II through today. I want to learn how they coped during wartime, whether ownership changed, how they survived during such a traumatic time."

Angelina perked up. "This has been in my family since immediately after the war. During the war, this building was used by the Germans as a beer hall."

"Do you know who owned it before the war?"

"It was under lease until the Nazis came here. The family disappeared like so many during that time. We were lucky to get the lease after the war."

"What kind of business was it before the war started?"

"I think a beer hall, like during the war."

Another strike. Francesca worked selling meats during most of the war. She certainly didn't run her business out of the Germans' beer hall.

Sophie heard cheers, wolf whistles, and the sound of a loud motorcycle from outside. She and the other patrons walked to the door to see who incited the commotion.

A bright yellow Ducati motorcycle entered the piazza. It skirted the edge with a roar and stopped in front of the imposing stone building with a turret.

Two people sat double on the motorcycle. They dismounted and removed their helmets. The driver wore a short, black skirt and a form-fitting knit shirt. The woman shook out her long, curly brown hair and carried her helmet in one hand. The stunning driver could strut down a Milan fashion runaway or Beverly Hills sidewalk and be right at home.

The man who rode behind her turned and waved at the group of young men who loitered outside the market. His eyes landed on Sophie for a second. He had close-cropped black hair, sexy stubble on his face, blue jeans, and a black T-shirt.

Both riders looked about Sophie's age but were infinitely cooler.

The woman grabbed her companion's hand and pulled him along with her into the building with a turret.

"What is that?" Sophie asked Angelina, pointing to the building.

"It is the Palazzo Comunale, an important government building in Montepulciano. The Nazis used the space as their base during the war in this area."

"What is it now?"

"It is the same as before the war. The city is managed there and you can get permits and licenses."

"Like marriage licenses," the self-proclaimed boss of the sandwiches said. He winked at Sophie and nodded, as if letting her in on a secret about the couple who scampered into the ancient building.

Engaged or not, having that sexy Italian man look her way made Sophie wish she'd gotten up in time to put on makeup.

54

That night, Sophie and Will decided to visit a nearby tasting room with underground caves. The man at the entrance, about Sophie's age, spoke excellent English and welcomed them inside.

The man explained this was not a winery, but a location for aging wines produced by one of the area's Vino di Nobile Montepulciano producers. This vino must be aged, he told them, for two years from the January 1st following the harvest, with a minimum of twelve months in oak.

They walked downhill into the cave. Sophie held Will's arm, praying the smooth stone surface would not be slick. She did not want her neighbor to fall.

They walked farther into the cavern. The humidity increased as they walked downhill, and the air became colder.

The vintages were aged in musty rooms where long rows of large wooden barrels lined the walls. Sophie and Will stopped to read the small instructional signs on the self-guided tour. The rooms spilled over, one after another, winding deeper and lower into the cavern.

They opted to follow a path that shortcut the remainder of the cave and passed into the tasting room at the end.

The greeter offered to pour them a sample, but Sophie thought food before wine would be a better option.

He suggested a trattoria nearby and directed them to follow the road that sloped down from the cave.

Will and Sophie walked a short distance and passed through an archway in the wall. This opened into a broader road—the main shopping street, according to the man in the tasting room.

Sophie kept her eyes on Will and worried about the uphill trek to return to their hotel.

Will, however, was full of energy, perhaps due to his time riding instead of walking earlier that day.

They settled into their chairs in the small trattoria, which held no more than a dozen tables. Will ordered a bottle of wine for them to share with dinner.

They started with a mixed plate of bruschetta: tomato, a dark paste of olives, and a savory one of boar, white wine, and raisins on thick slices of toasted bread.

Sophie couldn't decide which one she liked best.

They opted to split a pasta course and ordered Pici pasta with breadcrumbs. Their waiter explained that the rolled-by-hand Pici noodle was a traditional Montepulciano food.

Once their bowls sat before them, Sophie understood what he meant when he described it as a typical rustic dish. Pici noodles looked like fat spaghetti. With a simple sauce of garlic oil and breadcrumbs, the lightly coated homemade pasta soothed their souls and quenched their appetites.

"Joe Able," Will said, "is not a good driver. Way too jerky if you ask me. He did show me some pretty countryside, though."

"Where did you go and what did you see?"

"Oh, we went all around. We first drove by the Temple of San Biagio, just outside of Montepulciano. The church was made with travertine, Joe said. A real pretty honey-colored building. Shaped like a cross and very famous, too."

"Was the inside as lovely as the exterior?"

"We didn't go inside. We sat in the Fiat, and Joe told me about it."

He didn't look disappointed at the touring omission.

"Where else did you go?"

"Mostly we drove in rural areas. I was 100 percent lost. It was right nice territory, though. The vineyards were all pretty, and we saw rows of cypress trees, and olive groves, too."

"You rode in the car all day?"

"Of course not. We went to another little town, San Quirico d'Orcia, and had lunch there. Joe and I ate outdoors on a patio—a gorgeous scene. We had wine with lunch, but only one glass. After lunch, we rested in our chairs and looked at the view for a long while before we came back."

"Does that mean you and Joe napped?"

He chuckled. "I don't know about him, but I think I might have closed my eyes for a few minutes."

No wonder he's spunky and rested. They napped away the afternoon.

"Did you know that Etruscans settled this whole territory? And that the Medicis picked Montepulciano for a summer residence?"

"No, I didn't know that." Sophie tried to hide her disappointment. Joe had filled Will with interesting historical facts but didn't do a thing to find Francesca.

"I imagine I could tag along with Joe and keep out of your way for one more day. How about it?" His eyes twinkled.

"Do you have plans for anything specific?"

"No, just wandering down the road, seeing if I remember anything. Joe said he'd meet me in the Piazza Grande at ten in the morning."

"Oh. So you already planned it, did you?" Will looked stronger, more rested, and happy. She didn't mind if she got stuck with more dead-end queries at the stores in Montepulciano. She could wrap up the search here tomorrow and the following day go with them.

"Oh. One more thing."

"What's that?"

"Joe said there was a small chance that Margherita might need a bit of help from you tomorrow, like to run an errand or something. That OK with you?"

His hopeful face left her no choice. "Of course."

As long as I don't have to cook.

55

The next morning, Sophie and Will waited for Joe at a small outdoor table in the Piazza Grande. Their empty espresso cups sat before them. Joe's old Fiat pulled into the piazza's limited parking area.

Sophie walked over and thanked Joe for driving Will around, adding that she would also enjoy seeing the surrounding countryside. "Perhaps tomorrow?"

Joe nodded but didn't address her request. The good news was that he fired up the car without a word about Sophie helping Margherita.

He started to drive, but then stopped.

"Say, Chef Sophie, Margherita could use a bit of help today. She's giving a proposal to one of the local wineries. They're a big producer and want to start exporting their wine to the U.S. Would you mind stopping in to see her now?"

Joe pulled away—his hand waving good-bye through the open car window—before Sophie could ask what the "help" might entail.

Sophie stopped at the few shops that were open on her way to the school. The oldest establishment started doing business in 1948. Many of the businesses in Montepulciano, she realized, began operations after World War II.

Margherita was bustling in her kitchen. A lively fire was burning. She selected a log, added it to the fire, and rearranged the logs to elongate the flame.

"*Buongiorno,* Sophie. I am happy to see you. Joe sent you, no?"

"*Buongiorno,* Margherita. Joe said you might need a little help today. Do you need me to run an errand for you?"

Margherita waved her hand. "No, no. You can help me in the kitchen. I must finish my proposal, but I also need a few bites ready for the meeting."

Sophie gulped. *Cook?* She remembered her boastful, false claim to Joe. *This is bad—very bad. A few bites? I hope she wants something easy, like slicing and plating cheese and washing grapes.*

"I'm happy to help you, but I don't know how you like things done. I am a little nervous because you're a professional chef."

"Tsk, tsk. Don't be silly. This is easy. Slices of cheese. Simple."

Sophie hoped her relief didn't show on her face.

"The tomatoes are beautiful and ripe. Please use them to make bruschetta. I built a fire so it will be ready for you."

Bruschetta? Sophie had eaten bruschetta with a tomato topping but had no clue as to the ingredients that went into it. *Where does a blazing fire fit into the process?*

She swallowed. If she started with the cheese plate and took her time, perhaps Margherita would take over and whip up the bruschetta herself.

"Sure. Why don't I start with the cheese while you go do your computer work? That way if I have questions on the bruschetta, you'll be back here to answer them. Now, if you'll just show me which cheese you want to serve, I'll—"

"No, no. Start with the bruschetta, so the flavors have time to marry."

Time to fess up. "Margherita, please tell me exactly how you'd like the bruschetta prepared, step by step."

Margherita turned and bustled through the industrial kitchen like a whirlwind, shaking her head all the while.

"You start making a dice of the tomatoes. About this big." Margherita demonstrated by pinching her thumb and index finger. "Then you salt them." She nodded to Sophie. "Not like you Americans would, but lots of salt. I'll bring my computer in here, in case you have more questions."

Sophie felt the burn of embarrassment on her face. "Thank you."

A large bowl of Roma tomatoes sat on the island. Sophie brought the bowl to the sink. She knew to wash them before cutting. She could thank Russ for that. He had berated her once for slicing an apple at his apartment without scrubbing it first.

She carefully transferred the tomatoes into a colander

in the sink and sprayed them, making sure they were all clean.

She had just finished cutting the first tomato into a dice on the butcher block when Margherita returned with a laptop under her arm.

She stood next to Sophie and looked at the massacred fruit, which resembled more mush than dice. Margherita set down her laptop and put a hand on Sophie's arm. "You don't know how to make bruschetta, do you?"

Tears welled up in Sophie's eyes. "I'm sorry. The only thing I know how to cook is macaroni and cheese from a b-box." Her hand flew to her mouth, and she stifled a sob.

Margherita drew Sophie to her in a hug. "Shh. It's OK. We'll manage."

"I'm sorry I let you down."

"It's fine."

"Can I help you with the proposal, while you cook? Is that possible?"

Margherita nodded, her lips pressed together. "It is the only way the appetizers will get prepared."

Margherita quickly logged in, showed Sophie the proposal, and described the changes to be made.

"I can fix this," Sophie said.

Margherita raised an eyebrow.

"I do know how to prepare proposals. That's not a lie."

They both laughed. The tension broke.

Margherita became a calm but fast bruschetta-making machine. She smiled and hummed and explained the reason behind everything she did. To Sophie's surprise, it wasn't even that complicated.

First, cut an "X" in the base of the Roma tomatoes.

Dip them in boiling water for 30 seconds.

Pull them up with a slotted spoon and submerge the tomatoes into a dish of ice water.

Peel off the skins.

Cut the tomatoes lengthwise into halves, then again into long quarters. With a paring knife, remove the seeds and membranes.

Slice the quarters into thin strips and then cut them crosswise into little pieces.

Place the tomato dice into a colander in the sink, heavily salt the tomatoes, and gently stir them.

Let the tomatoes drain.

Sophie worked on the laptop. She looked up when Margherita walked by to wash her knives. The cheese was sliced and plated beside a platter of purple-fleshed figs, halved and drizzled with honey.

Sophie completed the proposal and Margherita went to print it. She directed Sophie to the back courtyard to collect basil.

Together they washed, dried, and cut the basil into a chiffonade. Margherita had to show Sophie how to create the thin strips, of course.

Margherita dumped the drained tomatoes and basil together into a glass bowl and added olive oil.

Sophie had thought Margherita had an overly generous hand with the salt until she saw what happened with the olive oil. The chef poured what seemed like a small pitcher of oil over the tomato mixture.

Margherita winked at Sophie. "Now we leave it to marry. I will go to change. You can toast the bread."

I can definitely run a toaster. "Of course." Sophie looked around. "Where is the toaster?"

Margherita laughed and clapped her hands. She pulled Sophie to the fireplace and motioned to the fire, calmed now into embers and low flames. "Here. This is what you use."

Margherita pulled out a long-handled wire basket that opened like a book. She demonstrated how it slid into support posts and rotated 180 degrees to roast both sides.

Margherita explained that immediately after toasting both surfaces, one side of the bread should be rubbed with the cut side of a garlic clove. Toast the next batch, rub with garlic, and repeat.

"You will add the tomatoes to the bread only when the guests arrive." For the first time today, Margherita looked nervous. "Can you do this? No lies."

Sophie looked at her and grinned. "It's like s'mores. This I can do. Go get ready."

Like s'mores? Not hardly.

56

Within the first minute of trying to balance the wire basket on the supports, Sophie realized she needed to hold the handle in place, as it wouldn't rest by itself on the bracket.

Sweat beads formed on her forehead.

Halfway through toasting the thick slices of bread, four at a time, quickly rubbing the cut garlic over the hot slices, and rushing to toast the next batch, she was a disaster. Sweat drenched her blue cotton T-shirt and soot streaked it with black.

Strands of hair stuck in wet clumps to her brow and the side of her face.

The odor of garlic on her fingers could ward off vampires.

"*Ciao*, Margherita," a woman's voice sounded from the entry.

Sophie prayed Margherita would appear to usher her business prospects into the dining area that doubled as a conference room.

Sophie listened for the sound of Margherita's footsteps.

The last batch of toast was almost done to crunchy

perfection. The trickiest part of the whole process involved dislodging the handle from the support. Sophie wiggled it loose, lifted it up, and ...

"*Ciao,*" a man said from behind Sophie.

Sophie straightened up and tried to turn toward the man, but the basket threw off her balance. It slipped out of her hand and, with the toasts still trapped inside the wire container, landed in the fireplace embers.

"Oh, no," Sophie said. The toasts were ruined.

"It's my fault." The man grabbed a towel from the counter and, using it as a potholder, helped her raise the basket out of the fire.

"I suggest you dump those in the trash before Margherita gets here." The woman who had entered with the man walked into the kitchen and wrinkled her nose.

Sophie wanted to say something witty, or apologetic, or anything, but she couldn't.

Not because she was mortified by dumping the last batch of bread into the embers, though she was.

And not because she looked sweatier and dirtier than if she'd been working in the field on a ranch under the hot summer sun, though she did.

No, Sophie was tongue-tied.

The striking Italian couple she saw running into the town hall, perhaps to get a marriage license? The very same duo stood in front of her.

"Don't worry," the man said. "Isabella and I promise to eat only a few of the bruschetta, so we won't run short." He smiled at Sophie.

He slid the garbage can beside her and urged Sophie to drop the ruined pieces inside.

"See? Your secret is safe with us. I'm Niccolò, by the way, and this is Isabella."

"Sophie." She gave them a weak smile. She couldn't muster more after broadcasting that she was as useful in the kitchen as pocket lint. "No need to cover for me. Margherita will know instantly that the platter is four short." Even if the chef didn't count them, the odor of burnt toast hung heavy in the air.

Sophie gestured to the dining room. "Perhaps you should have a seat in there while I finish up the food."

The handsome man put a hand on the woman's back to guide her. He turned before he stepped out of the kitchen and winked at Sophie.

Sophie scooped the tomato topping onto the still-warm bread. The fragrance of garlic meeting tomato and basil made her want to stuff one into her mouth immediately.

She decided to carry the platter into the dining room so the guests could eat them while they were still warm.

Margherita met her at the kitchen entrance, on her way to the meeting.

"I thought I'd take these to your guests before I leave."

"Let me," Margherita said, taking in Sophie's face and shirt. "It was hot by the fire, no?"

"Yes." *Please, don't say anything about the smell of burnt toast.*

"*Grazie.*" Margherita smiled with warmth. "Sophie, go home and take a shower."

"Believe me, I will. I hope the presentation goes well."

Margherita kissed the air in Sophie's direction and carried the bruschetta into the dining room to greet her guests.

On the way out of the cooking school, Sophie passed a mirror and made the mistake of looking at her reflection.

Her appearance was worse than she imagined.

Hair and shirt sweaty and plastered to her skin.

Black streaks crossed her top over her braless breasts. The clinging, grimy fabric made her look like she had competed in a muddy, wet T-shirt contest.

At least this shirt is blue, not white. Why did I think leaving my bras at home to save luggage space was a good idea?

57

A shower and clean clothes restored Sophie's appearance but did not alleviate her embarrassment. She sat on the balcony off her room and tried to convince herself the day's events hadn't been as bad as she remembered. She failed.

She got caught in a lie by Margherita, proving definitively that she couldn't cook.

She dumped the last batch of toasts into the ashes, showing her ineptitude in front of the prospects Margherita hoped to impress.

She looked like an unattractive Cinderella covered in soot from a furnace.

Sophie wanted no more men in her life after the devastating breakup with Russ.

Until today.

The Italian man who came to her rescue was handsome with an athletic build, friendly, kind, and spoke English. His eyes sparkled with humor.

Sophie made a fool of herself in front of him. The fact that he wasn't available didn't make her feel any better.

A brisk knock on the door pulled Sophie away from her pity party.

Will stood there holding a small bouquet of wildflowers in a coffee mug. "For you, Miss Sophie."

His kindness was the best thing that happened all day.

She offered him a glass of wine on her balcony. Even though entertaining her elderly neighbor in her hotel room might not seem proper, the delightful sunlit terrace provided an inviting spot to chat. Neither of them was eager to see Vincenzo after their earlier run-in.

Sophie thought about Vincenzo's crazy words. He claimed that wartime butchers killed both animals and people. He boasted that no one in Montepulciano would help them in their search.

Sophie refused to put credence in Vincenzo's claims.

One thing troubled her, though. Perhaps a mere coincidence, but no one in the city had given them any useful information. No one offered any clues about wartime meat markets or the people who owned them.

Will described his day with Joe. They covered a little more territory today, he explained. He mentioned a nearby town or two and the picturesque countryside they had driven through.

"It sounds lovely," Sophie said. She couldn't hide the wistfulness in her voice. She'd suffered through a hot, disastrous day while Will ambled around Tuscany.

Will tapped the rim of his glass to hers. "Tomorrow I'm getting you out of this town. We're going exploring."

"What about Francesca?"

"We'll stop in the butcher shops and markets we see and ask questions."

"That's the plan?"

"Yes, indeed."

She sipped her wine. Will's attitude switch from a hellbent search to "exploring" puzzled her. "What was the best part of today?"

Will gazed upward at the sky above the open courtyard. "Seeing how gorgeous it is here."

Sophie kept quiet, hoping he'd continue.

He took a tiny sip. "The Rockies are my favorite place on earth."

He rubbed his hands together. "I loved the days training with the 10th Mountain boys. Until I got to Italy, I thought the Camp Hale exercises were the hardest challenge I'd ever know."

Will swallowed hard. "I hated Italy. I've never been so scared." He shuddered.

He wiped his eyes with a shaking hand.

He gulped from his goblet. "Today I saw something else. This part of Italy looks exactly like the photographs in your guidebook: plains, rolling hills, olive groves, and vineyards." He nodded. "The crops getting ready to harvest are the opposite of the harsh, cold winter I remember."

Sophie didn't know what to say. She wanted to ask more about his time here, the battles he endured and his time with Francesca.

Will never gave her specifics. Sophie suspected his war years were too painful to recall.

Did a lifetime of denial and compartmentalization blur the memory of his time in Italy?

Will I be able to coax out the details?

58

They met Joe the next morning in the street outside their hotel.

"It's a grand day, isn't it?" Joe rubbed his hands together. "Let's go. The car's around the corner."

Will climbed into the front seat and Sophie sat behind him.

Joe eased the vehicle through narrow streets that wound downhill.

The calming colors of the continuous buildings varied from a weathered gray to beige to a deep salmon. Red-hued bricks set in arched patterns framed the rectangular doors that interrupted the tall facades.

Sophie marveled at the charm of this hill town. Arches appeared everywhere—above doorways and windows, around passages between streets, and even in the inlaid designs on the face of the city's fortified perimeter.

Pink and red begonias spilled over the window ledges above their heads. Ivy tendrils hung from small ridges along the wall. The colorful plants softened the hard surfaces of the passageway.

Sophie saw a bright light and distant trees ahead through an open archway.

"Where are we headed today?" Will asked Joe.

"We're heading to Pienza, in the Val d'Orcia."

"Is it far?" Will said.

"No. Only twenty minutes. Fifteen if I take out bicyclists that happen to be in my way." Joe grinned at Sophie.

Sophie refused the bait. "What's the Val d'Orcia?"

"You know we're in the Siena province, right?"

"I thought we're in Tuscany." Will looked sideways at Joe.

"We are, but the region of Tuscany is made up of provinces. This is Siena."

Will looked around at the chalky, rolling hills dotted with vineyards and shook his head in confusion. "Looks like farms to me, not Siena."

Joe swerved to the shoulder and slowed to a stop. A car whizzed by them on the two-lane road. "Climb out of the car on the shoulder side."

Joe walked around and joined them on the shoulder. He squatted down and drew in the dirt adjacent to the pavement. He scratched out a squiggly shape, long and narrow, that tilted left at the top.

"There are twenty regions in Italy. This," he said, pointing to his drawing, "is the province of Siena, which is only one part of the Tuscany region."

Joe drew a dot in the top center quarter. "The municipality of Siena."

On the right side, in the lower third of the territory, he drew another dot. "Montepulciano."

Next, Joe drew a line on one edge of Montepulciano that portioned off the lower right side of the territory. "This is the Val di Chiana, the Chiana Valley. It stretches across part of two provinces in Tuscany, Siena and Arezzo, and two provinces, Perugia and Terni, in Umbria."

"I will show you the Val di Chiana when we return to Montepulciano. It is where the famous Chianina cattle are raised. *Bistecca alla Fiorentina*, the Florentine T-bone steak, is made only from Chianina cattle and is served bloody rare."

Joe drew a short, wide oval to the left of Montepulciano that extended beyond the border of the province. "This valley, the Val d'Orcia, is where we head today. It is a World Heritage UNESCO site," he said, nodding with pride, "and runs from here to the Mediterranean. Photographers from around the world come to take pictures of the Val d'Orcia."

Back in the car, Joe nonchalantly draped his right hand on top of the steering wheel. He stuck his left elbow out the open window.

Sophie clenched her teeth in the back seat, thankful only a few cars shared the curvy, two-lane road with them.

"Pienza was started initially by the Etruscans. One important man born here, Piccolomini, was responsible for creating this ideal Renaissance city. In 1458, Piccolomini became Pope Pious II.

"The pope built a palace in this town of his birth, the Palazzo Piccolomini, next to the cathedral."

Joe glanced over his shoulder at Sophie. "Pienza is noted for its beauty, the Renaissance patterns, and trapezoidal-shaped piazza. It's also famous as a place of great romance and tragedy."

Romance and tragedy?

59

J oe refused to explain more but promised to elaborate when they stopped to eat.

"This," Joe swept his arm to encompass the trapezoidal court of Pienza, "is the Piazza Pio II. Bernardo Rossellino designed this piazza, which marked the inception of Renaissance urban design."

Sophie was surprised at Joe's knowledge. The piazza's floor was composed of a pattern of large squares. Red bricks spanned the ground at an angle, with each section bordered by light-colored stone.

Joe pointed to the cathedral and explained its architectural styles. "Rossellino created the white travertine outside facade in the Renaissance style. The inside, however, has Gothic elements, modeled after an Austrian church.

"The pope named the Duomo for the Assumption of Mary," Joe said. He walked up the steps.

Sophie expected Joe's dissertation on history and architecture to continue inside, but he stopped at the stand with multilingual brochures. "Deposit the fee, grab a brochure, and away you go. My tour stops here."

Sophie and Will walked inside. She studied the pamphlet.

The juxtaposition of polished wooden pews and a light-filled interior created a magical place. Sophie lowered her hand. She didn't need to read about the cathedral. Now, she only wanted to soak in the warmth that surrounded her and to capture the memory of this lovely space. Italy transformed Sophie's thoughts about churches. She found tranquility and beauty in the country's cathedrals.

The structure had a rib-vaulted ceiling in each of the three naves, which together resembled a cross. Sunlight poured in from windows on three sides. The pale, soaring columns and the pearl-colored main altar made the inside bounce with light.

"I've had enough," Will said. "You can stay if you want. I'm going to find Joe and have a cup of espresso. Maybe a pastry, too."

"I'll only be a bit longer," Sophie said. "Why do you want to leave so quickly?"

"I like little chapels, simple ones, better."

"We haven't seen any smaller than this."

"No. I mean in general, I like little chapels. They're more private. Intimate."

"Describe what you mean."

"One of my ski buddies is a rancher in Grand County. He built a chapel on his land. All his kids and grandkids were baptized there. I went up for a couple of them. "

Sophie wondered why he looked at the floor when he spoke.

His focus turned to her. He pulled out the snarl that he wore every day back in the apartment in Denver. "You needn't worry about finding us. I'll watch for you to come out."

If you're trying to be nice, you should use a kind voice instead of one that snaps at me, Will. I can find my own way around. She again kept her thoughts to herself. "Thanks."

At lunch, Will announced he and Joe would visit the butcher shops close to the piazza and ask if anyone knew Francesca.

"You," Joe said to Sophie, "may want to go to the Palazzo Piccolomini. The palace is the place of great romance and great tragedy."

"A love story? I assume, or hope, that was after the pope died."

Joe laughed. "Long after the death of the pope. It was used in a famous motion picture. Can you guess which one?"

Sophie shook her head. "I have no clue. Which one?"

"*Romeo and Juliet*, directed by Franco Zeffirelli."

Sophie held her breath. She had seen the film many times, the first with her mom once when she was sick and home from school. Her mother had adored it. Sophie watched Zeffirelli's version at least once a year.

She could hardly contain her excitement. "I know it well. Which scenes were shot here?"

Joe grinned. "The one with Juliet in the beginning in her—"

"Red dress?"

Joe nodded. "A few other scenes were shot in the building, too, including when Romeo and Juliet meet by the well during the Mask Ball. The dancing scene was filmed elsewhere, but they could have used the building's courtyard. It looks like it."

Sophie couldn't believe it. She loved the views of young Juliet running through the family palace and her glow when she meets the dashing Romeo—filmed right here in Pienza.

"Do you mind if I go to the palazzo while you try the meat markets?"

"Hell, no," Will said. "I'd rather spend my time looking at cuts of beef and pork and hanging prosciutto than touring another building."

"Same for me." Joe allowed Will to pay for the meal without any attempt to help cover the cost. "We'll drop you off, and you can stay there until we're done with the Francesca search. Be sure to check out the view from the loggia and garden. It's gorgeous."

How will I feel in that space? Every time Sophie saw the film, she cried. No, it was more of a full-on weeping session. The movie reminded Sophie of all that had been stolen from her.

60

Sand-colored travertine cloaked the exterior of the palace. The building, unremarkable except for the two floors of expansive windows, was incongruous with the lively frolicking gala where Romeo and Juliet first came in contact.

Adjacent to the residence, a white round well stood, similar in color to the city's cathedral. Two decorative columns and a crossbar topped the elaborate "Well of Dogs."

Sophie reran the film, *Romeo and Juliet*, in her mind.

Shakespeare established the feud between the Capulets and Montagues. He then introduced the fated lovers when Romeo, the son of the Montagues, crashed a glamorous party hosted by the Capulets.

Sophie dashed into the building.

The thick walls shielded the inside from the day's heat. A sign noted Pope Pius II used this as his summer home. She stepped, almost reverently, into the inner courtyard.

Sophie raised her eyes to peer at the balcony on the piano nobile floor, where the hall opened to rooms on the perimeter. This is where Juliet ran when her mother called to her and first spoke of an arranged marriage.

Sophie scanned the court. The other tourists entering the palazzo had disappeared.

She was alone.

She moved to the center of the courtyard's inlaid stones. She raised her arms until they extended straight out from her shoulders. She closed her eyes and remembered the orchestra's lilting music. Her torso and arms swayed in time to the tune.

Sophie opened her eyes and skipped around the circle of imaginary dancers. She pictured the whirling, twirling exuberance of the movie character Juliet. Sophie spun around and around with her arms held high.

"Juliet, I presume?" A woman's voice interrupted Sophie's twirl.

Sophie stumbled as her feet tangled from the abrupt stop to her dance. Her face reddened and she turned to face the woman who'd caught her dancing.

No. Not her.

Sexy Isabella's lips curled up in a smirk. Niccolò stood next to her.

"Don't worry. You're not the first American woman who imagines herself to be Juliet." Isabella's face bore a superior-looking smile. "Do remember that poor Juliet lost her love and her life."

Romeo remained true to Juliet. It was bad timing and bad luck that made Juliet lose her lover.

Two well-dressed couples entered. Isabella turned and carried on a soft conversation with them.

"The hanging gardens are famous. The view is spectacular," Niccolò said. "You may want to go there next." He pointed to doors that led outside.

Is this a dismissal, so his friends won't associate me with him? His face appears kind, not dismissive. Maybe he is offering me a face-saving escape.

Sophie bolted out the wide doorway leading to the garden.

The sophisticated grounds definitely belonged on the property of someone rich and powerful. Groomed bushes and hedges bordered precise pathways, which radiated from the central stone wellhead. The beauty and symmetry of the layout brought her a momentary sense of relief.

Sophie looked through one of the three arches in the ivy-covered rear wall. The breathtaking Val d'Orcia fell away below. Clumps of cypress and deciduous trees spiked up from the tans and greens of the rolling land.

An Italian villa graced the side of a hill. Tall cypress trees along the driveway created a regal entry to the sunset-colored home. Rows of grape vines dotted the slope above the house.

The distant, dusty-blue hills rose above the horizon. It reminded Sophie of the Colorado Rockies' foothills in the golden period of twilight, her favorite time of day.

Sophie heard Isabella's voice grow near. *She's bringing her companions out here. Why couldn't they have gone to an upper floor?* Sophie refused to subject herself to another confrontation. She dashed to the outer pathway and followed it around until she found an exit.

Sophie gazed over her shoulder at the mansion tied to her memories.

At the end of the path, Niccolò stood by himself. His fiancée's voice grew louder. *Isabella is coming this way.*

Niccolò lifted one hand to his lips and blew Sophie an air kiss.

What is that about? Sophie didn't wait to find out.

Joe and Will sat at an outdoor bistro table on the perimeter of the piazza. They had espressos in front of them and appeared to be people-watching more than visiting.

Joe's face bore an easy-going smile.

Will's face told her more than that his customary scowl had melted. He faced the piazza with glassy eyes and lips that drooped at the corners.

Is Will doubting the success of our mission, or is his disengagement caused by something else?

61

After they returned to Montepulciano, Sophie and Will rested in their rooms until dinner. Tonight, they wanted to try the new trattoria Joe recommended. They walked by Margherita's school on the way back to their hotel after dinner.

Two women with British accents wandered out of the school and up the street toward the central piazza. Margherita stood in the doorway, thanking them and wishing them a good evening.

"*Ciao*, Margherita," Sophie said.

"*Buonasera*," Margherita said. "You visited Pienza today. Did you enjoy it?"

Will straightened his shoulders. "Yes, we did. A pretty little town, but no leads, unfortunately."

Margherita nodded. "Tomorrow you may have better luck. Joe will take you to Montalcino. After the war, some people moved between the cities."

Margherita gave a firm nod, with her arms crossed over her ample chest. "You can purchase my supplies." She reached into her pocket, retrieved a folded piece of paper, and handed it to Sophie.

Sophie looked at the list. "Coffee and prosciutto? Can't you buy these here?"

"Of course." Margherita threw up her hands to emphasize the point. "This coffee is a special blend that one of my return students particularly requests. It is stocked by the bar next to the piazza in Montalcino. I called to make sure they have some. My butcher friend received a shipment of a special prosciutto from Parma. It is made in limited quantities and will sell out quickly."

She pointed to the paper. "Here is the address for my friend. Don't shop from another store or my friend will be angry. Joe will drop you off and then go to a winery to pick up bottles for a big dinner here."

Sophie agreed but was not happy about using her time for Margherita's tasks.

They were being used as pawns. Margherita dangled the news about people moving between the two cities to entice them to go to Montalcino.

What Margherita wanted was for Sophie and Will to do her shopping.

The only positive thing about running errands was that they could ask Montalcino storekeepers about Francesca. Those queries, however, seemed doomed. The farther they traveled from Montepulciano, the less likely they would uncover clues about Francesca.

The next day, the warm, brilliant morning and the smile on Will's face buoyed Sophie's spirits. They joined Joe at his table near the piazza.

"Will," Joe said, gesturing to a chair, "wait here. I have something to show Sophie."

He took Sophie's arm and walked her across the piazza toward the Duomo. "I forgot to tell you something about this place.

"Here," he swept his arm out, "this piazza was where they filmed the crowd scene for *The Twilight Saga: New Moon*." He bobbed his head with a self-satisfied grin.

"I read the books but didn't see the film."

"All those movie stars gathered right here."

Sophie listened to the sounds of the morning.

She watched an elderly woman walk past them, chattering in Italian to a young boy. Tourists discussed directions and sites in multiple languages.

A waiter from the market carried out a cappuccino to a patron. The saucer clinked against the table when he set it down. Friends called out to each other in passing.

Sophie liked the Piazza Grande as it was, with centuries of history behind it, and its present-day and future place in the workings of a city.

The Piazza Grande doesn't need a movie to make it a memorable place.

Joe's grinning face redirected her thoughts. She took the gracious route. "Thanks, Joe."

Joe described today's plan. "We will go by Pienza again, and then through the charming city of San Quirico d'Orcia. We can stop for a coffee before heading on to Montalcino."

"How long will the drive to Montalcino take?" Sophie asked.

"Only forty-five minutes, plus however long we're in San Quirico d'Orcia."

Sophie knew she needed to control their schedule as much as she could. "Let's not stop on the way. If we have energy after our shopping, perhaps we can on the way back."

Sophie glanced left and right as the tree-lined road wound uphill toward Montalcino. The city's walls of pale yellow, mustard, and burnt orange contrasted with the orange-gray of the corner towers' upper reaches.

The need to protect themselves drove Etruscans to build these ancient cities on hilltops. The strategic position gave them a military advantage.

Their road suddenly converged with several streets into a crowded switchback intersection of massive trucks and autos with scooters that darted in between. Sophie caught her breath.

How can people ride motorcycles and Vespas through these tight intersections with vehicles going every which way around them?

Joe pulled off the road. A skinny street ran uphill from where he parked.

"OK," Joe said. "You've got the list for Margherita, right?"

"Sure do." Will tapped the chest pocket on his shirt.

"Walk up," Joe pointed to the cobblestone street, "and you'll reach the Piazza del Popolo, by the Duomo. You'll see a place near the piazza to purchase an espresso. They have Margherita's coffee. No need to pay for it, she's got an account. They'll speak English and can direct you where to go for the prosciutto."

Will got out of the car. "Let's go. Time's a-wasting, Missy."

They agreed to meet back in the same location in three hours. Joe eased his car into traffic and drove away to pick up the wine for Margherita's dinner.

Sophie and Will strolled up the cobblestone street.

Several windows caught Sophie's eye, but she was on a mission: Pick up Margherita's supplies, check out all the meat markets, and, if they were lucky, grab a quick lunch.

She saw a tall, narrow stone building with a bell tower on one side. A round-faced working clock adorned the tower.

Retail establishments lined both sides of the street.

Archways marked many of the doors and openings. Ahead on the right, Sophie noticed a cafe, with small metal outdoor tables and chairs.

"Here's our coffee spot," Will said, pointing to the cups in front of a young couple outside. "Right where Joe said it'd be."

Will stepped back to allow Sophie to enter the store first.

Ebony and white tiles covered the floor. A long, beautiful, polished wooden counter, topped with white and gray marble, spanned almost the entire length of the business. Wooden open cabinets at the rear were filled with bottled wines, candies in large glass jars, boxes of sweets, small packages of coffee, and flavored syrups.

"*Buongiorno,*" said the solid-looking brunette woman inside. "May I help you? Would you like a coffee or something to eat?"

They learned the store had not only drinks but also panini sandwiches and small salads. Will and Sophie placed their order and then sat at a bistro table outside.

The woman came with their espressos. Will thrust the photo of Francesca under her nose.

"Do you recognize this woman? She's older now. In her eighties or nineties."

The woman shook her head, looking surprised at his question.

Sophie asked how long the storekeeper had been in Montalcino.

"I come from Austria, and am here only for the summer."

"We are to pick up coffee beans for Margherita Baggi, who runs a cooking school in Montepulciano."

The Austrian shook her head. "I can't help you. The owner's granddaughter will return soon." The Austrian smiled. "She may know."

Sophie thanked her and said they would wait. The Austrian walked inside.

"Sheesh," Will said. "She's no help."

Sophie patted his arm. "She is only here for the summer. You practically accosted her with the picture. A gentle approach might be better."

"Fine." Will crossed his arms over his chest. "You talk to the butchers. I'll wait here. We don't want to miss the granddaughter."

Sophie ate most of her salad. Will devoured his small sandwich.

She offered him the remainder of her meal and went into the bar to learn the locations of the butcher shops. There were only two in the city center.

Back out in the sunlit street, she found Will with his head tilted down on his chest, asleep.

It's all on me. The errands, looking for Francesca, and getting Will back to the U.S. healthy.

Life has been that way for a long time. It's my responsibility to take care of myself and make all the decisions. Mine alone.

62

One meat market was close to the Duomo, but the other was on the outer rim of the walled city. Sophie rushed to the farther one first only to find the business closed for the day.

I walked all this way hoping for information about Francesca. It was all for nothing.

Sweat beads dotted her forehead as she trekked back up the cobblestone streets. She prayed the next store—the one that had Margherita's prosciutto—was open.

Surely, Margherita knows the hours of her friend's shop. She wouldn't send us to pick it up if the store might be closed, right?

Anything seems possible in Italy. Anything that can go wrong, that is.

She sighed with relief at the open door. Rows of prosciutto shanks hung from the ceiling. Two middle-aged men in white aprons stood behind a refrigerated case.

"Buongiorno," one called out as she walked toward them.

The other man gazed at her in silence.

Sophie smiled and asked if either of them spoke English.

"Of course. In Montalcino, we almost all speak English, Spanish, and German."

"That's a relief. We certainly wouldn't have much of a conversation with my Italian."

Both men laughed.

Sophie explained about the errand for Margherita, and thankfully, they nodded their heads.

The older man grabbed a prosciutto shank that hung off to the side in the back. He secured the meat in a giant slicer on the rear counter. A thick wooden block formed the base of the cutter, with a tall, curved arm and metal pin to hold the shank in place. A tiny wire shaved the prosciutto off in thin, delicate slices.

The apparatus reminded Sophie of the old Victrola record player her mother had inherited from her parents.

The older man spoke. "This prosciutto is very special. We only get one or two of these each year. They come from Parma, but are aged longer than most, with a particular method of cure."

The second man meticulously layered the prosciutto between coated papers. The sizable stack, which weighed only 500 grams, was then wrapped in a white paper.

The man who ran the slicer wrote something into a ledger by the cash register. "This will cost our friend, Margherita, but she will pay us. She always does."

"Are you the owner?"

"Yes."

"How long have you owned this business?"

"My family started here before the war." His eyes looked off to the side. "Those were hard years. Germans came into Montalcino. They demanded we feed them."

He shrugged. "After the war was over, the hard times didn't end. No one in Italy had money." He rubbed his nose. "We," he tapped his chest with his palm, "our family, we survived. My father kept the business going until people had money again to purchase food."

Sophie played his words over in her head.

Were they German sympathizers? They had been allowed to remain open during the war, which, at a minimum, gave the appearance of aiding the Germans. Perhaps that was why the townspeople hesitated to frequent this place after the war.

She nodded in response to the man and pushed away her thoughts. *I need to stop suspecting people of aiding the Germans. It was wartime and people did what they needed to do to survive.*

The man puffed up in pride. "The visitors that rent expensive villas, they all come here for our meats. They are our best customers."

"The other store like yours in town—how long have they been open?"

"Not long. Twenty years."

Sophie showed the man the photograph of Francesca. "This woman worked in a butcher shop in Montepulciano at the start of the war. Her name is Francesca Polvani. She may have moved to Montalcino after the war was over. She would be in her eighties or nineties now. Do you know her?"

He studied the picture. "No. I don't know anyone by that name. I'm sorry. I can't help you."

Sophie nodded a farewell and left. She walked back to the coffee shop.

A striking Italian woman in her twenties sat next to Will with an espresso cup in front of her.

Sophie pulled a chair from the next table and sat beside Will. She extended a hand to the woman. "Hello. I'm Sophie."

The beauty's dark eyes sparkled. She clasped Sophie's hand between both of hers. "Mr. Mills spoke of you. I am Luisa. My pleasure."

"It's nice to meet you."

Luisa jumped up from the table. "*Scuzi*. I am sorry. Let me get you a drink. A refreshing glass of Vermentino? This lovely white wine from Tuscany comes from the coastal area."

"*Grazie*," Sophie said.

Luisa disappeared inside.

Will turned to Sophie. "She's pretty, isn't she? Her grandmother owns this place, and she runs the business."

Luisa brought out three stemmed glasses of white wine and a small dish of potato chips. She joined them at the table and lifted her glass in a toast. "*Salute*."

"I was telling Luisa, here, about Francesca," Will said. "She loved the story."

Luisa leaned forward. "So romantic. An American soldier coming back to Italy to find his love from long ago."

Sophie wondered if he shared the rest of the story. The part about him fathering a child.

"I wish I could help." Luisa shook her head. "I'll tell my mother and grandmother your story. My *nonna* is Francesca, too."

Will's head spun to face Luisa. "Your grandmother is named Francesca?"

Luisa smiled. "Yes, but she is not your woman from the war. *Nonna* moved here after my grandfather died. In the 1950s, I think. They came from Pisa, not from around here."

Will's crestfallen face said it all.

Luisa patted Will's arm. "I will ask them if they know of your Francesca. How shall I reach you?"

Sophie exchanged mobile numbers with Luisa and gave her Joe's cell number, too, as he would be a local call. She thanked the young woman and asked for the check.

"Margherita's coffee will go on the school's account." Luisa stood and walked inside.

Sophie followed her and offered her credit card to pay for their drinks and food.

Luisa declined Sophie's attempt to pay. "Put away your card. I'm afraid finding his Francesca will be difficult. I admire him, though, for his determination. This small gesture is all I can do to help him."

Sophie hugged Luisa. "Thank you."

A Francesca *did* live in this area, but she was not Will's love. Luisa, while well-meaning, only underscored the futility of their search. Luisa told them the name "Francesca" was one of the most popular female names in Italy.

63

It's fortunate the route out of here is downhill. Sophie looped her arm through Will's to walk to their meeting place with Joe.

The road curved at the base, and to her relief, Joe's car was parked in the "no parking" spot where he had dropped them off.

"*Ciao*," Joe said. "Did you get Margherita's prosciutto and coffee?"

Sophie held up the bag. "Absolutely."

Luisa, not Sophie, remembered the coffee. She gave Sophie a crisp green and white bag, into which Luisa tucked the coffee and the prosciutto. The bag was tied with a matching green ribbon.

Joe grinned. "I managed to not drink all the wine he offered at the vineyard, only one bottle." He winked.

Sophie studied Joe's face. *He looks sober.*

"Would you like to drive by a distinguished estate on the way home?"

"We're tired," Sophie said. "Perhaps another day."

"Speak for yourself." Will's grumpy persona had returned. "What's the name of this place?"

Sophie's eyes darted to Will. *It's not like him to opt for more sightseeing. Had he visited something similar during the war?*

"Villa La Foce. It's only a short distance. We needn't stay long, but the property is quite lovely."

Sophie started to object, but Joe silenced her with a wave of his hand. "We're going there. You'll thank me after."

Joe shared its history.

"The villa itself was constructed in the late 15th century as a hospice for merchants and pilgrims. Iris and Antonio Origo purchased the land and buildings in the early 1920s. They updated the operations and brought modern agriculture methods. The garden is pleasant if you like that sort of thing."

Will muttered something Sophie couldn't understand. She saw Joe glance at Will.

Will spoke in a loud voice. "I remember the name."

Sophie's eyes widened. *Once again, I find out he's not telling me everything.* "What do you remember?"

Will rubbed his forehead. He shook his head. "Can't recall."

Sophie didn't know whether to feel sorry for Will or be furious with him.

"Did Francesca mention it?"

"Maybe. Anthony, her brother, or his friends also might have told me about it."

Joe slapped one hand against the steering wheel. "I

thought you might be interested, Will, because of its role during the war."

They're both speaking in riddles. "What role?"

"The war years brought a hard and confusing time for the people here. The Germans forced young Italian boys to the front, they occupied the towns, and took the best of everything—food, lodging, vehicles, and livestock.

"The Italians didn't consider the Allies heroes. The Brits and Yanks dropped bombs on Italy's trains and harbors, including Pisa. Bombs sometimes don't land where they're aimed. Children who lost parents, women who lost their homes, these people had no place to go. Some came and took refuge at La Foce."

Will's head nodded. "That's what I heard."

Sophie's heart lifted with hope. "Were you there, Will?"

Will's brow furrowed. "Francesca hid me. She saved my life."

Will's trembling hand, not a handkerchief, wiped his mouth. "As soon as I could move without either bleeding to death or passing out from the pain, I worked my way to the coast."

He continued in a soft, slow voice. "The weather was starting to break. It was early April. We'd gotten word of fierce battles at the front, with awful casualties.

"The brass stationed some U.S. soldiers at Livorno, so I went there. I figured they'd patch me up enough for me to go back and fight with the 86th."

Will looked out the side window. "I was wrong. I did the wrong thing." His palm cupped the back of his neck like a sudden pain had erupted there. Will's shaking hand dropped to his lap.

"I should have gone north straightaway, to rejoin them and help break through the line in the Po Valley. Our troops sent those Germans running. On May 2nd, when the Nazi surrender in Italy happened, I was in Livorno.

"Part of the 86th charged on ahead and met up with the boys in the 44th Infantry coming south from the Battle of the Bulge. A couple of days later, on May 7th, Germany surrendered."

Will thinks he made the wrong decision because he went for medical treatment instead of dragging his battered, wounded body to the front. If he could barely walk, he wouldn't have been much use at the front.

"No." Will's voice rose, now louder and stronger. "I wasn't at La Foce."

Joe continued his story. "Italians caught harboring Allied troops or Italian deserters from the German fronts could be killed and their property confiscated. Brave individuals on the estate hid these soldiers anyway, at great risk to themselves."

"I want to see this farm." Will's tone left no room for discussion.

64

Joe spoke in a conversational tone, apparently unmoved by Will's confession. "My great-uncle fought in the war. Peter was the reason I started coming to Italy."

"Did he tell you about his war years?" Sophie said.

"All he'd say is that he hated the Nazis. He was wounded in Italy.

"My mum hailed from England but moved to the U.S. when she married my dad. She and I spent summers with her relatives in the U.K.

"My uncle and aunt rented a villa here in the summer during my teenage years. They let me tag along with my cousins. Those were fun times and along the way, I fell in love with Italy."

Joe drove on and the three of them fell into silence.

Sophie tried hard to stay alert, but the warm temperature in the rear seat made her sleepy. Her eyes closed.

Joe's voice snapped her awake. "Villa La Foce, Sophie. You might want to wake up and see it."

He parked the car on a hill overlooking an enormous pale mustard-colored villa and an impressive formal garden outlined by hedges and trees.

"I never imagined something like this." Will's quiet words came out slowly. "It must have looked like paradise to those who hid here."

Sophie echoed Will's serious tone. "Thank you for showing us this, Joe." Unfortunately, seeing La Foce didn't bring them any closer to finding Francesca.

"Let me take you to some of the most photographed trees in Italy." Joe started the engine.

A short distance from their panoramic view of the villa, Joe stopped the car and pointed out the window. "Recognize it?"

Sophie certainly did. A row of tall cypresses snaked alongside a road in a zigzag up the hillside. A wheat-colored field provided the backdrop and contrast for the trees that appeared on many of the Tuscany websites Sophie had surfed before this trip.

She jumped out and used her cellphone to photograph the curvy line of trees. Her pictures may not look like those she saw on the Internet, but they were hers and documented that she was here.

"We'll head back now. There's one more historic site to see." Joe's fingers tapped a silent tune on the steering wheel.

"Is it far out of our way?" Even though tempted to stop, Sophie feared the toll on Will.

"No. It's almost directly in our path."

"Is it another estate?" Sophie said.

"No. A church. A small country chapel."

Will straightened up from his slumped position. He turned toward Joe. "Let's go.

⁓

Maize-colored valleys stretched out beside them. Lines of tall cypress trees dotted the landscape and added interest the way rhythm variations liven a song.

"Up ahead on the right." Joe pointed to shapes that broke the horizon in the distance. "See those dark spots with something tan between them? That's the *Cappella della Madonna di Vitaleta:* The Chapel of Our Lady of Vitaleta."

Sophie gazed at the blip in the landscape and the fields that cascaded from it. "The chapel stands lost and alone on the hilltop."

Joe nodded. "That's why it's so picturesque, right? Do you want to stop for a photo?"

"Is the building open? To go inside?" Sophie said.

"Not today. There's no car out front, which means it's closed."

"I would like to stop for a picture."

"I know the perfect place." Joe stopped the car at a point where the trees framed the building and the hills fell away on both sides.

Sophie and Will got out of the car. She took her photos and checked the digital screen to make sure she liked the images.

Will stood next to the car and stared at the church.

"Do you recognize it?" Sophie said.

He looked around in all directions. "The harsh winter gave us frostbit toes, hard ground to sleep on, and sucked the energy from us. The landscape was gray, with bits of white, where snow clung to bushes and trees. Nothing looks like what I remembered." Will's arms hung by his sides and he stared at the chapel.

Why does this structure capture Will's attention? It's too small to have secretly harbored POWs.

Sophie promised herself she would research the church's history at their hotel while Will napped.

The car pulled away from the photogenic site. Will's head pivoted to keep the pretty spot in view until it was no longer visible.

What is Will thinking?

65

Joe parked his car in the Piazza Grande.

The soft rumbling of a car announced a vehicle's approach from a nearby street. A black Mercedes-Benz E 300 sedan drove into the piazza and stopped next to them.

Niccolò emerged from the car. His face radiated with a smile. "*Buongiorno.*"

"*Ciao,*" Joe said.

"*Buongiorno.*" Sophie got out of the car and smiled at Niccolò. "No motorcycle today?"

"The Ducati is Isabella's. I actually prefer something bigger, like this. Of course, the car is Isabella's, too."

A kept man, are you? Sophie chided herself for her thought. It wasn't her business if Niccolò lived off his girlfriend.

Sophie's mind flashed back to when she was ten. Uncle Ted, whom Sophie considered a know-it-all bore, declared it was as easy to fall in love with a rich man as a poor man. Therefore, he said, with a wine glass raised in a mock toast, "Marry a wealthy man."

Sophie's aunt, her mom's sister, lowered her head when her husband imparted this advice. Mom's family had been "comfortable," according to her mother. To Uncle Ted, that apparently meant "rich."

There may be a good reason Niccolò doesn't have his own transportation. Sophie tried to convince herself that this handsome Italian who spoke beautiful English wasn't a gigolo.

Will opened the car door and tried to get out. He sighed and sank back against the car seat.

Niccolò hurried around Joe's Panda. He placed one arm behind Will and helped him out of the car.

"Please tell me about your drive today, sir," Niccolò said to Will. "Where did you go?"

"Val d'Orcia."

"Please tell me more," Niccolò said. "I'll walk with you to your hotel, and we can visit on the way."

Will's grouchy face returned. "I can walk to the hotel myself. I'm not dead yet."

Niccolò backed up, raising his hands like he had been scolded.

Sophie mouthed a word silently to Niccolò: "Sorry."

Sophie rested her arm inside Will's bent elbow. "Would you mind if I steady myself on you, Will? Riding in the back seat made me a bit queasy."

"Fine. I'll help you." Will glanced back at Niccolò. "Humph." He scratched his chin. "I can tell you what we did today if you want to come by in the morning. I'll be in the piazza at eight o'clock, if you are really interested."

Sophie held onto Will's arm with both hands, to keep him close to her side. His collapse against the car seat worried her. She hoped she could catch him if he fell.

"How are you feeling?" Sophie said in the hotel elevator.

"Fine. How are you?" Will's tone smacked of sarcasm.

The man is insufferable. They stopped to collect their room keys. "How about we meet here to go out for dinner at 7 o'clock?"

"Nineteen hundred hours. Roger." Will grabbed the long key attached to the equally long brocaded fob.

"Do you ..." Sophie almost inquired if he needed help but decided she wouldn't know how to help if he asked.

Sophie had been an only child. Aunt Mary and Uncle Ted's two children were born after they'd shipped her off to boarding school in the East. She had no experience taking care of others.

She pictured the mystical house of worship that appeared to nudge Will's memory. Maybe she and Will could go there on another day and see if it was open.

A pang of frustration shot through her. *Will he ever share his full story?*

66

After Will's door closed behind him, Sophie returned to the common area for her room key. She needed something to drink and fresh air.

She tiptoed down the stairwell to keep her exit quiet.

In front of the little bar across the piazza stood Niccolò, Margherita, and Joe. Deep furrows etched Margherita's brow. Her hands sliced the air furiously to punctuate her conversation.

Joe tried to interrupt a few times, but each time Margherita silenced him with a chop of her hand. Niccolò stood silent, with an empathetic expression on his face.

Sophie didn't think a cheery greeting was appropriate, given Margherita's demeanor.

Niccolò nodded up and down, in agreement with Margherita's torrent of words.

Sophie walked up to them. She stood a few paces away, close enough to hear without intruding.

Joe glanced her way. "Here's our solution. Sophie can do it."

Do what? Sophie raised a quizzical eyebrow at Niccolò.

Joe put his arm around Margherita and kissed her cheek. He murmured quiet words to her, then pressed a twenty euro note into her hand and nudged her toward the coffee shop.

Margherita disappeared inside. Joe's demeanor changed immediately. "We have a problem."

"What's wrong?" Sophie asked. "Is there anything I can do to help Margherita?"

Joe shuffled his feet. "There is. It should be no issue for you, Chef Sophie."

"Go on," Niccolò said. "Tell her, Joe."

Margherita reappeared alongside the young man who tended the counter. They each carried two gelati. The young man handed cones to Sophie and Niccolò and retreated inside.

Joe said, "Everything is better with gelato." His smile encouraged them to agree.

"Come." Margherita headed down the street toward her school.

Joe fell in beside Margherita and licked his gelato.

"Shall we?" Niccolò pointed ahead at Joe and Margherita.

Sophie walked beside Niccolò and allowed a gap to develop behind Joe and Margherita. "What's going on?"

"Margherita's father called. Her mother has surgery tomorrow in Rome. Margherita said it was an emergency operation." Niccolò placed his hand on Sophie's forearm to stop their movement.

He waited for Joe and Margherita to move farther ahead of them. "She wasn't clear about the nature of the procedure, but her father is quite worried. The way Margherita acts, I suspect Mamma is not doing well. Margherita, of course, must go to be with her. She wanted to drive tonight, but Joe has convinced her, I think, to wait until early morning."

Joe had called her "Chef Sophie." A distressing thought popped into her mind. "Does she have a class scheduled?"

"No. That bit is good. No classes for the next week."

"What help does she need?"

Niccolò nodded at her with encouragement. "She is to host a small dinner party tomorrow night."

"Dinner party? Can't it be rescheduled?"

Niccolò gazed down the street like he saw someone he knew.

An ominous feeling washed over Sophie. "Niccolò?"

"Don't worry, Sophie. You can do it. It is only one meal, which will soon be forgotten."

In two short sentences he had gone from absolute faith in her to assurance the guests would soon forget her mistakes.

"Who will be there?"

His face lit with a smile. "I will."

"Who else?"

"Isabella." His lips curled up in a tentative smile. "See? It's a friendly group. We're your friends."

"Tell me everyone." Sophie glared at him.

"Besides us, Isabella's parents and two other couples are coming, an Italian wine distributor and an American importer, both with their wives."

Blood rushed from her head. She swayed sideways.

Niccolò's arm circled her back. He leaned her against his side to steady her. "Sophie? Are you all right?"

A dark circle narrowed her vision. The gelato cone slipped from her hand and tumbled to the stones below. She gulped air to fight off the lightheadedness. Her eyes drifted shut.

Strong arms swept her up. She relaxed and let her head rest against his chest. *He smells like a luscious mix of wine and cedar.*

He walked with her and she felt herself lowering and realized Niccolò sat down. His palm rested on her forehead. She opened her eyes.

"Are you OK?" His face showed concern.

She moved her head—slowly—and gazed to the right, and then the left. They were sitting on a long seat in front of a pastry store. "I think so. I'm sorry—"

"No. I need to apologize. I shouldn't have let Joe assume you would do all the preparations on your holiday."

Does he think I am so concerned about "my holiday" that I won't help Margherita, someone I consider a friend?

Sophie sat up straighter. She slid off his lap and sat next to him. "I'm not one to fret about my vacation when a friend is in a pinch. That's not why I almost fainted. When I get anxious, I get lightheaded and, if I don't get control of it, I faint.

"Thank you, though, for preventing me from falling. Oh, my gelato!" She spun her head to look for it. A cat bent over the sticky goo on the ground.

"No, no. I did not mean that the way it came out. You," Niccolò used his fingertips to turn her head toward him, "are the person who is willing to travel 10,000 miles to help her neighbor find his wartime sweetheart. You are kind-hearted."

The touch of his hand on her jawline sent a shower of sparks through her body.

I can't let him affect me this way. He's Isabella's fiancé.

"I can do it, of course." Sophie's usual bravado kicked in. This was a truth or dare moment.

Dare I keep to my claim about my kitchen prowess and try to bluff my way through it? Or should I be honest and admit that I can't even boil eggs without that ugly greenish ring appearing around the edges of the yolks?

How about a partial truth?

"I'm not familiar with Margherita's kitchen and wouldn't know what to prepare for such sophisticated visitors."

Niccolò chuckled. "Simple Tuscan dishes is all we want. That is what Margherita promised. Sophie, it will be fine. They will know about Margherita's unexpected journey, and that you kindly offered to take her place."

"I think postponing the evening would be best."

"They leave the next morning."

"There are many excellent restaurants in Montepulciano."

He shook his head. "They want a home-cooked meal." His eyes locked on hers. "I overheard Isabella's mother and Margherita talking. The school isn't doing well. This was to be Margherita's big pitch for a recurring association that would keep her solvent."

"Can't Isabella or her mother cook?"

He laughed. "Isabella and her mother, she told me, have a philosophy. Her line is, 'We make divine love, wine, and dinner reservations.' "

Niccolò confirmed his relationship with Isabella with that quote about making love. Sophie stood and stepped away from the bench and the man's magnetic pull.

I want to help Margherita. I'll buy a box of pasta and a jar of sauce, toss a salad, and presto—a Tuscan menu.

Despite her tendency toward false confidence and claims of expertise, Sophie had doubts.

"What time do you think Margherita will leave? She'll be able to get me started, won't she?"

"Perhaps." He gave her a skeptical, crooked smile.

67

Sophie tossed and turned all night. She devised her game plan.

At four o'clock in the morning, she got up and showered, knowing full well that if time allowed, she wanted to shower again before the guests arrived.

The entire time the cold water poured over her, she kept reminding herself of Niccolò's words about the guests having short memories. *It is only one meal, and I'll likely never see them again.*

The breakfast room was dark, empty, and absent of anything resembling food when she stopped to leave her key on its hook.

Sophie used the flashlight app on her phone to guide her way through the dark streets. She didn't go straight to Margherita's but instead walked away from the hotel in the opposite direction.

She walked downhill to a parking lot their driver passed their first day in Montepulciano. She remembered that it sat on the crest of a hill, with an expansive view of the countryside. This little detour would cost her precious time, but the peaceful vista, she hoped, would give her inspiration and strength for the day.

She was right.

Sophie walked to the edge of the space, where a low stone wall separated the gravel lot from a steep decline that fell away into a beautiful valley.

The black night softened with the sunrise and the sky was a pink-hued gray. The rolling slopes and vineyards and trees took shape and color as everything brightened with daylight.

One day. One dinner. Afterward, Will and I can leave.

Warm light filled the kitchen in Margherita's school. The door was unlocked.

Sophie called out to Margherita.

Silence answered her.

She walked to the back courtyard, expecting to find the woman picking herbs in her garden. Joe sat at the table with a coffee cup in front of him and an unsettled expression on his face.

"Good morning, Chef Sophie. Didn't expect you this early, but it's a blessing."

Sophie's stomach did a somersault. His words rang of a bad omen.

"I think I need coffee and food. Then I'll be ready to dig in. Is Margherita packing for her trip?"

He shook his head. He pushed up from the table. "I'll bring you an espresso."

He retreated into the building for a few minutes and

returned carrying a cappuccino-size cup and a small plate with a hard roll and two slices of prosciutto.

"Eat first. Then we'll talk."

"How did you make the coffee so fast?"

"We make it on the flame, to make a larger amount at one time. I gave Margherita a double before she left."

"She left?" Sophie's heart plummeted.

"Sorry about it, but she was quite anxious to go to her mum."

"Did she write out tonight's menu?"

"Sure did. It's inside. Ah, but I wonder if it might be a bit much for you to handle by yourself."

"You're helping me, aren't you?"

Joe glanced at his wristwatch. "I'll be off soon. I promised Will I'd take him for another drive today."

"No. No driving with Will. You need to help me with the preparations."

"Can't. Margherita has two requirements of me that I must do or she will throw me out to the street."

He grinned and pumped one fist twice against the palm of his other hand. "That's the first thing."

Sophie blushed.

"The second," he stood and picked up his drink, "is to keep out of her kitchen unless she is there to supervise."

Sophie jumped up from the table. "No. I need you."

"Come on. I'll show you where things are. After that, you're on your own."

The calm she found from looking out at the landscape evaporated like a ghost.

Joe opened the refrigerator and showed her the meat intended for tonight's dinner: wild boar chunks, marinated overnight and ready to be made into a sauce.

"That's it? Where's everything else?"

"Margherita didn't have time to shop. She needed to call her father, her mum, the priest. Many phone calls."

Joe set his dirty dish on the end of the work surface along the back wall, close to a deep double-bottom stainless steel sink. He pointed to it. "This is where you wash the plates. The first bin is for soap, and the second is for the rinse. The sink with only one basin is to use for food preparation."

"No dishwasher?" Her voice squeaked.

"Americans and their conveniences." He pointed underneath the counter. "These two dishwashers are for glasses. Everything else is done by hand."

He tilted his head toward the doorway. "Time to go."

"Wait. I need an Internet password." *YouTube will have to be my guide.*

Joe's face turned quizzical but he gave her the login information. He patted her back. "Buck up. You told me you have the skills to cook anything."

"That's not what I said."

He walked toward the door and waved. "*Ciao.*"

Joe was gone before she could ask when he'd be back. He hadn't washed his dishes or left her money to shop for groceries.

Her lips trembled. Her eyes welled with tears.

The entry door opened.

"*Buongiorno,* Sophie." Niccolò stood under the archway to the kitchen. He held a large bushel basket in his arms.

"Why are you here?"

Niccolò deposited the wicker container of produce on the counter. He turned to her and placed his palms on her shoulders.

What's he doing?

He leaned in on her left side and gave her a quick kiss to her left cheek, and then a matching one to her right.

He stepped back and gestured with his hands. "I brought every vegetable I thought you might need. Later, when the shops are open, I'll buy fruit."

He studied her troubled face. "Let me guess. Margherita left before you got here."

"Yes."

"I suspected as much and I know that Joe is worthless in the kitchen. That's why I'm here."

She ran one finger over a glossy eggplant, majestic in its deep purple. *It'd be nice—very nice—to have Niccolò here.*

He tucked a strand of hair that had fallen over Sophie's face behind her ear.

In a husky voice, he said, "How about we start cooking?"

68

Niccolò reached into the basket and pulled out a small wireless cylinder-shaped speaker. He put it in the center of the butcher-block counter. In moments, the sound of a tune Sophie loved filled the kitchen.

"Is this OK?" he said. "It's one of my favorites. I figured we needed something that would give us upbeat energy to tackle the cooking. I'll pair your phone, too, and you should pick the next artist."

"I love this song."

He sang along and rummaged through the under-counter storage baskets until he found aprons for them.

"Joe showed me the wild boar that we're supposed to use for the sauce."

Niccolò grabbed knives off a magnetic strip on the back wall. "We better get that boar simmering, or it'll still be like shoe leather at dinner."

He directed her without being obvious. "How about you dice the carrots, and I'll do the onions and celery? It'd be a bad start to the day if I made you cry so early in the morning, right?"

He pulled the carrots out of the basket, put them in a colander in the single bottom sink, and rinsed them with the large flexible spray arm. He left them there, grabbed a peeler, and in rapid strokes peeled each one, leaving the peelings in the colander.

Next, he washed and trimmed the ends of the celery and diced one stalk into quarter-inch cubes. "Does this look about the right size to you for the mirepoix? We'll want the vegetables all the same size, and I want to make sure that I dice these the same as you do with the carrots."

Sophie had no clue what mirepoix was, but Niccolò explained what to do and how to do it without making her feel like a dummy.

He pointed to the even cubes of celery with his knife. "Italians call this onion-celery-carrot dice, which is sautéed in olive oil, *soffritto*, which sounds more playful than mirepoix, don't you think?"

Sophie laid a carrot on the butcher-block counter, next to where Niccolò stood.

How should she hold the vegetable to prevent it from rolling? It'd be bad form to slice her finger instead of the carrot.

OK. I can do this. It's just a carrot. Sophie cut off the ends first. Then she grabbed the large end and lowered the knife lengthwise down the middle.

"Stop!"

The urgency in his voice made her freeze.

His hand covered her knife hand and raised it away

from the carrot. "I know a trick to make this easier and safer."

Sophie's face reddened.

He explained his movements during the process. "First, trim off one long side, to create a stable base. Then, with the flat side down, cut the carrot crosswise into about two-inch lengths.

"Next, cut the sections into strips as wide as the dice you want, flip them on their sides, and as they're too thick, you can slice them this way." He repeated cutting the smaller sections lengthwise until he had square strips of carrot.

He created the small dice by holding the carrot strips with his fingers and, using his knuckles as a protective guide, chopped the strips into small pieces.

She diced the carrots, but not nearly as fast or smoothly as Niccolò. He handled the onions and the remainder of the celery. Piles of tiny, even squares sat before him.

Niccolò teased her in a gracious manner while he taught her the technique.

"You know a lot about cooking," Sophie said. "How did you learn?"

"Both of my parents are physicians in Milan. My grandmother picked me up after soccer practice. I loved being in her kitchen—it smelled heavenly, she let me steal food, and she talked nonstop." Niccolò grinned.

"When I started college at Northwestern, I was lonely and homesick. I craved the warmth of her kitchen. I decided to recreate my favorite Italian dishes and bring a little bit of Italy to Illinois.

"I asked my grandmother to mail me her recipes, at least the basic ones. I read cookbooks, too, to supplement what I learned from watching her. I practiced every weekend at an upperclassman's apartment. I cooked, and my friend and his roommates bought the ingredients, including the wine.

"When I want something, I go after it."

He poured some olive oil into a Dutch oven, turned the heat to a low setting, and added the vegetables. "We'll let this soften before we add the meat."

He hummed along with the newest song as he gave the soffritto a quick stir with a wooden spoon.

Next, they worked on the pasta—wide pappardelle. Niccolò used a scoop to measure and transport flour to the wooden counter. He made a white pile that resembled a mountain more broad than high.

"Something isn't quite right," he said. He stood back and studied the mound. "I know." He patted the flour on the sides, with no noticeable difference in the shape after he finished.

Niccolò reached one floured hand toward her and patted the tip of her nose. "That's what it needed." He laughed.

Sophie stuck two fingers into the flour mountain and returned the favor of flouring his nose.

He grabbed his phone off the counter and encircled Sophie's shoulders with his other arm. He pulled her snug against his side and snapped a grinning selfie of the two of them with their white noses.

Niccolò turned his face toward hers. His dark eyes tugged on hers like a siren's song.

Her lips tingled. She jerked herself away and pretended to cough. Sophie rubbed her hand over her nose, to rid herself of the flour and, hopefully with it, her attraction to him.

She couldn't fall for him. He was Isabella's fiancé.

What is he doing? How can he cheat on Isabella, the sexy Italian goddess?

Niccolò was flirting.

Sophie loved every second.

I can handle this. Enjoy the attention and know this for what it is—flirtation that is going nowhere.

69

The day of cooking with Niccolò flew by. The wild boar braised all day in the Dutch oven. Its luscious aroma filled the room.

He taught her how to mix the eggs into the pasta flour with a fork, and how to knead it until it reached the proper elasticity. Niccolò explained why the pasta needed its rest. He declared when the pasta rested, they should rest, too.

He raided Margherita's wine cellar and came back with a bottle of Vernaccia di San Gimignano. "Look what I found. This lively white wine received the first Italian DOC designation."

"A glass of that sounds perfect."

After Niccolò poured the wine, he cut a few slices of Salame Toscano and washed a handful of ripe figs.

Sophie and Niccolò stood by the kitchen island. They snacked on the food, sipped their wine, and chatted about recording artists they enjoyed.

"Did you move back to Italy right after college?" Sophie asked.

"I went to grad school in Chicago. I had no plans to return to Italy until I started doing strategic planning and business development for the winery owned by Isabella's father."

Isabella is not only gorgeous but wealthy, too. By marrying Isabella, Niccolò not only gets a bride but potentially future ownership of an Italian winery.

"I needed this wine break, but now we should finish preparing tonight's dinner." Sophie hand-washed their wine glasses to make sure there would be enough clean for the evening.

Niccolò made sure all the food items were prepared before they left to dress for dinner. He walked Sophie to her hotel, and then left for the winery.

Back in her room, Sophie hugged herself in the shower and thought of the easy camaraderie she shared with Niccolò.

The thought of serving Isabella, her father and mother, their VIP guests, and Niccolò unnerved her, yet Sophie believed in herself. She could handle it.

She only needed to plate the food and carry it in. Even the salad sat ready to assemble. Sophie had prepped the table, complete with fresh flowers and candles, before she left.

Niccolò stopped along the way to her hotel to buy biscotti to serve with Vin Santo wine. He thought of every detail. Sophie knew she could never have pulled off this dinner without him. He shouldered all the real work.

He did this all without being asked.

Sophie allowed her wet hair to fall to her shoulders in its natural wavy curls. She chose her outfit, a short black skirt, ballerina flats, and a white peasant short-sleeve blouse.

She inspected her image in the mirror. *Not Isabella, but not bad, either.* Her blouse could be worn on top of her shoulders or pulled down to bare them. *Definitely down.*

She straightened her skirt to align the side seams with her body. *I don't remember it sliding off-center before.* Sophie stuck her hand inside the waistband along her hip. The last time she wore this, a few months before the trip, the garment fit too tightly to accommodate her hand.

Thank you, Francesca. Our search for you up and down the Montepulciano streets toned me up around the waist and hips.

At the cooking school, she finished the last preparations: chilled liters of bottled water placed on the sideboard, candles lit, and appetizers ready to serve as soon as the guests sat down and the Prosecco had been poured.

Sophie finished with fifteen minutes to spare.

She heard the sound of a motorcycle cut its engine outside, next to the kitchen.

Niccolò walked in. He wore a black short-sleeve, crew-neck shirt and black jeans.

He nailed it. He created a look both sexy and fun-loving. The twinkle in his eyes tops it off.

Niccolò gave an appreciative wolf whistle.

She blushed and reminded herself that Italian men considered flirting an art form. *Niccolò's actions don't mean anything. He's got the hottest girlfriend around.*

"You look beautiful. Not at all like you've been cooking in a hot kitchen all day." He walked over to her, touched the cap of her shoulder with one hand, and gave her a kiss on each cheek. "I came early to see if you needed help with anything."

His light clasp sent shivers through her body. She smiled and stood her ground, so close she could lean forward and kiss him. Her lips prickled with the thought.

Sophie smiled. "Thank you. On both counts. I think I'm OK, but maybe that's because I don't know what I'm doing."

"The dining room looks great. The flower arrangement is perfect—casual, yet festive."

"Thank you. You did the hard part. You picked out the flowers and greens."

Niccolò looked at her with a quizzical expression. "You're modest. I like that."

She laughed. "Sometimes. Look at the trouble I got into when I told Joe I cooked."

His hands flew up to punctuate his words. "I won't touch that one."

Voices outside the door grew louder. Their guests had arrived.

Niccolò's hands cupped her cheeks. His lips touched hers in a soft, quick kiss. "For luck." He smiled, turned, and retreated to the arched, open entrance.

What am I supposed to do now? He definitely kissed me. Sophie stayed in the kitchen, to allow Niccolò to meet the dinner party outside while she tried to compose herself.

Sophie stepped into the small, walk-in refrigerator and closed the door behind her. *Maybe this will cool me down.* It didn't erase the thrill of Niccolò's touch. She exited the cooler with a bottle of Prosecco in her hand. Sophie set it on the counter, took a deep breath, and went to meet the guests.

Niccolò, thankfully, put himself in charge of pouring the evening's selection of wines. He matched each course with the appropriate wine.

The guests wanted a "typical Tuscan meal." Margherita, however, had designed a multicourse event, probably to impress them with her cooking school.

Tomato and basil bruschetta, pappardelle with wild boar, mixed vegetables that—with Niccolò by her side—they had roasted earlier in the kitchen fireplace, salad, and a cheese course. Vin Santo and purchased biscotti would close the meal.

Sophie carried in the first bowls of steaming pasta. Niccolò jumped up and ducked into the kitchen.

Isabella stared at Sophie.

Sophie returned to get two more bowls. Niccolò

pulled her close to him in a hug and whispered in her ear. "You're doing great."

He grabbed two bowls and waved for her to precede him to the dining room.

Isabella scowled. Sophie avoided eye contact with her.

Isabella's mother and father greeted Sophie with warm smiles.

Sophie sampled each course in the kitchen. She didn't know what she'd do if they didn't taste right, but it seemed like an appropriate task.

Joe rushed through the entrance and came straight into the kitchen.

"How's it going, Sophie?" He kept his voice low. "I walked Will back to his room, and he's resting."

Joe's worried look alarmed Sophie. "Is Will feeling all right?"

Joe brushed off the question, with a distant look in his eyes. "Tired. We drove around today. Only stopped once or twice.

"Look, Sophie, Margherita called. Her mamma came through surgery fine, but her pa is a mess with worry. I am going to Rome to be with her. I'm leaving right away."

"Oh, poor Margherita. I'm so sorry to learn that."

He nodded. "She cried the entire time we spoke on the phone. I'm sorry, but I won't be here to drive you and Will anymore. I need to be with her." His brows furrowed.

"Don't worry about us. Please let Margherita know that we will say a prayer for her mother and father."

"Will do. If I don't see you again, it's been a pleasure to meet you and Will."

Sophie's heart sank. Joe's departure meant their transportation left, too. This would halt their search for Francesca, the search that was going nowhere.

She hugged him and patted his back. "Thank you for all your help. For being our friend and, of course, our driver. Even though we didn't find Francesca, you gave us a lovely tour."

Joe gave her a double kiss. "I hate to abandon you and Will."

Sophie tried to hide the devastation she felt. "Please drive safely."

He turned to leave.

With a moment of clarity, Sophie realized she didn't know where Joe and Will had driven today.

"Where did you go today, Joe?"

He stopped and looked back at her. "Where we went yesterday. La Foce. The chapel. Montalcino."

Sophie's eyes widened. "He asked to go back to the same places?"

Joe nodded. "He got out a few times and walked. Like he was looking for something or trying to remember."

She grabbed his arm. "What did he say to you about these places?"

Joe's sorrowful expression answered her before he spoke the words. "That nothing looked like what he remembered."

70

Sophie couldn't enjoy the accomplishment of the successful dinner party.

Joe left, and with him, our only form of transportation. Will didn't see anything that looked familiar.

She was furious with herself for letting Niccolò flirt with her—he was taken. *What was I thinking?*

She smiled at the dinner guests when she served the courses but kept her eyes away from Niccolò and Isabella.

She washed dishes through the evening, so only those from the last course would remain.

She didn't let Margherita and Joe down. That was the important thing, Sophie tried to tell herself. *We don't have any reason to hire a new guide and keep looking.* She fought back the urge to cry.

Finally, the guests readied to leave. They all stopped by to thank her, which boosted Sophie's spirits a little.

She watched the group through the kitchen window. Isabella put one hand on Niccolò's waist. The stunning Italian stepped in closer to him.

Isabella looked through the window at Sophie, and

then back at Niccolò. Isabella's hands slid up his arms to his shoulders, and then she kissed him.

He hugged Isabella. Isabella tossed her hair, walked over to the American importer, and hooked her arm through his. Everyone except Niccolò walked up the street.

Sophie smiled when Niccolò strolled into the kitchen. "Thank you for your help and expertise today. You saved the dinner." She tried to keep her voice friendly, but nothing more.

He crossed the room in a few broad steps and grabbed her waist. He hoisted her up. "You were fantastic."

He set her down and pulled out two clean glasses. Niccolò ducked into Margherita's cellar and came back with an unopened bottle of Vino Nobile di Montepulciano Riserva.

He uncorked the bottle and poured two glasses. Niccolò offered Sophie one. He touched her glass with his. "To you, Sophie. Marco and Owen couldn't keep their eyes off you, of course, and the food and service were perfect."

Sophie sipped the wine. "Thank you, but I was only your peon helper."

"No, not true." He stepped in closer and pulled her glass from her hand. He placed both goblets on the counter.

What is he doing?

He pulled her into him and tilted his head down to kiss her.

"Stop." She pushed him away.

"I'm sorry. Did I overstep the boundary?"

"You have a girlfriend. One that you kissed in front of the kitchen window." She flung her hand in that direction. "A girlfriend, lover, fiancée. What do you think I am? An easy American girl you can sweep off her feet because you're a handsome Italian? That I don't care if you're cheating on your gorgeous lover?"

"You're wrong, Sophie."

She grew angrier by the second. "Isn't that why you volunteered to help? Because you thought you could flirt your way into my bed? Or was it because you thought I couldn't cook and you needed to save Isabella's family from embarrassment with their important guests?"

Her voice and fury had risen with each accusation. "Which is it, Niccolò? Or is it both?"

He leaned back against the counter. His face split with a grin and he erupted with laughter.

She picked up a wooden spoon and shook it at him. "Don't you laugh at me!" Her lips trembled. Tears sprang to her eyes.

"Shh. I'm not making fun of you, dear Sophie. I'm laughing because you are completely wrong."

Niccolò raised his hands into a "surrender" position. "Promise not to attack me with the spoon, and I'll explain." He picked up her wine glass and offered it to her. "Here. I think you need a glass of fine Italian wine after your work today."

She exchanged the spoon for the wine. She downed one big swallow, and then another. Not acceptable wine etiquette, but at this point, she didn't care.

He didn't touch his glass. "One thing at a time. You were brave and generous to offer to help Margherita with this dinner."

"Joe volunteered me for the job."

He waved off her comment. "Doesn't matter. You agreed to help."

"I," he shrugged, "guessed you cooking a Tuscan dinner might be ..." He searched for the proper word.

"A challenge?"

"Yes, but I came this morning because I wanted to spend the day with you. We could have gone to one of the fine *ristorantes* in Montepulciano. I convinced Isabella to keep the reservation here because I wanted to be with you."

His attempt to explain himself infuriated her even more. It left only one reason for him to spend the day with her. To finesse his way from guiding her in the kitchen to leading her into bed.

Sophie reached for the wooden spoon.

Niccolò's hand covered hers, trapping both her hand and the spoon, on the counter. He shortened the distance between them.

His other hand raised, and his fingers silenced Sophie's lips. "Shhh. Please. Let me explain about Isabella."

Sophie stepped back away from him and pulled her hand out from under his.

"Explain? Explain what? That she's your Italian girlfriend and I could be your American girl? That a fling with you would be a vacation romp for me? That she allows your indiscretions?"

She gulped in air and blinked her eyes to stall the tears "Or is it—"

"Sophie. Stop."

Her lips trembled. Fury boiled inside her. Her fingers itched with the urge to slap him.

He spoke in a steady voice. "Isabella is not my girlfriend."

"You kissed her moments ago in front of me."

"Sophie, Isabella kissed me. There's a big difference."

"You looked like you enjoyed it."

Niccolò lifted his eyebrows. "Is that so?"

Sophie glared at him. "Yes."

A smile flickered across his face, but a pensive expression quickly replaced the smile. He stroked his chin, like a thoughtful professor.

"Sophie, please give me a chance. Pretend to kiss me like Isabella. I think this will answer your questions."

"OK."

Niccolò stood in front of her with his arms at his sides. "Can you reenact the scene between Isabella and me?"

She remembered every instant of the kiss. It scorched her like a branding iron and left its mark.

"Start with when she kissed me."

Sophie placed her palms on Niccolò's shoulders. A shudder ran through her. She leaned in and pretended to kiss him, but stopped short of meeting his lips with hers. "See? You kissed her."

"Sophie, please do exactly the same thing again."

"What's the point?"

"Please? Again?"

Sophie did as he asked.

Rest my hands over his shoulders. Lean forward and pretend to kiss his lips.

Niccolò's hands cradled her cheeks. He met her lips. The warm tenderness of his mouth sent a shock of desire through her.

He pulled back slightly and then kissed her again. This time, he did not pull away. Her eyes closed and she let herself surrender to the moment.

His lips retreated slowly from hers, but his fingers didn't part from her cheeks. Niccolò's eyes locked on hers. "I kissed you. I did not kiss Isabella. Do you see the difference now?"

Sophie nodded.

Her lips trembled. She wanted his lips on hers again.

She forced herself back to a thinking reality. "But she has been your girlfriend, right?"

"No. Isabella wanted a relationship more than merely friends and business associates. I never allowed it. I don't have a girlfriend. The last time I dated anyone was before I started working for the winery, about a year and a half ago.

"The first time I saw you in the piazza, you intrigued me. You're pretty, of course, but more than that, you looked genuine. Then I saw you dancing in the courtyard in Pienza. I had to learn more about you. Today was my chance to do that. My attraction to you is real, Sophie."

A mischievous grin lit his face. "What about you? Are you hiding a boyfriend, lover, partner, or husband from me?"

His question broke the tension that hung over the room.

Sophie shook her head. "None of the above. No boyfriend or dates since the beginning of the year."

The remainder of the bottle of wine disappeared. They shared their personal stories, joked, and, of course, interjected a healthy measure of kissing between the conversation and the sipping of their wine.

Niccolò held Sophie's hand on their walk to his motorcycle. Her cell phone rang.

It was Vincenzo.

Will had fallen down the mansion stairs.

71

Niccolò climbed onto the motorcycle and Sophie got on behind him. Niccolò ignored the speed limit on the way to her hotel.

When they arrived, the stairway was empty.

Sophie ran up the stairs, with Niccolò right behind her.

Vincenzo had moved Will, with the assistance of the elevator, back upstairs to the lounge. They found him there, slouched in a chair with an untouched cup of tea before him.

Will's eyelids drooped and his mouth gaped open.

Sophie knelt beside him. She rested her palm against his forehead and asked Vincenzo to bring him bottled water and a glass. He wasn't running a fever, and his eyes, although weary, looked normal.

Vincenzo poured the water. Will gulped it down. In response to questions from Sophie and Niccolò about what happened, he said, "I tripped."

After two glasses of water, he looked at Vincenzo and said, "Now I need a whiskey. Neat."

They all laughed.

Will drank the shot of whiskey in one long pull. He nodded at Vincenzo, ignoring his feud with the man, and gestured to his glass. "Another." Their feisty friend had returned.

Sophie tried to object, but Niccolò put his hand on her arm. She understood his signal. *Let him drink the whiskey. What does Will have to look forward to?*

Will, weakened from his day of touring, sat and sipped the second shot. Probably to keep his mind off his own failed day, he asked a few questions about Sophie's day in the kitchen.

Will's normal color seeped back onto his face.

Niccolò described for Will the dishes that Sophie prepared.

"Thank you for rescuing Sophie," Will said. "I know she can't cook a lick, so you had to be the one doing all the work."

"I only stirred a few things." Niccolò went behind the bar and rummaged in the cupboard below. He held up a bottle of Brunello di Montalcino for the others to see.

"You've been hiding this, Vincenzo," Niccolò said. A shadow flickered across Niccolò's eyes.

Vincenzo shrugged.

Niccolò brought out three glasses and tossed euros on the counter. "This will cover the bottle plus some." He pointed one finger at Vincenzo. "It's enough. Don't add a charge to their bill."

Vincenzo looked affronted. "No. Never. I would not do such a thing." He busied himself rearranging the glassware on the shelves.

Sophie invited Will and Niccolò to move to her balcony. "It's lovely. The cool night air will be refreshing." A nod from Niccolò confirmed that he knew her invitation was to remove them from Vincenzo's hearing.

Will sat in the wicker chair, and she and Niccolò sat side by side on the love seat.

Niccolò gave Will a small portion of wine. "You downed two whiskeys, Will."

Their elderly friend snorted but offered no other objections.

"What's the deal between you and Vincenzo?" Sophie asked Niccolò in lowered tones. She didn't know if their voices would carry to another floor.

"Townspeople suspected Vincenzo's father of collaborating with the Germans. Rumor has it that's how his father hung on to this mansion during the war. It may not be true, but I don't trust him."

Sophie thought back to how he hovered around them, close enough to eavesdrop. She nodded her agreement.

"There are rumors and stories about other families, too. One of the markets in town changed ownership during the war. The family that had owned it for generations at first refused to sell their food to German soldiers."

Sophie tried to hide her excitement. "Where is it located?"

Niccolò described the market.

Joe and I stopped there—the place where his eggplant juggling prevented any useful inquiries. I need to go back. "Will you go there with me, to interpret?"

"I'm going, too." Will leaned forward in his chair.

"I'll take you both if you want to go," Niccolò said. "I don't think it will be helpful, though. The original owners, good people, declined to sell to the Nazis.

"German guards stood at the front door to prevent others from entering. The owners had no choice but to do business with the Nazis, who then announced they would no longer pay for food—it was theirs to take."

Will spoke with measured words. "What happened to the family who owned it before the war?"

"The day the Germans confiscated all the food, the family disappeared. The next morning, when the troops discovered they had left, the store was given to a collaborator."

"Is the current owner a descendent of the collaborator?"

Niccolò nodded.

Will leaned forward in his chair. "Maybe the good people, the ones with principles, were Francesca and her father."

"The night you made bruschetta," Niccolò said, smiling at Sophie, "Margherita told me about your search for Francesca, and that one of your clues had to do with a butcher shop.

"The next day, I asked Isabella's *nonna* about Francesca and stores that sold meat here prior to the war. She didn't remember Francesca but told me about this particular business. I asked around but couldn't find anyone who knew what happened to the original owner, or Francesca.

"Stories of merchants driven out by the Germans are similar across Tuscany.

"Even if this was Francesca's family, the trail ends. I'm sorry, Will. I didn't say anything to you because I didn't learn anything useful."

"Thank you," Sophie said, squeezing Niccolò's hand, "for talking with Isabella's grandmother and asking around town to help us." Niccolò had done this for them after their one brief meeting.

Will's dejected face made Sophie ask about his drive today. She wanted to learn why he wanted to repeat their tour from the day before.

"Will, today you asked Joe to return to the places we had already seen. Why?"

"I ... I thought I recognized something." Will shook his head. "But nothing looked like I remembered."

Sophie reached over and patted Will's knee. "It was a long time ago. Wartime. I'm sorry we haven't found Francesca."

Will bit his lip and looked away.

Sophie hesitated. She hated what this meant. "Now that Joe is gone, we don't have local transportation.

Perhaps we should think about whether it's time to go home." Even as she said it, her heart ached—for Will and for herself. *Going home means leaving Niccolò.*

Will's eyes dampened with tears. He reached for his handkerchief.

Niccolò leaned forward and spoke to Will. "Let me take you tomorrow. I'm caught up on my work and can easily take the day off. One last trip, wherever you want to go, Will."

Sophie kissed Niccolò's cheek. "Thank you." *One more day together.*

"Would you like to go for a drive tomorrow? Do you feel up to it?" Sophie worried about Will's strength and health.

"Hell, yes, I'm up to it." Will pushed up from the chair. His face paled at the sudden change in posture.

"Will—" Sophie stood and reached for him.

He raised his hand to stop her and sank back down into the chair. "I'd go right this second except you two lovebirds have hardly put a dent in that wine. You may need help with it." His lips curled up in a weak smile.

"Where would you like to go?" Niccolò asked.

"Maybe we want to try heading over toward Montalcino again." Will scratched his head. "I'll look at the map tonight and come up with a plan."

Does he remember something about Montalcino? Or does Will merely want to keep looking, however fruitless the search?

Sophie's hand rested on Niccolò's thigh. An over-whelming desire to spend every moment with him swept over her.

Can I blame Will for wanting to find Francesca?

No, I understand his passion. The truth is, I'm falling in love with Niccolò.

72

The bright morning sun that bathed the piazza greeted Sophie and Will.

Niccolò drove into the piazza moments later in Isabella's Mercedes. He got out of the car and greeted them by kissing both of Will's cheeks and Sophie's lips.

Will described today's route to Niccolò. It wound through the countryside and ended at Montalcino.

They stopped at Pienza for an espresso and hard roll. Will insisted on sitting at an outdoor table. "The chilly air is refreshing," he said. Will studied each person who walked past them.

Sophie sipped her espresso. "Do you think Francesca might live here?"

"Don't know. But I figure we should keep an eye out. We might get lucky."

Sophie exchanged a glance with Niccolò.

Will had no interest in walking the streets or talking to the shopkeepers who bustled around and opened their stores.

"Let's drive on." Will paid for their drinks and food over Niccolò's objection and started off toward the car.

Sophie hung back with Niccolò. She looped her arm inside his. "I'm afraid this is a feeble exercise. A half-hearted attempt at continuing the search, but not likely to discover anything."

Niccolò stopped walking and turned to face Sophie. "Can you blame him? Not wanting to give up on reuniting with his love?" He bent his head and kissed her. His voice turned raspy with emotion. "I can understand why he won't let go."

Sophie wanted to sink into his arms and stay there for weeks. Or longer. She fought the urge to cling to him here in the square. "I understand, too."

Niccolò draped his arm around her. "His route heads to San Quirico next."

Will directed Niccolò to detour and follow the gravel road to the Chapel of Our Lady of Vitaleta.

Sparks raced over Sophie's neck and chest. *There must be something here that Will remembered. Something he kept secret.*

They drove as close to the building as possible and walked the rest of the way.

"Look," Sophie said, "it's open." She and Niccolò walked faster.

A veined brownish material covered the facade of the church. Sophie stopped and ran her hand over it. "The stone is lovely."

"It's Rapolano from Tuscany. Travertine. I love the stones and marbles of Italy. Someday, I'd like to incorporate some of them into my home."

Sophie cocked her head. "You know about both Tuscan wines and rocks?"

He blushed. "I love architecture and the building elements that give it character. I'm a geek that way."

"Not a geek. Oh, look." Sophie pointed above the door's lintel, where a small rose window graced the space. "A rose makes sense for a chapel that held a statue of Our Lady."

They tiptoed into the dark cavern. It held a single nave. Out of reverence, Sophie made the sign of the cross before she walked down the aisle. Niccolò did the same.

He walked beside her and grasped her hand.

"Sophie! Niccolò! I need you!" Will's loud voice came from somewhere outside.

They bolted out.

Will wasn't near the car. They ran around the building to the back. Will knelt by one of the cypress trees, head bowed.

Sophie dropped to her knees next to him.

Tears ran down Will's cheeks.

Sophie placed her hand on Will's back. "What is it? Does your chest hurt?"

Will's trembling lips gasped air. "They're gone. They're gone, Sophie."

She clutched his arm. Niccolò knelt on the other side of Will. Will's back shook with sobs. Niccolò wrapped his arm around the frail, elderly man.

"We'll help you to the car, Will. Get you to a doctor." Sophie tried to assess his condition.

"No." Will grabbed Sophie's hand. "The flowers. The flowers I left for Francesca are gone."

73

Will swiped at his tears.

Sophie and Niccolò helped him to his feet.

Will asked Joe to return here. He left flowers for Francesca.

She wanted to pummel him with questions but held them for now. Sophie led Will to the chapel.

Will stood inside the entry and blinked his eyes, to adjust to the change in light. He walked up to the front of the nave.

I joined you on this crazy mission to Italy, Will. But you didn't tell me everything.

"Have you been in here before?"

"No."

She walked up and put her hand on Will's shoulder. "Let's go outside. The fresh air might be better for you. You can sit on the step in front. We need to talk."

Will faced her. His stern face broadcast a warning. "I guess so." They moved outside and he sank down on the steps, gazing at his hands clasped in his lap.

Sophie stood in front of Will. *Be careful or he'll withdraw.* "Did you leave blossoms here yesterday when you came with Joe?"

"Yep."

"Why didn't one of you tell me?"

"Joe was sleeping. He didn't see me pick the wild-flowers."

Sophie blew out an exasperated breath. "You left wildflowers by a country chapel that you've never seen before in the hopes Francesca might find them?"

Will lowered his eyes. His chin dropped to his chest.

Her words hurt him. Sophie knelt by her neighbor.

"Will." Sophie rested one hand on his knee. "I'm sorry."

She softened her voice. "You said you didn't remember this chapel, yet you left flowers here. Why this place?"

He didn't answer.

"Will, it may not have been Francesca. It's possible whoever opened the building saw a wilted bouquet and threw it away. If you weren't in this spot during the war, she would have no reason to be here."

He raised his eyes with a defiant look on his face.

"Francesca had every reason to come here." He stood, caught his breath, and stomped away.

"Will, wait."

Niccolò stepped in front of her. He wound his fingers through hers. "Let him be. It goes against his grain to share the details of his time with Francesca. He's kept his past secret for seventy-five years."

Seventy-five years. A long time to love one person.

She nodded in agreement. Will needs time before he'll agree to reveal more about this place.

Niccolò kissed the tip of her nose. "Blame destiny, not Will. What if you had come here first and found Francesca before I met you?"

Sophie caught her breath. *Never meet Niccolò?*

"Will," Niccolò called out to him, "we're going to head back inside for a few minutes. When you're ready, come get us."

Will bent to pick a new handful of wild blooms.

Niccolò rubbed his palm over Sophie's back. "He's too frail to walk to any town. I have the car keys. Let's go inside and give him some privacy."

They walked inside.

Niccolò brought her to him and lowered his lips to hers. Sophie wanted it to never end.

After he pulled his mouth away, his thumbs traced tiny circles on her skin. "I would never lie to you in a church."

"Don't you always tell me the truth?" A sense of panic rose in her.

"Of course, I do."

"Why did you say that? About a holy place forcing you to be honest?"

"Shh." He touched her lips with his fingertips. "I have always spoken the truth." He stopped to think. A grin spread over his face. "Except about your cooking skills."

She relaxed and chuckled. "That's fair."

"I want to talk about us. About what happens when you return to the States."

This is it. It's over. She blinked three times in succession.

"You look sad. Why?"

"I don't want this—us—to end." Sophie choked back a sob.

"Why do you say that?" Alarm underscored his words.

Can I tell him my secret? The horrible thing about me that no one knows?

Her words spilled out. "I know this magical thing between us will end." She swallowed with effort. "If ...if distance doesn't kill our relationship, then I will."

"You would do that? Why?"

She embraced him in a swift movement and backed away. "I don't want to be apart from you. I want 'us' to continue." Her lower lip trembled. "But I'll do something, or more likely say something, that drives you away from me." Tears trickled down her cheeks.

His face showed his confusion. "Why do you think this will happen?"

"Because I drove away every person I ever cared about."

"No, it can't be true. And even if it were, I'm different. I'm strong."

"You need to understand this about me, Niccolò." She let her tears fall unchecked. "I finally figured it out this year."

He brushed the water off her cheeks. "Figured what out?"

"Something happened when I was a child. It wasn't a one-off. I drive away everyone I care about."

"I'm not everyone."

"The boyfriend I had at the first of the year? Well, I fell hard for him. Opened up to him."

He opened his mouth to speak, but Sophie waved him into silence.

"I told him I wanted to marry him and have four kids." She ached with the humiliation of Russ proposing to someone else after she bared her soul to him.

"Do you still care for him that way?"

"No." She did imagine a possible future with Niccolò but had learned to keep her mouth shut regarding dreams of marriage and children.

"Sophie, you're not the first woman, or man, who has said something like that to a lover prematurely."

"Oh, but I do this—I say or do something—and chase away every boyfriend."

"I'm sorry. You can't own this. There are two people involved."

"I'm telling you, I don't mean to, and I hate the consequences, but I'm horrible. I do it. I drive people away. Somebody always gets hurt."

"I'll take the risk. Now can we talk about what happens after you go back to the U.S.?"

Her breath quickened as the damning truth created waves of nausea in her stomach. She ran to one of the windows to hide her face from him. Her shoulders shook. She sobbed into her hands.

He moved behind her and encircled her waist with his arms. His warm breath brushed her ear. "Let's talk about us. You and me."

"I'm horrendous. You don't want to be with me."

"I do want to be with you. Now and in the future."

"You don't know what I did."

"Tell me."

She inhaled a long, deep breath. "I killed my parents."

74

Niccolò kept his arms around her middle. He snuggled her closer against his chest and whispered in her ear, "Tell me."

"I was eight and an only child. I didn't consider myself spoiled, but I was. We lived in Chicago. I had a four-day school holiday over Martin Luther King weekend. We planned to go to Telluride, Colorado, for two days of skiing."

Sophie's spine turned into railroad tracks for the Icy Express. "A girl from school asked three friends to her home for a sleepover. I wasn't one of the popular kids. I had never been invited to stay overnight with a friend.

"I begged my parents to postpone the ski trip.

"Dad had made all the arrangements, including flights on a charter airplane. He gave my mother the getaway as a Christmas gift.

"I told them to go without me. That I'd..." Sophie's voice broke. "I'd rather be with my friends than go with them."

Sophie stared out the window. The scene was not a field dotted with wildflowers, but frosted glass and snow-covered shrubs and trees. Her parents walked to a black car parked in front of their house. They turned around, looked back at her, and waved good-bye while she watched through the dining room window. Sophie felt her aunt's hand on her shoulder. She shamefully remembered what she had asked her aunt. "Can you drive me right now to my friend's house?"

Niccolò didn't move or speak.

"The worst thing? I accused them of not loving me." She bowed her head. "The night was awful. The other girls played games but didn't teach me the rules, and they gossiped about kids in a mean way. I called my parents from my friend's house and pleaded with them to come home the next day, two days early."

She shivered. Niccolò's arms tightened around her.

"I found out later the news stations forecast snow for the day I wanted them to leave. My parents insisted on coming home. The pilot's family wrote a letter to me a month later. My mother convinced the reluctant pilot to ignore the storm warnings.

"Sleet peppered the wings and windshield minutes before they boarded it. The maintenance man who cleared the flight for takeoff said he'd seen similar conditions and those other pilots managed to get above the storms without mishap.

"Mom and Dad's charter crashed on takeoff.

"Years later, I checked the Telluride newspapers. Sunny, calm skies blessed the original day they were to return home."

Tears she thought she had exhausted long ago coursed across her face. "I never told them I loved them."

She clamped her eyes shut, but she couldn't escape the truth. "I killed them."

Niccolò pivoted her body to face him. He kissed her eyelids. "You didn't need to say that you loved them. They knew you did. Horrible accidents happen every day. You didn't cause it."

She nestled her face in his neck and sobbed. He held her and rubbed her back. The warmth of his body seeped into hers.

He lifted her face. His solemn eyes commanded her attention. "Their death was not your fault. They loved you more than anything, and you loved them back. It was a tragic accident. You are a good person, Sophie. You can forget all that nonsense about driving me away. I won't let you."

They turned at the sound of Will's cough. He stood in the entry. "I'm ready to tell you about Francesca. About why I know she might come here."

Will approached them, a handkerchief in his extended hand. "Looks like you need this, Miss Sophie."

Sophie murmured her thanks and swiped her cheeks with the white, pressed cloth. She patted her face to clear it of tears.

"Let's go." Will walked outside to where they had found him earlier. A fresh handpicked bouquet lay on the ground. Behind Will, a cypress tree stretched toward the sky like a ballerina.

Will moistened his lips with his tongue. "Francesca's brother drove me to this area from up north, after the battles on Riva Ridge. He rejoined his buddies near Montepulciano. Anthony asked Francesca to tend to my wounds until I regained my strength.

"Partisans stashed Italian deserters in sheds, cellars, and in the woods all around here. I was the first Yank Francesca had seen.

"There were two of us she nursed and protected—a Brit and me. German fire brought the Brit's bomber down. Nazi bullets wounded him after he crash-landed."

A sliver of a smile flickered on Will's lips. "Partisans repaid those Germans and left none to tell the tale. I asked Francesca, and she admitted she shot her share of those Germans.

"I adored that girl. Of course, I wanted to sleep with her."

He pursed his lips. "Now don't you go thinking that I was a rake, only wanting in Francesca's britches. I loved her, and she loved me back. War can snuff out life in a second. You don't dillydally around with silly things like a courtship."

Will squatted by his arrangement and put the brightest blooms on top. He stood and spoke in a raspy voice that broadcast his emotion. "Francesca was a good Catholic girl. She wouldn't make love with me because we weren't married. I tried to explain that we might die the next day or the next hour, but she wouldn't change her mind.

"Her brother and his friends headed for the mountains up north. Anthony told me about points of interest nearby before he left. He described where the Germans bunked and concealed themselves for ambushes, the La Foce estate, a handful of other farms, and the nearest cities. He also mentioned this church."

Will gazed at the fields. He spoke in a slow cadence. "I asked Francesca to bring me here after dark. The building was locked, but we came here—to the outdoor chapel formed by these trees. I convinced her that we could bend the rules in wartime. We said our own vows in God's presence." His chin dipped in one firm nod. "We married each other right here, in this spot."

He set his jaw with determination. "That's why Francesca would come here if she heard I was looking for her. It's why I left a bouquet."

Will's lower lip trembled. "Francesca found my flowers."

75

The next morning in the piazza, Sophie and Will sipped espressos and watched for Niccolò to arrive.

Sophie's cell phone rang. Niccolò apologized. He couldn't be with them today. Something came up at the winery, and he couldn't leave.

Their high spirits crashed. Will slumped in his chair. Sophie had a hunch about the cause of this crisis. Her money was on Isabella.

Sophie stood. "Come on, Will, let's go for a walk."

"What's the point?"

"We can get some exercise and fresh air."

Will pushed up from the table and grumbled to himself. The Piazza Grande buzzed with people.

Sophie saw Joe enter the piazza from a side street. He raised his arm in an energetic wave of greeting.

Joe sauntered over to them and gave Sophie and Will each an Italian double kiss. "Splendid news. Mamma is recovering. She has breast cancer. The cancer is all gone now, with the surgery. Gone." He slapped his palms together twice.

"Margherita's father thinks everything is a secret." Joe threw up his hands. "He didn't explain to Margherita about her mother's disease or the likely prognosis. Mamma came home and is doing quite well. Margherita will be back tonight. Let's go to the school. We can have a coffee, and you can tell me about the dinner you prepared."

Over coffee, Sophie told Joe about the success of the party. She kept the story brief because Will fidgeted and checked his watch every five minutes.

Joe agreed to drive them to the chapel.

Today, the church door was locked.

The wilted blossoms sat where Will left them yesterday. Will grabbed the arrangement and stomped off toward the field of wildflowers. He flung the dead plants into the meadow. Will bobbed up and down and selected replacements. He placed the new bouquet in the spot where he wed Francesca.

Back in the car, Joe spoke. "I want to go to La Foce."

"I wasn't at La Foce," Will said.

Joe ignored Will and guided the car toward the beautiful estate.

"I didn't go there."

Joe grinned at his elderly companion. "Doesn't matter, Will. We're going because I want to show you something."

Will grumbled to himself.

Joe pulled the car to the shoulder when they reached the property. They looked out on a view of vineyards and distant gardens. "I did some research while I waited for Margherita at the hospital."

"About Francesca?" Will asked.

"No. About my family."

Will waved him off. "You're English."

"Scottish-American. My mum was English."

Will grunted. He looked out the window.

"Remember how I first came to Montepulciano?" Joe said.

"Your family came here on vacation, right?" Sophie tried to compensate for Will's lack of manners.

"Right-o. My great-uncle, Peter, brought his entire family here on holiday every year. I tagged along for several years when I was a teenager."

"I'm beat." Will's growly voice returned. "I'd like to go back to the hotel. I am tired of driving around for no good purpose. We should rest now. Francesca *will* go back to the church. We can check later today."

"Will," Sophie spoke with a gentle voice, "you realize someone other than Francesca might have picked up your flowers two days ago. Maybe whoever opened the building found them and threw them away—"

"No. Francesca found them. No one else. I know it." He glared at Sophie. "Don't say that again. You're wrong." He looked out the window. "Let's go back to Montepulciano."

"Joe," Sophie said, "please excuse Will. We want to listen to your story."

Will's voice rose in volume. "Speak for yourself! I don't want to hear it."

Joe chuckled. "Too bad, mate. It's my story and my car. You could go for a walk, I guess, but I think you'd rather listen."

"Doubt it." Will crossed his arms.

Joe reached over and patted Will's arm. "You never know, Will. My story might involve Francesca."

76

Will looked at Joe with skepticism.

Joe scratched his chin. "I told you about my English great-uncle, who suffered wounds while fighting in Italy. I wondered why Peter started taking his summer holiday near Montepulciano. I suspected there might be a connection with the war. I made some phone calls. My great-uncle passed away ten years ago, but my great-aunt is still living.

"Turns out, Peter was in the RAF. He was my hero when I was a teenager—strong and brave, plus he sported a wicked sense of humor. I got those traits from Peter." Joe swelled with pride at his self-acclaimed attributes.

"Maybe the humor," Will said.

Joe ignored Will. "The RAF planes, though out-numbered by the German Luftwaffe, held off the Nazis in 1940 in the Battle of Britain. Any way you look at it, the Allies wouldn't have won the war without the RAF and U.S. Army Air Corps. Only one in four of the fighter-bombers completed their tour of duty without being shot down.

"The Germans hit Peter's bomber when he flew inland to take out some bridges. The plane went down not far from here."

Sophie leaned forward. "You said you learned something about La Foce and, perhaps, Francesca?"

"I only want to hear about Francesca." Will's tone broadcast his impatience.

Sophie squeezed Joe's arm. "Please tell us the entire story."

Joe picked up the tempo of his story. "Peter told my great-aunt that he would have died several times over if a handful of people hadn't taken significant risks for him."

Will listened. His eyes bore into Joe.

Joe nodded at Will. "Francesca treated Peter's injuries."

Will grabbed Joe's arm. "She took care of him?"

Joe nodded. "Peter brought his children and grand-children here to show them where he hid during the war. He wanted to thank the people that saved his life—the workers of Villa La Foce and Francesca."

"He found Francesca?" Will's fists pumped the air. "Man, spit it out!"

Joe shook his head. "I'm sorry, Will. Peter tracked down one of the farmworkers from the estate, but no one else. Not Francesca. He looked for her over the course of several years but came up with nothing."

Will's face slackened. "No clues?"

"No."

"Francesca hid Peter at Villa La Foce?" Sophie said.

Joe shook his head. "No, but not far from here. Peter and my great-aunt explored the area by foot their first year here, she said, and he re-created his path to the estate."

Joe rested his hand on Will's shoulder. "Peter credited several people for saving his life: Francesca, her brother, the people who risked their lives to feed and hide him in the outer buildings here, and even one American."

Joe looked at Will. "A Yank named Willy carried him several miles to La Foce. Uncle Peter wouldn't have survived without his help. Was that you, Will? The American named Willy who helped my uncle?"

Sophie gasped.

Will shook his head. "No. No. Can't be. I didn't know a Brit called Peter."

"Did you know him by his nickname, Stubbs?"

Will's eyes widened. "Stubbs? Your uncle was Stubbs?"

Joe clapped his palm against the steering wheel. "Bloody right. It *was* you."

Will spoke in a soft voice. "I thought he died. All these years, I thought I killed him."

Sophie grabbed Will's shoulder. "Will, what happened?"

"My duty was to rejoin the 86th. I was too busted up to fight. I could only hobble."

Will looked out the front window. His voice grew quieter. "Francesca had gone hunting. I planned to leave that day for Livorno, and she wanted to send me with food to last the journey."

His head lowered and he drew a slow breath. "I left before she returned. I heard gunfire not far from our hiding place. Germans, I figured. I needed to go before the Nazis found us. I refused to leave Stubbs, though. He couldn't walk without help. Francesca said if she didn't come back from a hunt, to go to La Foce."

Will stared at Joe. His voice trembled as he spoke. "I helped Stubbs get close to the property. I had to leave him. German patrols walked the road so I couldn't carry him across it to get all the way there. They would have shot us both.

"I left him. I left Stubbs by a tree and gave him my knife. I reckoned his wounds would kill him if the Germans didn't find him first."

"Will, you saved his life," Joe said. "Workers from La Foce found him and brought him to an outbuilding. They concealed him in a space they created underneath the floor. They fed him and kept him alive. They protected him until the end of the war."

Joe rubbed Will's arm. "You saved Peter's life."

77

William reached over for Joe's hand. "Thank you. All these years, I thought I was a coward to leave him." He shook his head. "I didn't kill Stubbs."

"Bloody hell, no. You saved him. You brought him here."

Will opened his mouth but couldn't seem to find the words.

"I'm sorry I didn't find any clues to locate Francesca. I rather think it's splendid, though, finding out you were the Yank that carried Peter to safety."

Will smiled at Joe. "I'm not good with words, but finding out about Stubbs, well, it means the world to me. Thank you. Will you tell us more about him at dinner tonight?"

"Love to." Joe grinned. "Peter took us boys on the best adventures. The kind we never told our mums about."

Will chuckled. "I can believe that." He lowered his head and rubbed his eyes. Will turned toward Joe. "I bet Stubbs looked real hard for Francesca. I think he was sweet on her, too. On the way back, let's stop at the chapel."

They reached the small sacred building. Will asked Joe to wait in the car.

Sophie and Will walked to the spot by the trees that held his precious memories.

Will bent down, picked up his latest bouquet, and tossed it toward the field.

"This is hopeless," Will said. "Stubbs couldn't find her, and that was only a few years after the war. How can I find Francesca now?"

Sophie's heart ached for him. She stretched her hand out to him, but he shifted away, out of her reach.

A few paces from the car, Will stumbled. He crumbled down and landed on his side.

Sophie ran to him and dropped to her knees beside him. Joe bolted from the car to help.

"I'm fine. Just tripped over my own big feet." Will sat up. "My arms are a bit scraped, but that's all."

His forearm had road rash. His skin had been scratched off, but nothing appeared to be bleeding. He didn't want attention and accepted only minimal help up.

Once they were all back in the car, Will spoke. "You're right, Miss Sophie. Whoever opened the church yesterday threw the flowers away, not Francesca. We're not going to find her."

"I'm sorry, Will," Sophie said.

"This was only a foolish old man's idea." Will fumbled with his seat belt, unable to fasten the strap.

Joe reached over and latched it for him. "You found out about Stubbs. That's something."

"Right." Will said, "Thank you for that." His voice sounded hoarse. "Can we go back now?"

"I'm tired, too," Sophie said, which wasn't the truth. She wanted to see Niccolò.

Joe accompanied Will and Sophie to their hotel. He left after Will was in his room.

Sophie found herself too restless to sleep or read. She decided to go for a walk. She opened the room's door and froze in place.

Niccolò stood there with his arm lifted to knock on her door. His face lit up.

Sophie grasped his hand and pulled him into her room. She closed the door behind him and jumped into his arms.

Niccolò crushed his lips against her. Sophie guided them both to the bed. He supported her back as he lowered her down.

His mouth was everywhere. He kissed Sophie's lips, her eyelids, her cheeks, her earlobes, her neck. Slow, soft, nibbling kisses.

Sophie trembled. Shivers prickled her skin and danced down her spine.

His hair carried the heady musk scent that permeated the aging room at the winery, but Sophie didn't mind. The magical process that for centuries turned grapes into wine resulted in a powerful pheromone.

She had enough of his agonizing, gentle kisses. Sophie used her body weight to flip him and reverse positions. "It's my turn now." Niccolò sucked in his breath when her mouth traced the tender skin where the collarbone meets the neck.

She clutched his shirt, tugged upward, and hurled the garment to the floor.

Her head bent over his chest. Sophie continued, alternating between kissing him and teasing him with her tongue.

Niccolò groaned. He bent forward and flipped her over. "You have to stop now."

His chest rose and fell with his panting breath. "You need to quit, or I won't be able to stop short of making love to you."

She pulled her blouse over her head and sent it to join his shirt on the floor. "I don't want you to stop."

Don't stop. Not now. Not ever.

After they made love, Sophie curled into Niccolò's side, with his arm around her, holding her close. She wanted this moment to last forever.

He moved first. He turned to kiss Sophie's lips. His kisses increased in intensity as he climbed above her again. He lifted his head. "I want to explore every centimeter of you." His lips moved from her face to her neck in his pursuit.

Their hunger eventually overwhelmed their desire for making love.

Outside, they strolled toward the Piazza Grande, with Niccolò's arm over her shoulders and her hand in his back jeans pocket.

He took her to a tiny trattoria. Niccolò knocked on the door. Even though the trattoria wasn't open for business until tonight, a man about their age looked out the window and unlocked the door. He waved them inside.

Niccolò and the man exchanged double kisses. They had met soon after Niccolò moved back to Italy, Niccolò explained. He asked his friend for salumi and today's special crostini.

The owner's eyes bounced from Sophie's face to Niccolò's. With a broad smile, he showed them to a table away from the windows.

The owner brought out a bottle of Rosso di Montepulciano. He buzzed away after pouring the wine and returned with a board of thinly sliced salumi, thin triangles of Pecorino Romano cheese, and small toasted bread, spread with a light brown paste. He winked at Niccolò and disappeared into the kitchen.

Niccolò clinked his glass against Sophie's in a toast. "To you."

After she sipped, Sophie picked up a crostini and eyed the topping with skepticism. "What are the main ingredients in this?"

Niccolò grabbed one and ate the appetizer in two bites. "It's chicken liver pâté and is delicious. You better try your piece soon, or I'll steal it for myself."

She laughed and took a bite. "Oh, my. It melts on my tongue."

He chuckled. "We can order more when he comes back."

"Please."

Between sips of wine and nibbles of the salumi, cheese, and crostini, she shared Joe's story about his great-uncle. "Will saved the RAF pilot's life. All this time, he thought he had been responsible for killing him." She shook her head. "No wonder Will was conflicted about coming back to Italy."

Sophie shared Will's realization that he wouldn't find Francesca. "I'm worried about him."

"I'm worried, too." Niccolò held her hand. "Sophie, I wanted to be there with you this morning. I'm sorry I wasn't. Isabella's father called an emergency meeting today about our export plan, which is my responsibility. I'll work here only one more month. After that, I'll be based out of the U.S. and will come back to Italy only as necessary."

Sophie's heart surged. *He'll be in America?*

"I don't want to lose you." His squeezed her hand. "Chicago is a lovely city."

I will never move to Chicago. I'll convince him to choose another city.

"When you return to the States, I'll have Will home and settled. What if we talked about the merits of Chicago then?"

Sophie's cell phone rang.

Joe's words spilled out. "Can you and Will come to the school? Now? We have visitors with questions about Francesca."

78

Will's walk said it all.

His shuffled gait had gotten a shot of adrenaline and transformed into something that resembled a slow race-walk stride. He held his back straight and pumped his arms. Will's face smacked of determination. It also broadcast his fear.

Niccolò and Sophie walked with Will between them, in case her neighbor tripped. Niccolò gave Sophie a nod behind Will's back that seemed to say, "Whatever we learn, I'm here for you."

Will stood outside the school and stared at the entry. He squeezed his hands together and nodded at Sophie. "Let's go."

Sophie walked in first, with Will only a step behind her.

An empty kitchen greeted them, but the sound of voices in the courtyard led them outside.

The light in the garden washed over Sophie and warmed her face. Luisa sat at the table with Joe, along with a man Sophie didn't recognize. The lovely barista from Montalcino jumped up from the table.

Luisa rushed to Will and kissed him on each cheek, followed by a quick hug. Sophie got the same warm greeting.

Luisa dipped her chin at Niccolò with a coy smile. She arched her back enough to enhance his view of her low neckline.

"Luisa," Sophie said, "this is Niccolò." *She's flirting with him. How will he react?*

"It's nice to meet you, Luisa. I'm Sophie's friend. Her special friend." Niccolò demonstrated this by sliding his arm around Sophie's waist and snuggling her against him.

I love this man.

Luisa tucked her arm under Will's elbow and led him to the table. "This is my father, Paolo."

Paolo stood and shook hands with Will, Sophie, and Niccolò, a solemn expression on his face.

Sophie sat next to Will, with Niccolò on her other side.

"Luisa told me of your search for a woman named Francesca," Paolo said. "Please tell me what you know about her."

Sophie let Will tell his story. He left out that Francesca had a baby and that he had married her at the Cappella di Vitaleta. Sophie couldn't blame him for his omissions.

Sophie asked Paolo a question. "Did you grow up in this area?"

Paolo's face displayed no emotion. "In the Val d'Orcia."

Sophie remembered Joe's lesson. That meant the region that contained Montalcino, not Montepulciano.

Sophie smiled at Paolo. "Have you heard about Will's Francesca?"

"What was her given name?" Paolo said.

"Francesca Polvani." Will stared at Paolo's face. "Do you know her?"

Sophie did the math in her head. "She would have been in her twenties or thirties when you were young."

"Francesca Polvani? No."

He's not much of a conversationalist. Sophie wondered why Paolo had troubled to come here. It was Luisa's doing, she suspected. The young woman who befriended them might have hoped her father could help them.

Will slumped over. His head landed against the table with a thud.

Sophie reached for him. "Will!"

79

Luisa ran into the kitchen.

Niccolò jumped up and pressed his fingers against Will's neck. He sat beside Will, put his hand under Will's head, and eased the elderly man off the table. Niccolò cradled him against his chest.

Will's face turned ashen.

"Call a doctor, Joe." Sophie rubbed Will's arm. "Now!"

Luisa came back with a damp kitchen towel. She held the cloth to Will's forehead.

Will stirred. His eyes opened, and he coughed. It was the sound of a feeble person.

Joe explained a doctor could come here or meet them at the hotel. Either way, it would be close to an hour. He offered the use of his motorized wagon, which he used to haul supplies within the city of Montepulciano.

Will, his arms shaking, braced his palms against the table and pushed himself away from Niccolò's chest. He moaned.

"Easy, Will," Sophie said. "We're going to have a doctor look at you. Let's go back now so you can lie down."

"Cancel the doctor." Will shook his head. "I'm not having some Italian doctor poke and prod me. They'll probably try to put me in a hospital. I'll go to the room now, but only because I want to call the airlines. I'm going home tomorrow."

Sophie didn't agree with anything he said, other than getting him to a place where he could rest.

"I'll get the cart." Joe hurried out.

Sophie heard a vehicle approach the school. She hugged Luisa and shook Paolo's hand and thanked them for coming to visit with Will.

A cross between an open-sided golf cart and a sawed-off truck sat in front of the school. It was narrow with a high-sided bed, designed to navigate the ancient streets with a load in the back.

Joe and Niccolò helped Will into the passenger seat.

Joe drove uphill toward the Piazza Grande.

Sophie and Niccolò jogged up the street behind them.

They brought Will to his room. He insisted he was fine, demanded that Joe call off the doctor, and announced he was going to pack. Sophie, Will said, should gather up her own clothes and call the airline to book them on a morning flight.

"No." Sophie crossed her arms over her chest. She looked at Niccolò for support. "Tell him he's crazy to think he can fly across the ocean one day after a health incident."

Will glared at Sophie. "Listen here, young lady. 'Health incident?' Baloney. I know one thing: I nearly died here in 1945. I swore then, and I swear now, I'm not—I repeat, NOT—going to die in Italy. I want my feet planted on Colorado soil when I croak."

His chest heaved, and his face flamed red.

"Sophie, book me a plane and decide whether you're coming with me or not because I'm leaving."

Will slowed his breathing and blinked several times. "Stubbs survived. The thought of him haunted me every day. I figured I gave him a death sentence when I abandoned him."

He sighed. "We're not going to learn more here." His eyes pleaded with her. "Let's go home. Will you call and make the arrangements, Sophie? Please?"

Tears filled Sophie's eyes.

Is Will strong enough for the ten-hour trip over the Atlantic?

How can I survive without Niccolò?

80

Niccolò led her to her room and cradled her face in his hands. His lips pressed against her mouth.

Sophie backed away. Soft, delicate kisses were not what she needed now.

She pushed him onto the bed. Sophie straddled Niccolò and showed him the urgent, seeking kiss she craved.

He used his hands to gently, but firmly, raise her shoulders while pulling his lips away from hers. "Sophie, you know I want you, but we need to talk." He pulled her down on the bed beside him and tucked his arm around her.

Sophie curled into Niccolò's side. "Will's too weak to fly. Help me convince him to wait a few days."

Niccolò shook his head. "I saw it in his eyes. I think you did, too. He believes if he stays, he will die here. I say you go with him tomorrow. You can help him through the airports, make sure he drinks enough water, alert the attendants, get a wheelchair for him, that sort of thing."

Sophie bit her lower lip to stop it from trembling. She had to put Will's needs ahead of her own, but that didn't make leaving Niccolò any easier.

She nodded. "I'm concerned about more than Will's physical condition. It's also his heartbreak. The search for Francesca gave Will energy and hope. He's got nothing to live for now." Her hand flew to her mouth. "I didn't mean that."

Niccolò hugged her. "Shh. We both know what Will's thinking. That's why you must go with him."

"I don't want to leave you."

Niccolò tucked her hair behind her ear. "I don't want to be apart, either. I need to finish this phase of the big rollout here but will be back in the States in about a month. I'll take time off and go to Denver first before heading to Chicago."

"Denver?" Her voice sounded like she felt—a puppy gushing with unconditional love.

Niccolò's eyes sparkled at her. "Of course, I'll go to Denver. How else will I persuade you to move to Chicago with me?"

"I won't move there. I hate Chicago."

Niccolò's head cocked back like she'd slapped him with her hand rather than her words.

"I'm sorry. I can't think. I'm dreading the trip back with Will. I'm worried about how he'll be by the time we get home."

Home. She quit her job before they left for Italy. What would she do now? Play nursemaid to Will?

Sophie held Niccolò's hand. "Please forgive me for sounding like a nag. I may not be able to move because of Will."

Niccolò's face brightened with her apology. "Will's situation affects everything. Why don't we postpone this discussion until we're together?"

Sophie nodded.

Niccolò smiled. "Good. But I'm putting you on notice—I want to be with you."

He touched her lips with his index finger. "I love you, Sophie."

A staccato knock on the door kept Sophie from speaking.

"Niccolò, are you in there?" *Isabella.* The knocking grew louder.

"I'll be right out." Niccolò got up from the bed.

He extended his hand to help Sophie stand. He kissed her forehead and then opened the door.

Isabella flung herself at Niccolò and wrapped her arms around him. "The most wonderful thing happened." She pressed herself against him.

Niccolò stepped away from the hug.

Isabella tossed her long hair over her shoulder and smiled at Sophie.

Sophie forced herself to smile back.

Isabella rubbed her hands together. "What we worked and hoped for, dear Niccolò, has happened!"

Dear Niccolò?

Niccolò's eyes widened. Excitement lit his face. "What? Tell me."

Isabella nodded. "A very prestigious importer wants to bring us to the U.S. He can place our wine in all the important markets across the country. We need to set up everything in six months."

"YE-ES-SS." Niccolò fist-pumped the air.

"There is much work—overseeing the government filings, coordinating with production, and creating the marketing plan."

Niccolò grinned.

Isabella linked her arm in Niccolò's and urged him to leave with her.

Niccolò moved Isabella into the hall and muttered something to her that Sophie couldn't hear.

He walked back into the bedroom and closed the door behind him.

Niccolò clasped Sophie's hands. "I'm sorry. I won't be in Denver in thirty days. The winery hired me to expand our export market." He shook his head. "It's a crazy amount of work. I'll come to see you, but it'll be at least two or three months, or maybe—"

"Maybe longer." Sophie nodded, trying to keep her face neutral.

Isabella won.

81

Sophie got flights for herself and Will to go home.

Joe called with an invitation. Margherita was back from Rome, and she insisted on cooking a late dinner tonight for Will and Sophie.

Sophie packed but left out her dress for this evening and travel clothes for tomorrow. Her bag was a jumbled mess, but it didn't matter. She couldn't see what she was doing through her tears.

Niccolò is staying in Italy. With Isabella.

Water coursed over Sophie, from both the shower and her eyes. She tried, without success, to put him out of her mind.

Her cell rang. It was Niccolò. Margherita had invited him to join them tonight. "I'll come early to help Will into Joe's cart."

The distance between them created gaps in their conversation. Sophie kept her words to a minimum.

"I'll be there in thirty minutes. Is that OK, Sophie?"

"Yes."

Neither had mentioned the word "love."

Sophie stretched out on the bed and put a cold, wet cloth over her eyes to calm the redness. Her phone alarm went off after fifteen minutes. One glance in the mirror showed her trick hadn't worked. She finished dressing, walked to Will's room, and found him standing outside his door waiting for her.

He peered at her face. "Are we set for the morning?"

"Yes."

Niccolò waited for them on the ground floor.

He handed Sophie a small bouquet of wild roses. He gave her a double-cheek greeting and smiled. "You look beautiful."

Niccolò's greeting—perfect for a friend, but not a lover—tells me he wants to step away from me.

"Thank you for the flowers, but don't lie to me."

"I didn't lie."

"I look like a clown with my red, puffy eyes."

Niccolò grabbed her hands. "Not a clown. You are beautiful. Isabella's visit contributed to the state of your eyes, didn't it?"

Sophie nodded. *In more ways than you know.*

Niccolò helped Will settle on the seat and told Joe to go ahead. They followed the cart on foot.

Niccolò laced his fingers through Sophie's and folded her arm against his body. "One of my goals for the winery was to establish an export relationship with an American distributor, with a time frame of one year. It will take a massive effort to get everything done in six months.

U.S. distribution will be my responsibility afterward. My dream is to manage the global distribution for the company but maintain my base in the States."

Sophie swallowed and tried to sound happy for him. "Congratulations. What a fantastic opportunity for you."

"The good thing about working day and night, seven days a week, is that it will help me deal with missing you."

Sophie couldn't face him.

"Sophie. Look at me."

She blinked hard and willed herself to keep her eyes dry.

Niccolò stopped walking. "I love you, Sophie. I want—"

"*Ciao*, Niccolò." They had reached the school. Margherita stood in front of the door. She waved at them. "*Ciao*, Sophie." She led them into the kitchen, where Will and Joe sat by the fireplace.

"Come here, you two," Margherita said to Sophie and Niccolò, "I must give you hugs to thank you for hosting my party." She laughed. "And also for watching out for Joe while I was in Rome."

Margherita folded them in her fleshy arms, one after the other. Her warm embrace was the comfort Sophie needed.

"How is your mother?" Sophie said.

Margherita shook her head and clucked her tongue. "Mamma had surgery for cancer of the breasts. She is home now, getting strong.

"Do you know what Mamma said to her doctor?" Margherita's hands flew to her own large breasts. 'These?' Mamma said. 'Cut them off. I do not need them, and I want to live. At my age, they're flat like focaccia, anyway. My husband will still chase me around the kitchen because he knows I'll always let him catch me and make love with me.'" Margherita laughed.

Will coughed into his hand.

Joe moved beside Margherita and kissed her nose. "Margherita is like her mother that way. She always lets me catch her."

Margherita hip-bumped Joe. "Make sure it's always worth my while."

Joe puffed out his chest. "That's why she keeps a bloke like me around, you know?"

Sophie embraced Margherita. "I'm thrilled your mother is doing so well. I wish I could meet her. She sounds like a fighter."

"She is," Joe said. "Where do you think Margherita gets her spunk and sass from?"

Margherita blew a kiss through the air at Joe. She looped her arm through Sophie's and ushered her guests into the dining room. "No more visiting in the kitchen. It's time to eat."

Two platters of antipasti and bottles from the Valenti vineyard sat on the table. The platter of colorful bruschetta made Sophie's mouth water—vibrant pesto, fresh tomatoes with basil and garlic, and ripe figs topped with ruffles of prosciutto. The second platter held thin slices of cured meats and a variety of sliced dried sausages. Margherita gestured to the antipasti. "Please eat."

She told them her mother's disease had been found by a routine screening mammogram. "Mamma takes care of herself. I have a mammo every year, too." Her eyes bore into Sophie.

"I had one, even though I'm young," Sophie said.

Niccolò reached for Sophie's hand and squeezed it. His eyes asked her a question.

"I'm fine," she said.

"I volunteered to do Margherita's monthly breast exams, but she said I get too distracted," Joe said.

They all laughed. Margherita flicked one hand up in fake exasperation.

Will picked at his food. Margherita disappeared into the kitchen, and Joe replenished their glasses.

A few minutes later, Margherita brought in a creamy-looking spaghetti. It had a dusting of fine white cheese on top and flecks of black pepper. "*Cacio e Pepe* is Mamma's favorite."

She served Will first. "I heard how you saved Peter's life. You are a hero."

She ladled noodles into Sophie's bowl. "*Grazie* to you and Niccolò for making my Tuscan food. I hear it was quite successful. Now this, *Cacio e Pepe*, is one dish even you can make." She winked at Sophie.

Margherita entertained them all with stories about her mother as a child. Will's chin drooped twice. Each time he jerked his head up and pretended it didn't happen.

Sophie and Will declined the digestivo, an after-dinner bitter liquor. They hugged Margherita and thanked her for welcoming them to Montepulciano and for her friendship.

Sophie hated saying goodbye to Joe. With all his quirks, Joe endeared himself to both Will and Sophie. He drove them around in their quest, was a unique tour guide and interpreter, and, most important, solved Will's mystery about the Brit he long ago carried to Villa La Foce.

Sophie's lips quivered and her eyes filled with fluid when she thanked Joe. Will gave the man a heartfelt hug, a demonstrative gesture for the old veteran.

After they situated Will in his room, Niccolò and Sophie walked in silence to her suite.

Part of Sophie longed for him to come inside and make love with her all night. Another part wanted a quick kiss and even faster farewell.

In her room, Niccolò backed her up against the door. His lips pushed hers with a fierceness that shocked her. He pinned her head to the door with his insistent lips.

Sophie's purse slid out of her hand and hit the floor with a thud.

"Niccolò's impassioned lips moved to her ear. To her neck. He groaned. He whisked her up in his arms and laid her on the bed, his lips never far from a tender, sensitive spot on her neck.

A casual good-bye may have hurt less, but the memories of this night would linger in her mind and on her skin.

"Sophie."

She opened her sleepy eyes and looked at him. The first pale rays of pink light peeked through the window.

"I love you, Sophie."

She said what had burned on her lips for days. "I love you."

I want to marry you and someday have a houseful of babies with you, but that won't happen. Not now. You'll be caught up with this exciting dream-come-true job. There will be no place in your life for me.

He swept a wayward lock of her hair behind her ear. "I will come to you as soon as I can."

Sophie silenced him by pressing her fingers to his lips. She stared at him. A thousand words that were the wrong thing to say jammed into her mind. The right things to say? They'd gone into hiding.

"Sophie. Please say that I'm welcome in Denver."

"I'd love for you to be in Denver with me." She sat up and turned to face him. "Niccolò. Where is the importer's headquarters? Maybe you could live in that city."

"Yes, that is also a logical choice. Sophie, their head-quarters is in Chicago, too."

This time, it isn't me. It's karma that can't be changed.

Her one word, and the tone with which she said it, sent him out the door. "Go."

82

After Niccolò left, Sophie showered and put her last dirty clothes in the suitcase. Their driver would pick them up this morning and transport them to the airport in Florence.

She walked out to the breakfast room, though it was too early for the buffet to be set out for guests. They had to face Vincenzo to check out. Will sat at one of the small tables with his hands folded on top.

"Hello, Will. Did you have trouble sleeping, too?" His color had almost returned to normal. "How are you?"

"Good morning. I'm up to flying today if that's what you're asking. My mind woke me up, not my health."

"Are you worried about something?"

"No. Just thinking."

"About what?"

"Francesca."

Sophie nodded. She wondered whether his memories or regrets prevented his sleep. It would be at least an hour before they had a chance for coffee if they stayed there.

"I'd like to go out," she said. "The bar by the Duomo

may be open. Coffee would be nice. Would you like to come with me?"

He stood up, using his hands and arms against the table for leverage. His lips lifted in a thin smile. "It's damn depressing sitting here without coffee or food. Let's go."

She convinced Will to sit in the piazza while she went in to purchase their items.

The aromas of espresso and fresh pastries greeted her. Sophie bought drinks for them both and a slice of cake for Will.

Joe drove up in his cart and parked beside Will. He climbed out, kissed Sophie's cheeks, and clapped Will on the shoulder in greeting. "I'm glad I found you."

A white-haired, curved-back woman stopped and turned to stare at them with dark, fiery eyes. Sophie thought she had seen her before in Montepulciano.

The woman turned to the side and, with a jerk of her head and a hacking sound, she spat on the cobblestone street.

Sophie's eyes widened.

Will slammed his hands against the table. "Now look here—"

Joe grabbed Will's forearm and stood between the woman and Will. "Let me sort this out."

Joe spoke to the woman in Italian. He smiled at her and punctuated his words with both hands slicing the air.

The woman's head bobbed in their direction, and she chopped her hand through the air. Her spittle sailed to the ground for a second time.

This time Sophie held Will down.

Joe's tone and demeanor changed. His voice was firm and louder.

The woman answered him in a matching voice. She pointed at the Americans. Her words fired at Joe in a rapid stream.

Joe's words matched hers, both in speed and volume.

Sophie understood only one word: "Vincenzo."

Something the woman said made Joe nod his head, one bob of his head, and then another. His voice dropped in volume when he responded.

The tempo of the older woman's words slowed.

Joe gestured at Sophie and Will, but Sophie couldn't understand his words.

The woman nodded. She turned her head and stared at them.

Joe continued his long explanation.

Sophie thought one word Joe used several times sounded like mun-tahn-ya. *Mountains?*

The woman's eyes locked on Will. The stern mask over her wrinkled face cracked. Her lips curled into a smile. Without saying more, she strolled down the street.

"Why was she so upset?" Will said.

"She saw you at Vincenzo's home. She despises him. She hates him as only an Italian can hate. She told me Vincenzo's father was a Nazi collaborator during the war, which is how the mansion came into their family.

"By association, anyone who helps Vincenzo make a living today is supporting the traitorous family."

Will's hands formed into fists. "I fought with the Allies to liberate this country."

"I told her you are one of the brave Americans who broke the German line in the mountains."

Sophie patted Will's hand. "She smiled at you because you battled to end the Nazi occupation of Italy."

"She better understand it, or I'll go tell her myself."

Joe sat down at their table. "She knows you were on their side. I told her if you had known Vincenzo's family cooperated and aided the Nazis, you would have chosen another place to stay."

"Damn right," Will said.

"Italians hold on to a grudge forever." Joe rubbed his chin. "She told me something interesting about Vincenzo's father.

"His father went into the woods to locate partisans who hid there. He intended to turn them over to the Germans for profit. The father didn't come home for several days. Vincenzo found his body—his father's throat had been cut, ear to ear."

Sophie's heart raced. "Will, do you think..."

"Hell, yes. I bet it was my girl Francesca, or her brother, who slit the traitor's neck. Vincenzo spewed nonsense to us about the butchers of Montepulciano who cut up both animals and people. Now we understand."

"You're right," Sophie said, "and we know one more example of how Francesca and her brother were heroes." She spoke in soft words. "Unfortunately, it won't help us find her."

83

"I wanted to find you before you left," Joe said. "You're a popular guy, Will. Luisa called the school this morning and asked if you were still in Montepulciano."

"What does she want with me?"

"She said she and her father, Paolo, would like to see you again."

"Why?"

"Guess you'll have to ask them yourself. They're at the school now. I brought the cart to drive you there."

"This better be quick," Will said. "I'm leaving as soon as our driver gets here."

"Hop in, Sophie, we've got space for you, too," Joe said.

The narrow bench seat couldn't hold three. Sophie climbed into the small truck bed. "Let's go."

Margherita, Luisa, Paolo, and another woman were in the courtyard. The third woman, who looked older than Luisa and younger than Paolo, wore large sunglasses and a dress that highlighted her bust, cleavage, and hour-glass shape.

The woman's dark glasses and form-fitting garment reminded Sophie of Sophia Loren.

Paolo introduced them to his wife, Maura. The husband and wife shook hands with Sophie and Will.

Luisa hugged the two Americans.

Maura asked Will to repeat his story for her.

When he was finished, Maura asked, "Why did you take so long to search for this woman?" This question was one that Luisa and Paolo hadn't asked.

Sorrow accentuated the creases in Will's face and the pain in his eyes. "I had to wait until Marie, my wife in the States, died. I didn't want to disrespect her. Marie got Alzheimer's, and her health started to slip. I took care of her until the end, about a month ago." He wet his lips. "I thought about coming to find Francesca every day since I got her letter."

Will's chin trembled. He drew in a deep, slow breath. "I've had two big regrets in my life. Believe me, they've haunted me.

"You learn what it is to be a member of a team when you're in the military. The success of the team is most important. You never want to let your brothers down. Most of all, you sure as hell never want to be a coward."

A wet film covered Will's eyes. Agony wracked his face. "Like me." He grimaced. "A coward."

Sophie leaned forward, eager to defend Will from his own accusations. Paolo caught her eye and held up one palm.

"What did you do?" Maura asked in a quiet, even voice.

"It's what I didn't do. Twice I made a choice and took the coward's way out." Will's head bowed. He set his jaw and breathed in and out in short bursts.

"I didn't go find someone to care for Stubbs. I left him by a tree and hoped to hell someone would find him."

"He didn't die." Joe looked at Maura. "Stubbs was my great-uncle, Peter. He was an RAF pilot shot down over Tuscany. Will carried him for miles to get him close to Villa La Foce, a place to hide, and receive food and medical help."

Joe turned back to Will. "You left him, Will, but you picked a spot not far from the estate—a place a friendly person might find him. You saved Stubbs's life. You are a hero."

"I should have taken Stubbs all the way to the buildings. Put my body in front of his in case the enemy was there."

"OK, Yank. Why didn't you do that and go for the warm food and shelter?"

Will swallowed. His voice broadcast the torment behind his decision. "My job was to rejoin my unit, and if possible, return to the battlefield."

"Right-o. Your job was to not let your Army brothers down. You did the right thing, Will. Don't regret it."

Will didn't look convinced. He turned his gaze back to Maura. "The biggest regret I have—one that I'll carry to my grave—is that I was too much of a coward to come back for Francesca after the war."

Will's breaths turned shallow. His eyes went to another place, another time. "I nearly died here. More than once. That scared me more than anything about the war. I wasn't afraid of being killed. I knew I might be sent to the good Lord when I enlisted.

"After I was wounded, my head went kind of crazy. It sounds foolish, but I couldn't... couldn't bear the thought of dying and being put six foot under in a foreign land."

He blinked. The clarity returned to his eyes. "I'm a simple country boy. I wanted the dirt of Colorado on top of me, the red, white, and blue flying over my grave, and the good people of the state I grew up in around me.

"I didn't know then that some soldiers are brought home for burial. I thought if you died in Italy, you got buried here.

"Once Francesca got me healthy enough to walk, all I could think of was to rejoin my troop. I promised myself that if I survived the war, I'd never do anything to risk dying on foreign soil again."

His eyes stayed on Maura's face. "I was scared to go back to Italy right after the war. I was a coward that way. I met and married Marie shortly after I got home. A lot of G.I.s got married right after the war. I got Francesca's letter months later."

His lips formed a determined line. "I tried to convince myself that the war had turned me into someone else and that I lied to Francesca about how I felt, but that didn't happen. We loved each other and we both would have felt the same way without the war, I know it."

The truth gave Will strength.

He straightened his back, once again a proud soldier. "After I got her letter, I wrote to Francesca. I asked for her address and a place to wire money. Her letters only had a postmark from Montepulciano, no return address. I wrote every week to the church in Montepulciano and asked them to forward it to Francesca.

"I did that for two years.

"I don't know whatever happened to my letters. Francesca never answered them, and they never came back." Will curled forward and buried his face in his hands. The weight of his loss and his guilt crushed him.

Maura stood and walked into the school.

Sophie squeezed Will's hand. *You're not an evil person. Not a coward. And you're not alone.*

The sound of footsteps nearby made Sophie and Will turn.

Maura stood in the entry, this time without her glasses. Her eyes resembled those of the tiny, white-haired woman beside her.

Will stood.

The beautiful elderly woman spoke first. "You left me flowers."

84

Will moved to her. He reached out one hand, and then let it drop to his side. His voice quivered when he spoke. "Francesca."

She nodded.

Will moistened his lips with his tongue. He spoke to the woman from his past with a tender voice. "I always loved you. Always. I know you must hate me. I was married when I got your letter."

Francesca stood silent.

"I'm sorry that I didn't come back after the war. I wrote to you. Every week for two years. Did you receive any of my letters?"

"Yes," Francesca said. "I never opened them."

Will shook his head. "Why? Why, after you wrote to me, did you leave them unopened?"

"I had moved away. A friend sent them to me."

"Why didn't you read them?"

"I was angry and afraid." Francesca glanced at Maura. "Then I met a good man. A man who wanted to marry me even though I was a single mother to your child."

Maura lifted one hand to cover her mouth.

Francesca nodded at Maura. "Yes. This man is your father."

Francesca faced Will. "Once I was married, I couldn't open them. What would have come of it if I had? What if you had written to say you would bring me to America, or come to Italy? I was a married woman who made promises to someone else. I did what I needed to do, what was best for Maura."

Will nodded. "I understand. I did the right thing for Marie, but it cost me a lifetime of being with the woman I love. It cost me knowing my family." Tears rolled down his cheeks.

"Ma?" Maura touched Francesca's forearm. "Why didn't you tell me?"

"Cosmo, the good man that he was, took care of you like you were his. Nothing else was important."

"Has your life been good, Francesca?" Will said.

"Yes, and you?"

He thought about her question. "All right, I guess. I never forgave myself for leaving you."

Francesca took a step nearer to Will. She reached one hand toward his.

Will clasped her hand.

"I read your letters last night. It took me most of the night."

"You read them?"

"Twice."

"Why now?"

"I needed to know if I should come to see you."

Will reached for her other hand. "Thank you."

Francesca breathed in a deep breath. "I forgive you."

Will's knees buckled, and Joe and Sophie rushed to him. They eased Will onto a chair. Will bowed his head. His hands rested on his legs.

Francesca came and squatted in front of Will. Her hands covered his. "Will you forgive me for not opening your letters?"

"Would it have made any difference?"

Francesca pressed her lips together. "Yes, if I had read them before I was married."

Will stood and held Francesca's hands. Will stood two inches taller than his wartime lover. "It's not your fault, Francesca. It's mine. I should have come immediately."

Francesca shook her head. "I could have left for America." She clutched his hands. "Please. Will you forgive me?"

Will's hands caressed her time-wrinkled face. "My sweet Francesca." He kissed each of her cheeks in turn. "Of course I forgive you."

Luisa skipped over to her grandmother and Will. "This makes you my *nonno*." She hugged Will.

Maura moved in after her daughter stepped back. "You were a courageous soldier." She brushed her lips against Will's cheek. "I wish I had known you sooner."

"Me, too," Will said in a quiet voice.

Wracking coughs doubled Will over. He lifted his elbow and coughed into it. Blood and cloudy mucus splattered over his arm.

"Will!" Sophie dashed to him.

Niccolò entered the courtyard. A few rapid steps took him to Will's side.

Luisa darted to the kitchen and carried out damp kitchen rags. She wiped off Will's mouth, and then blotted the stains on his sleeve. Fear streaked her eyes. "You can't get sick, *Nonno*. I've only now found you."

Francesca kissed Will's forehead. "You are ill, *amore mio*. You should rest. We can visit you later."

Will responded with another wracking fit of coughing.

Maura appeared with a glass of water.

Will swallowed three gulps. He looked at Sophie. "What time is it?"

"Nearly time to leave, Will. Less than an hour."

Francesca's head jerked up. "What? Surely you can stay longer?"

Will coughed again. Now nonproductive, the dry rasping made Will shudder.

Niccolò knelt beside Will, with one arm over Will's shoulders.

Will motioned for Francesca to come closer. "I'm sorry, my sweet love. I must go home to die."

"We'll bring a doctor to make you better. Don't leave. I don't want to lose you again."

Will stroked Francesca's hair. "Thank you for coming to see me, and for forgiving me. I grew up with Colorado dirt under my toes, and that is how I'm gonna go out of this world." He looked at the people circled around him. "I'd like you all to leave now. I want to say a proper goodbye to my girl."

Tears, hugs, and kisses followed. Everyone left Will and Francesca alone.

Maura, Luisa, and Paolo sat in the dining room. Sophie and Niccolò went into the kitchen. Joe and Margherita walked out to the street.

Sophie opened her mouth to speak. Niccolò silenced her with a demanding kiss.

This doesn't change anything.

85

Three weeks later, Sophie stood under an overcast Colorado sky beside Will's "Over the Hill Gang" ski buddies. Will's flag-draped coffin was suspended over the double-deep plot that already held Marie.

The lilting, lonely sound of bagpipes accompanied the nine soldiers in full dress blue uniforms who marched in crisp formation to the burial site. Seven of the soldiers carried guns. The commander stood behind them and called out their instructions.

The first word Sophie couldn't understand, but the cry sounded like "Hey." The soldiers cocked their guns. "Aim." The rifles lifted.

"Fire." The crack of the bullets split the air.

Another command and they cocked their guns. Aimed. Shot.

Three times the weapons fired. Three times seven. Twenty-one guns for a veteran of the Second World War, one of the legendary 10th Mountain soldiers who fought the Germans and the weather in the treacherous mountains of Italy.

The commander and the uniformed, gun-bearing soldiers raised their hands with deliberation and held a salute. A beret-wearing soldier brought a silver bugle to his mouth. The mournful sound of *Taps* rang through the air.

Tears gushed down Sophie's cheeks. The tune ended, and the bagpipe resumed its piercing song.

The soldiers slowly lowered their hands to their sides. Two of them moved to the casket and with precision and respect, folded the flag. They walked to Sophie and held it out to her.

"Thank you." She accepted the Stars and Stripes triangle and held the fabric to her chest. The men saluted, pivoted, and returned to their places.

People drifted away from the gravesite.

Sophie forced herself to stop crying because she thought it might be disrespectful to shed tears on the flag.

One of the last riflemen approached Sophie. "Ma'am," he said, holding out his hand. "I collected the spent shells. Would you like them?"

"Thank you. I would."

Sophie stood alone by the gravesite.

Will, I think you died content. You found Francesca and she forgave you. You got to meet your daughter and granddaughter. I truly hope the facts convinced you that you were a hero, not a coward. We honored your wish to bury you in Colorado soil, next to Marie.

Thank you for being my friend and for allowing me to be part of this journey with you. I suspect you helped me much more than I helped you.

Will's attorney, a tall, thin man, walked up to Sophie. "I'll drive you home."

She nodded.

"Will instructed me to go over his will with you."

"Can't this wait? He's not in the ground yet."

He shook his head.

"I don't care about his will. He was my friend, and he's gone."

"I know. I hate to do this, but Will insisted."

Sophie studied his face. He didn't look heartless.

"You can say 'no.' You have the right. I must attempt to carry out Will's instructions, but this is your choice."

She fingered the pear-shaped sapphire that hung from her neck on a silver chain. "Will was stubborn."

The man smiled. "He certainly was."

"Did he say why we need to go over the will now?"

"He said his will would change the course of your life."

86

The attorney sat behind his desk in a burgundy, high-backed leather chair.

Sophie sat in a tufted chair facing him. She glanced at the row of diplomas on the wall and the mahogany bookcase behind him filled with law tomes.

Does he ever read those books, or are they for show?

Sophie's head hurt, and her eyes burned. A numbing fog surrounded her.

Why did Will insist on this torture?

The man tapped his pen against the document on his desk. "I'm sorry for your loss."

She nodded.

The lawyer shuffled a few papers. A close-lipped smile flickered over his face when he found the page he wanted. "Here." He held it out toward her. "This is for you."

Will's Catholic school-trained cursive ran in straight lines across the paper. It was a letter from Will to her.

Dear Miss Sophie,

I suspect you're crying. You should stop that now. I'm dead and with Marie, which is how it should be.

I found my beautiful Francesca and got to meet my daughter, Maura, and spunky grand-daughter, Luisa, because of you. No one could have given me a more remarkable gift.

I said, stop crying.

Sophie chuckled at this and wiped away her tears before reading further.

You were angry, and rightfully so, when I kept secrets about Francesca from you. I hid something else from you. I couldn't tell you before because I didn't know if my gamble would pay off.

I lost someone I loved, and you did, too. We were alike that way.

The day you told me you had to put Bangor down, I talked to those folks up at CSU about him. They said an experimental treatment might help. No guarantee. They offered to apply for a grant, but funding would likely be too late, they said.

I knew that dog was all you had. I gave CSU the money for his treatment.

You'll want to call them after you finish reading this. Now you understand why you needed to come to meet this "suit" immediately. You wouldn't want to take off somewhere and leave poor Bangor to the researchers. The experiment worked, and those lab rats will give Bangor back to you if you go fetch him.

Now you can drive with Bangor to Maine like you planned before I got in your way.

Sophie, you gave me back my love, my Francesca. You also gave me back my honor.

Thank you.

Your friend,

Will

P.S. I'm leaving half of my estate to Francesca, Maura, and Luisa. They're my family.

You will receive the other half. I figure it is enough for your road trip with Bangor, a house or a condo, and a wedding if you decide to marry someone. It'll provide you a good start in life. The rest is up to you.

P.P.S. Have a good life. Respect love for the gift it is.

I love you.

Sophie wept.

87

She gave Will's World War II skis to one of his "Over the Hill Gang" buddies, who accepted them with a nod and silent tears.

Will had already given Marie's good jewelry to Sophie. He said that he couldn't give his American wife's jewelry to his Italian daughter, now could he?

Sophie hid the jewelry in her underwear drawer. No one held an interest in her thongs these days, so she figured that was a safe spot.

A big truck from the Salvation Army would come in three days to clear out Will's apartment. They would empty most of her apartment, too. The items Sophie wanted to keep, like her "hope chest" and extra clothes, she hired movers to put in a storage unit she rented.

One item of Will's, though, Sophie wanted to keep for herself. He hadn't outright given it to her, but she chalked that up to a rare oversight on his part.

Sophie ran her palm over the lid of the box made of aspen wood. The box was kitten-smooth from its finely sanded construction and years of Will's hand being slowly drawn over its surface.

The first time she saw the box, roughly the dimensions of a piece of copier paper and about five inches tall, Will's palm drifted across the top. Once. Twice. The caressing stroke of a father on his baby's back.

The box itself wasn't remarkable, the type one found in any number of mountain gift shops that feature locally made crafts. Will spent most of his years skiing and hiking the Colorado Rockies. Aspen trees dotted the slopes with their silvery trunks and autumn blaze of sun-kissed golden leaves.

The barest whisper of a satin finish covered the box, with the typical blond aspen coloration except for one thread of a coffee-colored swirl.

Sophie sat at Will's round wooden table with the box before her. Bangor lay curled against her leg. His warm body comforted her in the empty apartment. She lifted the lid and removed the contents.

Will's honorable discharge papers from the Army, dated 1945.

The royal blue presentation box, with the title "Bronze Star Medal," made Sophie catch her breath. She lifted the cover. Inside, on the upper section of the gold fabric, rested a fabric ribbon bar and a lapel pin. They matched the prestigious award of merit, with a scarlet ribbon, split by a brilliant blue stripe and white edging.

The bronze star itself and its larger red ribbon pin were missing from the case. Will left the medal in Italy by Tom Hermann's grave.

She removed Francesca's treasured airmail letter, faded with age. Sophie pictured Will reading the fragile document through the years.

She recognized the last item in the box.

It was a long, narrow "to do" list, the kind that comes as a pad of pull-off sheets. A graphic of a quizzical-looking bulldog highlighted the top of the page.

Sophie gave this to Will with her answer about accompanying him to Italy. *Will kept the paper with his most prized possessions.*

She had written one word.

Yes.

88

Bangor—the one in Maine—was not what Sophie expected.

She didn't research it or even look at pictures of the port city on the Penobscot River before she arrived. Bangor was once the boomtown lumber capital of the world. Over-foresting, pollution of the river, and completion of the Transcontinental Railroad led to a decline in the importance of Bangor to the lumber industry.

She and her bulldog companion visited the tourist sites. They had their photograph taken by the thirty-one-foot-tall statue of Paul Bunyan and went to sites notable because of their role in books by its famous resident, Stephen King.

Sophie and Bangor sat beside the Thomas Hill Standpipe one afternoon. In a stroke of luck, today was one of the four days each year that the landmark opened for tours. Stephen King supposedly wrote much of the book, "It," sitting at the water tower's base. The only inspiration that hit Sophie was to figure out a way to carry Bangor up the stairs with her.

The 360-degree views made her climb up the one hundred steps worthwhile. Crimson and apple reds, fire and apricot oranges, gold and butterscotch yellows, emerald and chartreuse greens, tawny brown and bronze—the waves of hardwoods in their fall colors dazzled her.

A waitress in the diner where Sophie stopped for lunch recommended she and Bangor take a walk on the paths by the Bangor Waterfront.

Sophie drove to the park after lunch. Food trucks and people filled the grounds. A paved trail meandered through the grassy areas. An outdoor concert pavilion anchored one end of the park and a casino loomed large at the other.

Sophie and Bangor strolled down the walkway. Two women sped past Sophie. They wore business casual clothing and sneakers. Three whiskered men in T-shirts and jeans ambled in the direction of the casino.

A few people lingered by the trucks to buy food for a late lunch. A mother and a baby lolled on a blanket spread across the grass.

Loneliness bombarded Sophie. Tears wet her eyes. Her weeks with Will were only an eye blink of time. She missed him.

Sophie turned around and led Bangor back to her car.

One tourist destination remained on her list of places to visit. *Can I handle it?*

She searched on her phone and found the address and a description. Mount Hope Cemetery, established in

1834, was the second oldest garden cemetery in the U.S. *What is a garden cemetery?*

Scenes from the movie *Pet Sematary*, based on Stephen King's novel by the same name, were filmed there. She had rented the movie one Halloween. That was the first—and last—horror movie she watched alone.

The wooded, hilly acres surprised her. Ponds lay nestled between hills, and grottos peaked out from moss- and fern-covered slopes.

Curved-top grave markers clustered in small groups across the vast sections of grass and in the shady, leaf-strewn ground under the trees. The faces of the ancient burial monuments had been worn and whitewashed by time. A few of the groupings had turned black rather than white over the ages.

Sophie edged the car into a turnout and clipped on Bangor's leash. Her feet carried her uphill on one of the many footpaths. A large memorial graced the crest of the hill, and beyond it sat a cannon. She read the inscription. This monument honored servicemen who died or went missing in action during the Korean War.

Sophie and Bangor wandered farther into the sprawling park. She stopped to read the names and dates on a few of the headstones and found several that dated back to the 1800s. She traced the inscriptions with her fingers.

She walked on footpaths through the sunny, park-like lawn and the shaded trees in their autumn splendor. Bangor strolled with her.

She had no desire to find the locations of the scenes from King's movie.

Her breaths came slow and deep. A sense of peace and respectful honor for those who rested here cocooned her. Bangor looked up at her with his big, dark eyes. He felt it, too.

Sophie didn't know if the magic emanated from Mount Hope's garden cemetery design or stemmed from the centuries-old markers. This burial ground did not paralyze her with the traumatic memories of burying her parents, Marie, and Will.

Sophie and Bangor sat in her car. *What now?*

89

Sophie had pictured herself and Bangor standing by a lighthouse, peering out at the Atlantic Ocean together. She wouldn't find that in Bangor, as it sprang up along on a river, not the ocean.

Now, more than ever, Sophie needed to stand on the coastline and look out at the water. It was that vast body of water, and so much more, that caused the separation between her and Niccolò.

She refused to feel sorry for herself. Will gave her everything she needed to start a new life. What happened now and in the future was hers to determine.

Lighthouse research, Sophie decided, was in order.

The Fort Point Lighthouse in Stockton Springs beckoned vessels in on their way to Bangor. The photos of the lighthouse, though, didn't look like the one she had imagined before the trip.

Sophie's research led her to the West Quoddy Head lighthouse.

Not only did West Quoddy Head have a cool name, but it was on the easternmost point in the U.S. and one of only two standing lighthouses with the distinctive red and white bands. It was perfect.

Last year in Denver, without knowing its name or anything other than that it was pretty, she stuck a magazine photo of the West Quoddy Head lighthouse on her refrigerator. She had clipped off the description and only kept the photo.

Sophie couldn't find that picture when she packed up her apartment and sent most of her belongings to the Salvation Army. In her daze after Will's death, she must have accidentally thrown it away.

The sailor's landmark was practically in Canada, a suitable place for Sophie to decide where she wanted to go next and what she would do with her life.

The next morning, Sophie and Bangor drove to Lubec, Maine.

Sophie loved the tour of the two-hundred-year-old lighthouse. It was a clear day at West Quoddy Head. At the top of the watchtower, she contemplated the first keepers. Only hardy souls could be stationed here and entrusted with the responsibility for unknown vessels and sailors fighting the waves.

How frightening and lonely this post must have been. Sophie learned that about half of the time, fog draped the coastline here, making this a particularly treacherous stretch. West Quoddy Head held the distinction of being one of the first lighthouses with a fog bell.

Each lighthouse has a unique signature of flashing lights and fog signals. This candy-cane-striped tower called out to sailors with two white flashes every fifteen seconds and, when fog draped the rough, craggy coastline, two blasts on the bell every thirty seconds.

She was tired of hotel rooms and living out of a suitcase.

Sophie walked to the edge of the lighthouse grounds. Bangor trudged beside her on his leash. A chilly, damp breeze rolled in off the ocean. The smell of the salty sea filled her nostrils.

Where should she go to make a home? Will's generous gift made anything possible.

Bangor gave up smelling the grass. He lay content on the turf beside her. For Bangor, being with Sophie *was* home.

Sophie knew where she had to go.

She stood there, by the ocean's edge, and spoke to the crashing waves.

"We made it to Bangor, Will, and found my lighthouse. The ocean is beautiful and terrifying. Those early sailors were brave, to go out to sea, never knowing if they'd return.

"They were like you, Will. You went during wartime with your skis to the mountains of Italy. You risked everything, but you made it home."

Bangor stood. He woofed, low and short, at something or someone behind them. He pulled on his leash.

"Ready to go, Bangor?" Sophie took one more glance at the ocean and turned around.

Sophie dropped Bangor's leash and ran. Ran into Niccolò's arms.

They stepped back from their lingering kiss when Bangor wedged himself between their legs and plopped down.

Sophie stroked Niccolò's face. Tears rolled down her cheeks. "How? How did you know where to find me?"

He laughed. "I guess that's one question. I have a few, too. We need to correct an oversight first."

"What?"

"Don't you think I need to meet the other man in your life?" He knelt beside Bangor. After Bangor smelled his hand, Niccolò gave the dog a thorough rubbing, including his belly and behind the ears.

Sophie sat down next to Bangor on the grass.

She hadn't told Niccolò about her idea for a road trip, only that she sent Bangor to the research lab, one brief stop on the way to dog heaven.

She pointed to the ground beside her. "OK. You can pet Bangor, but start talking. How did you find me?"

"Will left a letter for you. He left me one, too."

"He did?"

"He told me if I didn't go to Maine to find you, I'd be a bigger fool than he had been. He even left me money to hire an investigator to find you. He also left me this." He held out Sophie's magazine photo of the West Quoddy Head lighthouse.

"I hired an investigator as soon as I got Will's letter and asked her to start looking in Bangor. Luckily, the P.I.

trailed you here. I arrived in Bangor this morning. I, ah," he grinned, "may have broken a few speed limits getting here."

Sophie shook her head. It was like a dream. Niccolò and Bangor here, with her, in Maine. She grabbed his arm and squeezed.

"I'm not an apparition."

She pulled back her hand. "Yes, you are."

"Sophie, I want to be with you. Always. It doesn't have to be in Chicago. We could live outside the city, and I'll commute. I'll commute each week by plane if the entire state is off-limits.

"I decided—"

He pressed his fingertips against her lips. "Shh. Please wait. I have only a little more to say, and it will be your turn."

"You don't have to do this, Sophie, but the winery will hire you, too, if you want. They're going to need new marketing and event planning people. They love you."

"Even Isabella?"

He laughed. "Isabella's father and I will persuade her."

Sophie followed the planes of his face with her fingers.

Will did it. He changed the course of my life.

Sophie touched her lips against his. "I decided before I saw you, it's time for me to go home. Home to Chicago. I'm going there with you."

ACKNOWLEDGMENTS

The Army 10th Mountain Division, the soldiers who fought on skis in World War II, has held my interest for years. Those of us who love the Colorado ski resorts can thank a few of these soldiers for creating, nurturing, and expanding the Rocky Mountain ski industry. My research for this novel included materials available on the Internet, books, articles, and in the stellar Western History Collection on the 10th Mountain Division in the Denver Public Library. The Allied victory in Italy would not have occurred when it did without the battles fought and won by the 10th Mountain Division soldiers.

It Happened in Tuscany is a work of fiction and the product of my imagination. Where real-life places and historical figures appear in this novel, the situations, incidents, and dialogues concerning those places and persons are fictional or are used fictitiously and are not intended to change the entirely fictional nature of this book. My imagination took Will Mills out of the Apennine Mountains and along the route through Italy where my story occurs.

My heartfelt thanks go to you, my readers, who make this possible. You have delighted me with your continued interest in my debut novel, *To Tuscany with Love*. I sincerely appreciate and am touched by and grateful for your excitement about and interest in *It Happened in Tuscany*.

Writers love reviews and ratings—they are how we spread the news about our work. Thank you for considering sharing good thoughts about my novel with your bookseller, or reviewing or rating my book on the online site where you purchased it, or on Goodreads.

My special thanks to Nick Zelinger, who created the beautiful, mysterious cover that raises a question about the soldier on skis as well as the lovely interior that transports us to Tuscany. My sincere gratitude to Michael Rudeen, copy editor, who not only kept me grammatical but wisely asked more questions and offered more comments than that function usually would dictate.

I sincerely thank the gracious, charming, and hospitable people of Tuscany for their warmth and kindness. Tuscany is my favorite place to visit, and I will return often.

I offer all of my friends and family, as well as those who watch and applaud from the next life, my immense gratitude for their love and constant support. I especially thank Brandon, Michelle, Nicolas, Gianna, Justin, Rachel, Avery, Nathan, Caitlin, Damian, and Courtenay for believing in me and understanding and encouraging me during the highs and lows of a writer's life.

Most of all, I offer my profound, everlasting gratitude and love to my dear husband, Ray, best friend and soul mate, inexhaustible reader, unwavering cheerleader, and dedicated physician delivering compassionate care to women—including me—on their journey with breast cancer. You are my world.

Gail Mencini is the acclaimed author of *It Happened in Tuscany* and *To Tuscany with Love,* a *Denver Post* bestseller. Gail has received numerous awards for her writing, including winning the 2014 Beverly Hills International Book Award in the Chick-Lit Fiction category for *To Tuscany with Lov*e and being named the 2014 Top of the Town Readers' Choice Author by *5280 Magazine.*

Gail grew up in DeWitt, Nebraska, and graduated from Wartburg College with a BA in Accounting and Economics. She earned a master of taxation degree from the University of Denver. Gail began her career as a CPA specializing in tax law, which later transitioned to full-time mother to four boys. A frequent visitor to Tuscany and a homegrown gourmet cook, Gail has toured Italy by car, train, bus, Vespa, and foot. Gail lives in Colorado with her husband, where she loves entertaining her family and friends, traveling, and spending time outdoors. Gail is a breast cancer survivor and a passionate advocate of proactive breast healthcare and is grateful every day for her many blessings.

Visit Gail's website to find *It Happened in Tuscany* and *To Tuscany with Love* companion recipes, reader discussion questions, and book club enhancement ideas. *www.GailMencini.com*

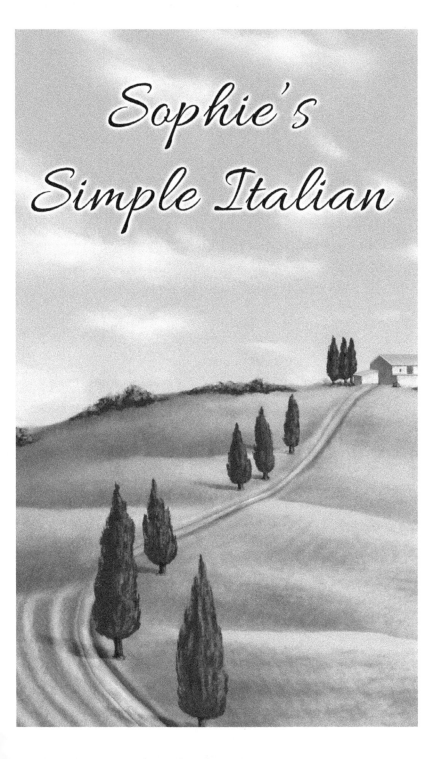

During my brief journey to Tuscany, I fell in love with the landscape, the people, the food, and the wine. And if you've read about my trip to Italy, you know about my experiences in a Tuscan kitchen. After I returned to the U.S., I wanted my home to resonate with the aromas and tastes of food that reminded me of the dishes that I loved in Italy.

Sophie's Simple Italian is a collection of recipes my Italian friends taught me that are easy to prepare. They have a limited number of ingredients, and yet capture the tastes I quickly came to love in Tuscany.

You can find more of my recipes by visiting *www.GailMencini.com.*

Salute!

Sophie

Arugula and Speck Salad
Serves 2

*This fresh salad is one of my favorites from Tuscany.
Arugula is listed on Italian menus as "rucola" or "rocket."
In Italy, this salad is made with bresaola, an air-dried,
salted beef. I adopted my recipe to use speck, a smoked,
aged ham, which I find to be more readily available.*

3 cups arugula
1 tablespoon Extra Virgin Olive Oil
1 1/2 teaspoon white balsamic vinegar
1 pinch of kosher salt
1 ounce Parmesan cheese, preferably
Parmigiano-Reggiano, shaved (see notes)
3/4 ounces speck, which is about
2 thinly-sliced pieces (see notes)

Wash the arugula and spin it dry in a salad spinner or
blot it dry with paper towels. Cut the speck into strips
that are 2 inches long and 1/4 inch wide. Mix the olive
oil, white balsamic vinegar, and salt together.

Shortly before serving, toss the arugula with the dressing.
Stir the speck matchsticks into the salad, and then gently
fold in the shaved Parmesan cheese. Serve immediately.

If you usually add freshly ground black pepper to your
salads, I suggest you taste it first—the arugula can be
quite peppery!

Notes:

If you are shaving the Parmesan yourself by hand, it is easier if you start with a 2- or 3-ounce chunk of cheese from which you shave off 1 ounce. My shavings, using a Y-shaped potato peeler, are irregularly-sized, thin curls approximating 1/2 inch wide and 1 inch long.

I buy speck in 3-ounce packages, which hold about 9 slices. I use 2 slices for this salad and serve the remainder with melon for an Italian breakfast or antipasto.

Spaghetti Carbonara
Serves 4

Spaghetti carbonara is a Roman dish. I wanted to learn how to make carbonara because it reminds me of Will. One story about its origin is that it was created during WWII when American troops advanced north through Italy. The American soldiers brought supplies of eggs and bacon to Rome. They asked the Italians to make these ingredients into a sauce. The key to a successful carbonara is to have your ingredients prepared and organized and to move quickly.

1 pound dry spaghetti
1 tablespoon olive oil
8 ounces pancetta, cut into 1/4 inch slices
3 large egg yolks, in separate small dishes
5 tablespoons Pecorino Romano cheese, freshly grated
5 tablespoons Parmesan cheese,
preferably Parmigiano-Reggiano, freshly grated
Freshly ground pepper
Salt

Bring a large pot of salted water to boil. Grate the Pecorino Romano and Parmesan cheese, preferably using the rough, raspy side of a box grater. Combine the two kinds of cheese and set aside for later.

Trim the large pockets of fat off the pancetta and discard. Chop the trimmed meat into a 1/4 inch dice. Combine the olive oil and diced pancetta in a skillet large enough to later hold the cooked spaghetti, and sauté over medium heat until the pancetta is mostly crisp, but not burnt. Remove the pancetta and set aside on a paper towel-lined plate. You should have no more than 2 tablespoons of fat remaining in the skillet. Spoon off and discard the excess fat, if any. Remove the skillet from the heat.

Cook the spaghetti for 2 minutes less than the package directions, reserving 1 1/2 cups of the cooking water. The spaghetti should be slightly less cooked than *al dente*. Return the skillet to medium heat.

Working quickly, add the drained pasta and reserved pasta water to the skillet. Turn the heat to low and use tongs to toss the pasta until it is heated through and cooked to *al dente*. Add the reserved pancetta to the pasta and mix.

Remove the skillet from the heat. Quickly add the yolks, one at a time, mixing after each addition. Add the cheese to the pasta and toss vigorously. Add freshly ground pepper and salt to taste. Serve immediately.

Amaretti Cookies
Makes 24 - 30 Cookies

These small cookies are crunchy on the outside and soft and chewy on the inside. I love them with a cup of espresso! The cookies get crunchier each day and, whether served alongside or crumbled on top, can turn a sliced pear or cup of gelato into an elegant dessert.

2 1/2 cups of almond flour
1 1/4 cup of superfine sugar, also called baker's sugar
3 egg whites
1/2 teaspoon of vanilla extract
1 teaspoon of almond extract
Parchment paper

Preheat the oven to 300°F. Line a baking sheet with parchment paper. Pulse the almond flour and sugar together in a food processor. (See note below.) Mix in the vanilla and almond extracts by pulsing for a few seconds. Add one egg white at a time and pulse between each addition to mix the eggs into the dough. Process the dough after the last egg has been added, stopping when it is smooth.

Wet your hands with water. Form the cookies by lightly rolling and patting teaspoon-sized amounts of dough between your damp hands, creating a smooth ball. Place the balls on your parchment-lined baking sheet. Bake at

300°F for 22 – 24 minutes, or until the tops are starting to turn golden brown at the edges. The cookies can be stored in an airtight container once they are cool.

Note:

If you don't have a food processor, you can make this dough using a spoon. It will be easier, however, if you use an electric mixer or food processor to add in the egg whites.

9 781938 592157